VENUS WITH PISTOL

VENUS
WITH PISTOL

*

GAVIN LYALL

THE
COMPANION BOOK CLUB
LONDON

This edition, published in 1971 by
The Hamlyn Publishing Group Ltd.,
is issued by arrangement with
Hodder & Stoughton Ltd.

*Made and printed in Great Britain
for the Companion Book Club
by Odhams (Watford) Ltd.*
Standard 6007713X
Deluxe 600871304
1.71

ONE

HE DIDN'T want to buy a gun. At least, not the kind I sell. You can tell.

He was thin, slightly nervous-looking, in a thick black over-coat and the sort of narrow-brimmed hat worn by fashionable spies in the movies.

For a moment he stood there, just inside the door, avoiding catching my eye. So I left him to it. After a while he picked up the pistol that I leave on the little table by the door for people to pick up and click if they're that sort of people.

He clicked it.

Then he coughed and asked: 'How much?'

I put on my professional expression and came forward and pretended to peer at it closely. It had only been there six months.

I gave a professional opinion: 'The workmanship isn't out-standing, of course, but it's in good condition and it's fairly rare of its kind.' Rare? It was probably unique. A non-rifled screw-barrel job with the original 1820 lockplates, a barrel cut down from something else around 1930 (I guessed) but nicely aged; 1950 vintage hammer and mechanism, and a butt carved out of bad oak a few years ago.

I mean, if that was *exactly* what you were looking for, you'd be dead lucky to find it, wouldn't you?

I said: 'This time of the year, I'd sell for twenty pounds.'

'The money's tight at this time of the year, is it?' He had a faint Irish brogue.

'Who buys antiques in January? Surtax payers buy antiques. This is the time they pay their surtax.'

He got a slightly craft look in his light blue eyes. 'You've paid yours yet?'

'That'll be the day. When they want surtax off me.'

He nodded absently. 'They're all saying that. Bad all round.' He eased past me towards my desk at the back of the shop. 'To tell the truth, it was about a sort of surtax I came to see you.'

I just looked after him.

He picked up the pistol on my desk.

I said: 'Put it down.'

He put it down. 'Worth a bit more than twenty pounds, is it?'

'A bit.' It was one of a pair of Scottish flintlocks I'd been fiddling with to see if anybody else had been fiddling with.

He grinned and looked around. 'Dreadful thing if somebody busted in here, bashed up your stock, done the place over a bit. Dreadful. Never get it back on the insurance. Difficult to value, this stuff, I'd say.'

The hammer finally clicked in my head. 'A protection racket? You can't run a protection racket in this part of Kensington.'

He was sensitive enough to look a bit ashamed. Maybe he'd had a difficult day. But he recovered quickly. 'A racket? Who said anything about a racket? Security, it is: security. A small down payment every month, you'll be safe as Buckingham Palace.'

'Charlie Good, I suppose?'

This time his eyebrows nearly knocked off his hat.

I patted his shoulder—I had to reach for it, him being a good bit taller—and said: 'Look, you check with Charlie about me. Tell him you saw me. I'll ring him myself later, when he's likely to be up.'

'I didn't say anything about it being Charlie,' he persisted.

'No, but it had better be, mate. If you're trying this little game on your own, you're in dead trouble when Charlie hears about it.'

That didn't frighten him, so he obviously wasn't a freelance. But he wasn't any genius, neither. 'Twenty quid a month,' he said. 'And it's cheap at the price, it is. Shall I tell them you'll be paying it?'

6

There was a little buzzing and crackling in my head, like a loose connection in a radio. This was a hell of a way to start the New Year.

'Look,' I said patiently, 'just piss off home and tell Charlie you've seen me and ask him does he really want me to pay. I mean, just do that.'

'You know Charlie, do you?' The message had finally arrived.

'What the hell have we been talking about the past five minutes?'

He nodded. 'I'll be checking with Charlie about it, then.' Just as if he'd thought of it for himself.

'That's a good idea,' I said.

'Not that he'll be out of bed, yet,' he added.

The doorbell pinged again.

My first visitor glanced quickly over his shoulder. 'Well, I'll be checking with Charlie then. When he's up, that is.'

'I wouldn't try it before,' I advised.

'Not a thought of it.' And finally he went.

I'd zipped back down the narrow shop to my desk and opened the big bottom drawer and got out the bottle before I realized the new customer wasn't clicking the pistol by the door.

'Second customer of the year always gets offered a drink,' I said, loudly. I found a second glass that was almost clean and started pouring.

He walked easily, almost elegantly, down past the tall narrow display cabinet that was really an old bookcase. It was dark by the desk, even with the desk lamp on. So I put on the working light, the bright twelve-volt I use for fiddling with guns under, as well.

He was slim, neat, and around five-eleven high. Long handsome-craggy features, a strong thin nose, sallow skin, dark eyes. All that, and the threequarter-length coat in some rich dark fur, taped him as Spanish, or maybe South American or something—except for his hair. It was curly and auburn.

I held out the second glass. He took it, sniffed it, smiled appreciatively.

7

'Single malt Scotch,' I explained. 'Christmas present from a customer who thought he'd cheated me.'

'Aye,' he said, 'and a verra good one, I'd say.' I just stared. At the voice more than the man It was thick and Scottish as a haggis.

He took a nibble at the drink, then smiled again. 'It'll be Mr. Gilbert Kemp, will it?'

I woke up. 'Bert. Gil to Americans, Gilbert to my enemies.'

He frowned politely. 'I dinna quite—'

'Sorry. I don't like my own name. Skip it. What can I show you? The stock's a bit low at the moment, but so's the prices.'

He took out a black leather card-case and dealt me one. It read:

Carlos MacGregor Garcia
Managua

I said: 'Managua,' sort of thoughtfully, as if that was the one moment in the year when I'd forgotten just where or what it was.

"Ye'll recall Managua's the capital city of Nicaragua,' he said politely.

'Ah yes.' I thought of saying something like Welcome to Britain, then remembered he couldn't have picked up that accent in the capital city of Nicaragua. So I just said again: 'Well, what can I show you?'

'Well, now, I'm not exactly buying. I have a little proposition.'

'Oh?' I sipped my single malt. 'Well, take a seat, then.' I found a rickety seat for him to take, and he sat down carefully.

He said: 'Mr Kemp—I believe ye smuggle art?'

I found I'd finished my drink. 'Do I? I mean, where did you hear that?'

He waved an elegant hand. 'Ye sort of learn these things, if it's your job. Do ye still do it?'

I poured myself another drink, then remembered to offer him one. He shook his head. 'Look, Mr Garcia—'

'MacGregor, if ye dinna mind. Ye'll recall the Spanish

8

custom uses both the patronym and matronym, but ye're always known by your father's name.'

'Sorry. But look: let's say I've done a bit, in the past, just for the sake of argument, I mean . . . well, what have you got, where is it, and where d'you want it to go to?'

'Will ye be taking on the job?'

'I want to know more about it first.'

'Aye. That's fair enough. Well now—I represent a certain person who's in Europe building up a collection for export.'

'To Managua?'

'Aye. But ye wouldna be doing that part of the journey. We reckon it's good enough if we can store it in Switzerland, then send it on as one big load.'

That made sense, of course. There aren't any Swiss art export laws. Once you've got it across the frontier into Switzerland—and there's plenty of frontiers into Switzerland—you can fly it to any damn place in the world and legitimate as lechery.

Wait a minute: he'd said 'one big load', hadn't he?

'Sounds like quite a collection,' I said. 'What've you got? And where?'

'Most of it isna bought yet.'

I frowned. 'You might not even need me. I mean, the art export laws aren't as tough as they used to be. Except Spain, Portugal, Italy.'

'Aye. But we think we'd like ye along. Anyway, it's a risk we'll take—and be paying for.'

I got up and walked around in a small circle—there wasn't room for more—behind my desk. 'You mean you just want me to come on the payroll and travel around for—for how long?'

'I'd reckon a month.'

'For a month, just so if you pick up something that needs my sort of exporting then I'll be there to do it?'

'Aye.'

I mean, it was bloody barmy. If they thought they needed me, they thought they were going to buy some pretty pricey stuff—artists even I'd heard of, probably. You can export all you like of the average stuff, from almost anywhere. And they were planning on just a month, buying that sort of picture. I

9

mean, I don't know much about sticking together a collection of Picassos and Matisses and Gainsboroughs, but I know it takes a damn sight more than a month. Unless you're really going to throw your money around.

Well, maybe they *were* going to throw their money around. So why should I duck?

I said: 'I don't much like leaving the shop. Closing it up.'

He raised his eyebrows politely. 'At this time of the year?'

'This time's when people sell their collections to pay their taxes. I could miss a lot of good stuff cheap.'

'Aye. Well—I can offer ye five pun' a day for yerself and five pun' for the overheads on your shop, and all your travelling and living abroad, of course.'

He waited calmly for me to grab at it.

I said: 'And a special rate for each job.'

A polite frown. 'I dinna see—'

'You should've seen. There's a lot of difference between getting a Picasso out of France and a bloody great statue out of Italy.'

'Aye. I think there'll no be any statues, but . . . I reckon we can accept the idea. Will ye be coming, then?'

'I suppose so. When? Where?'

'Paris, tomorrow.' He reached inside his coat again. 'There's a ticket for the aeroplane and fifty pun' for your first expenses. Ye'll be keeping a good note about them of course?'

I just nodded.

He stood up, and thought over his next remark rather carefully. 'Mr Kemp—do ye usually dress like that?'

'Huh?' I mean, what was this? I was even wearing one of my suits that day. Well, I suppose it was a bit worn at the cuffs and elbows, and maybe a bit too much gun-oil on the lapels— you shouldn't really wear light grey to fiddle with guns—but hell, it was a *suit*.

I said: 'I've got another suit. Sort of brown and green. Tweed I mean.'

He gave a little artificial smile. 'Aye—well . . . it's just ye'll maybe find yeself in some smart places.'

'Oh. Don't you worry about me, mate. I'll manage.'

'Aye.' Then he sighed. 'We'll meet on the aeroplane, then.' He held out his hand and I shook it and he walked away up the shop and out.

I just stood behind the desk staring at the bunch of francs, the BEA ticket and the visiting card. I picked up the card and automatically ran my fingernail across it to see if it was engraved. It was, of course. Pompous bastard. Telling me how to dress. Then I tore up the card and threw it away. He shouldn't have left it anyway. Bad security, if we were doing any undercover work—and art smuggling *is* undercover. Well, supposed to be.

Then I checked the airline ticket. It was in my name, so he'd been pretty sure of getting me. So then I counted the francs and it seemed about right. And a month was—say—thirty days, which was three hundred pounds with the overheads on the shop, plus the special rates for the real work. Well, that wasn't so bad. A lot better than I'd do staying here, in January, whatever I'd told MacGregor.

Provided I didn't land in some Italian jail.

Selling antique guns isn't a bad way to earn a living. At least the cheating's legal. And there's always the chance you'll pick up something really classy from some nit who doesn't know the prices, or maybe match a pair of handguns that've got split up. Not a bad trade. And then somebody comes and dumps a wad of francs and a ticket on your desk and you're out in the cold again. And you're scared—well, no, not scared, but . . . all right, you're scared. You might be getting a bit old for this sort of thing.

Christ!—you *are* getting old. You forgot even to ask the name of the people you're working for!

TWO

ANYWAY, the next day I was on the plane.

I'd stored my best guns at the bank, warned my landlord, turned off the water, packed two bags—the big smuggling one with the rigid frame, just about as big as you can get without it looking suspicious, and the small airline handbag affair—and at the last minute I even paid a few bills, then on the way to the air terminal I bought a couple of shirts which I'd been planning to do for months . . . and I caught the plane.

I don't like aeroplanes. Particularly I don't like jets. At least the old propeller thing made a decent noise so you knew the engines were really trying, and they didn't go up like bloody rockets, neither.

I'd teamed up with Carlos MacGregor in the final departure lounge (that's a hell of a reassuring name, too) and I let him take the window seat on the plane. I don't really want to know how far down it is.

We did the usual bit where the thing stands on its tail and the engines go all quiet as if they've stopped and the pilot's had a heart attack, and they're throwing soft piped music at you to get your mind off your short future . . . and somehow we survived it. The stewardesses started running around with little sandwiches and empty cups and ignoring people like me screaming for alcohol.

Carlos looked at his watch and said: 'Well, we're off on time.'

I said: 'Marvellous,' and went back to shivering. It was pretty warm in the plane.

He glanced at me, smiled gently. Then took out a black leather case and lit a rather long fawn-brown cigarette. Now I wouldn't even be able to smell when the engines caught fire.

Carlos took out a piece of paper, consulted it, and said: 'There's a room reserved for ye at the Montalembert. D'ye know it?'

'I think so. Over in Saint-Germain, isn't it?'

'Aye.'

'Well, fine. But isn't it about time I knew who I'm working for?'

'Aye. I'd 've told ye yesterday if ye'd asked. Dona Margarita Consuela Santana . . . well, it's a rather long name. Just say Dona Margarita Umberto.'

Somehow the name was a bit familiar. I frowned over it, then caught him looking at me, slightly amused. 'Ye'll remember her if ye ever followed tennis twenty years ago, Mr Kemp.'

Well, of course I hadn't followed tennis, but at Wimbledon time the papers and radio are full of it. There'd been a Margarita Umberto at Wimbledon the first few years after the war. She hadn't won anything, but the newspapers had liked her, they'd called her the Spanish Smasher or something. You know.

Carlos went on: 'She's a widow lady, now. She married Don Lorenzo—he was a big landowner and something of a politician —and he died just seven years ago.'

'And now she's spending her inheritance on an art collection, huh?'

'Ye might say something like that.'

'Just how much are you spending?'

He looked a little stiff about that. But then: 'Well, ye'll be hearing figures mentioned, no doubt, so ye'd best get the right one. It'll be around two and a half million pounds.'

After a long time I found enough breath to whistle. 'You shouldn't have to make do with a stack of dirty postcards on *that* money. Quite sure the lady wouldn't like to buy a few antique guns just to add variety?'

'I fear not, Mr Kemp.'

Then I got another thought. 'If anybody else knows that figure, you'll be up to your neck in every faker and forger in Europe.'

'Aye. So we'd appreciate ye keeping it a secret.'

'Don't worry, mate. I don't want her going broke until I've had my bite. I just hope she hasn't been bidding it up at Christie's and Sotheby's and places.'

'We have two experts who're doing the buying on Dona Margarita's behalf.'

'Well, where's she staying in Paris?'

'The Prince de Galles.'

'Nice inconspicuous little pub. What's wrong with the Ritz or the Crillon if you want to get noticed? The gossip columns check those places, you know?'

'Aye. We decided it would be impossible for her to make the trip incognito, as ye might say. And it'd be even worse if she were trying to hide and got discovered. Most suspicious. So as far as the newspapers are concerned, she's just doing a European tour, visiting some of the countries she played tennis in. She hasna been in Europe for ten years, ye know.'

Well, that made sense. Maybe I wasn't going to have to give Carlos the complete security lecture I'd planned.

'So me—and the buyers you were talking about—we stay somewhere separate and check in by phone? Is that the idea?'

'Something like that. We meet when we have to, of course, but we can be careful about that.'

So far, reasonable enough. Maybe even too reasonable. What's so reasonable about lashing out two and a half million on art? Give me that sort of money and just watch me spend it —but at least I'd spend it on things I chose for myself. I wouldn't hire experts to tell me how to get shot of it.

'This is an investment policy, is it? I mean—General Motors is worth five per cent more a year, but Picasso's worth ten? Right?'

A little formally, he said: 'The gallery, when it's finished and stocked, will belong to the people of Nicaragua.'

Oh really? I'd looked up 'Nicaragua' in the encyclopedia at the library the night before, and nothing I'd read suggested 'the people' owned much of anything. Still, once you've given it away you can't very well ask for it back.

Hell, it wasn't my problem. Maybe it was Dona Margarita's

idea of a snazzy memorial to her late lamented husband. Maybe it was a family tradition that you endowed a nifty piece of public works, and this would be a smack in the eye for Uncle Gonzales and his crummy old sewage farm.

And maybe two and a half million was just a drop in the bucket and it didn't much matter how you spent it. If so, I was keeping the right company this time.

Just then the plane gave a shiver and a lurch that always makes me think of headlines like Antique Gun Dealer Among Those Feared Lost. A stewardess came on the intercom asking us to please fasten seat belts since we had a reasonable chance of landing intact at Le Bourget in a few minutes.

THREE

WE SPLIT UP before the immigration desk, and I went and
dosed myself with a stiff cognac before going back into Customs
to pick up my bag. Carlos had vanished by then. I took the bus
into Les Invalides and a taxi on to the Montalembert.

It isn't the Prince de Galles but it's a pleasant enough hide-
out, and a lot nearer what I think is the centre of Paris than
the empty windy streets up by the Etoile. I gave my name and
passport and the desk clerk found me on his little list.

As the porter was picking up my over-size suitcase and finding it surprisingly light, the clerk added: 'Mam'selle Whitley
asked to be told when you arrived.' He had his hand on the
desk phone. 'Shall I do that?'

The name didn't mean anything to me (or did it? There was
a faint echo) but I've no prejudice against meeting unmarried
women in hotels, away from their families. In fact, it's my
favourite indoor sport.

I nodded. 'I'll be in my room.'

The room was just a room: comfortable-looking, slightly
old-fashioned. I didn't bounce on the bed or turn on the taps:
they should be okay in the Montalembert, and if they weren't
I wasn't going to draw attention to myself anyway. The only
odd thing was a large flat brown-paper package lying on the
middle of the bed.

I said: 'C'est pour moi?'

The porter shrugged, accepted two francs and left me alone
with it.

I knew what it was, of course: a picture. A bit over two foot
by three. Well, if it was on my bed . . . I started ripping off
the paper.

It was a painting of four old men sitting around a café table staring into their glasses, pulling on clay pipes and wondering what the hell to say next. Done in an easy, flat style in rather dull browns and blues and things. It was peaceful; the sort of painting you could hang on your wall and never notice any more than you'd notice the old boys if you were sharing the same café.

There was a sharp rap-rap on the door. I shoved the picture under the bed, shouted: 'Entrez!' and she entrezed.

She was almost my height; a round school-girlish face without much make-up, fluffy fair hair without much styling, unless not much styling was the style nowadays, and a bulky blue tweed suit with a black fur collar sticking up like an angry cat. You got the impression that her main interest in clothes was that they kept her warm.

I'd just started saying: 'Mam'selle Whitley, I presume?' when she saw the torn paper and said: 'Have you opened that?' A quiet American voice, presumably from the East Coast.

I shrugged. 'It was in my room. It could've been a late Christmas present.' I pulled the picture out and laid it on top of the bed.

She was looking at me with a sort of timid horror. 'But do you know how much that's worth?'

'Quite a bit, I'd guess. Cézanne, isn't it?' In the left-hand bottom corner there was a signature: P. Cézanne.

'We paid $550,000 for that.' She started nervously bundling it up again.

'Now, hold on a minute. If I'm smuggling that out to Zurich, and I suppose that's why it's here, I've got to get the frame off first. By the way, I'm Bert Kemp.'

'Elizabeth Whitley.' She held out her hand automatically; Americans don't do the smiling and nodding and shuffling that the British go in for before deciding you're worth a hand-shake. Her hand was small, neat, firm.

I said: 'I suppose you're one of the travelling experts.'

'Yes. I do the old masters.'

That made the name even more familiar. 'Wasn't your old man in this game, too?'

17

Wrong phrase, of course. She stiffened and said, a little coldly: 'Insofar as it's a game—yes. He was Benjamin Whitley at the National Gallery in Washington.'

I said soothingly: 'Thought I knew the name. I mean, he wrote a lot of books, didn't he?'

'Yes.' She turned back to the picture. 'Why do you want the frame off?'

'I mean, just look at it.' It was about three inches wide all round, and at least two inches thick. 'It'll more'n halve the weight and, without it, the picture'll go in my big case. And if the Customs do take a snoop, a frame makes a picture look more valuable. I can pass this off as something I knocked up myself in a wet weekend.'

She glanced at me, quickly and dubiously. 'With that signature?'

'Oh, I'll paint that over and sign it myself.'

'You'll do *what*?' The horror was a lot less timid.

I said: 'Just poster paints. I've got a kiddie's paintbox in my case. It washes off easy enough.'

She looked a little dazed. But hell, she ought to know *something* about the end of the art trade that doesn't get mentioned in the coffee-table books.

Then she shook her head slowly. 'Mr Kemp—'

'Bert, if we're going to be travelling around together.'

'Look—I'll be frank. I know it isn't your fault, but . . . but I just don't like your job. I wish we were doing all this entirely legally. And I didn't realize we had to take such risks with the pictures.'

I shrugged. 'I'm a necessary evil, you might say. I mean, I help make pictures more mobile. More people get to see them. I sort of help spread culture all over the world. Rather noble, really.'

She was looking at me, quite without expression. It was a good face for that: I mean, it couldn't do very much in the way of extreme expressions anyway. It just went on looking gentle and hopeful, like a new kitten.

'Anyway,' I added, 'we aren't taking any risks getting the frame off.'

'Do you know a lot about art?'

'Me?—not a bloody thing. But I know a bit about framing and things. I mean, that's part of my job.'

'Well . . .' She looked back at the picture. 'I'll take the frame off myself, if you don't mind.'

'Go ahead.' I gave her the double-ended flintlock screwdriver I carried for poking at old guns. 'I didn't know Cézanne counted as an old master.'

'He doesn't. I didn't find this; Henri Bernard did. He handles the Impressionists and moderns, but he's gone to Amsterdam.' She stopped yanking at the nails and turned the picture over again and looked at it. 'I still don't think if the Customs see this they'll think you painted it.'

'Why not? Customs men aren't art experts—they don't have to be. Art smuggling's pretty rare; I'm the only professional, far as I know. And this one doesn't look much. I mean not half a million dollars-worth.'

'I thought you said you didn't know anything about art.'

'I'm giving you the layman's view. Customs officers' view. *Real* art's a big fat naked bird sitting around a landscape and not minding the thorns in her bottom.'

She started pulling nails again, and said, maybe a little bitterly: 'You're going to get on well with our employer. That's about her view—only she'd like a couple of galleons firing their guns in one corner and the Imperial Guard fighting Waterloo in the other.'

'She's strictly tits and cannon school, is she?' I thought it over. 'Well, I know a bloke who can paint that stuff. I mean, he can really age it, too. Then all you need to do is swear it's a Titian or Goya or something and we'll all die rich.'

She was looking at me as if I'd turned into the Mad Monster of the Montalembert. 'Are you really *serious*?'

I shrugged. 'Just talking. But I do actually know him. When do I get to meet the Boss Lady, anyway?'

'Oh yes. Sorry—Carlos asked me to tell you: they want us to be on the steps of St Sulpice—d'you know it?—at three o'clock and they'll pick us up in a big black car.' She lifted the whole frame gently clear and stood up. 'It's all a bit like something out of a bad spy movie.' She glanced at me and almost said 'So you'll love it' but didn't have the courage, or maybe bad manners. Then she just nodded and hurried out.

I had forty minutes; St Sulpice was about ten minutes' walk away. So I unpacked my duty-free bottle of Teacher's, had a short reviver, scattered a few clothes and things around, then started picking the framing pins off my bed.

Which left me with a big fancy frame. Not worth much, but too much just to dump in a hotel bedroom without starting suspicions. In the end I kicked and pulled it to pieces, wrapped it up in the brown paper and then sat there sucking splinters out of my fingers until it was time to go out into the cold. I assumed Miss Whitley would find her own way, and prefer to.

FOUR

I STARTED FREEZING TO DEATH on the steps of St Sulpice
Church just before three. It isn't exactly the swinging centre of
Paris; the square was empty of everything except a lot of
parked cars, shops selling crucifixes and Madonnas and priests'
robes, and occasional pairs of clerics hurrying along holding
on to their hats.

Miss Whitley was late, but the car was later.

I said: 'Cold.'

She said: 'Yes.' She'd added a long and rather shapeless
black coat with the black fur of her suit collar half in and half
outside.

I said: 'Used to be a toy shop over on that corner. Sold some
rather good toy soldiers.'

'Oh yes?'

After my body temperature had dropped a few more degrees,
I said: 'It *is* a bit like a movie, isn't it? I mean, two lonely figures
waiting on the long steps. Long black car draws up. Back
window rolls down slowly. Edward G. Robinson pokes out a
tommy-gun. Rat-tat-tat. Two figures roll dramatically down
the steps. Car zooms away. Priests rush out of church, throw
up their hands in horror, hurry down to administer Last Rights.
Too late. One says to the other: "Ye'd best get on to Captain
Brannigan down at th' station house".'

'In an Irish accent?'

'Of course.'

She nodded. 'In case you hadn't noticed, the car's been
there the last half minute.'

It had, too: a big Mercedes 600. We scuttled down the
steps and piled in.

I said: 'You forgot the tommy-gun.'

Carlos looked blank. 'I did what?'

'Skip it.'

It was a long car, and roomy, even with me parked as bloody usual on the fold-down seat just behind the chauffeur's glass panel. The other three got the back seat, and plenty of room with it. We glided away, smooth as a bobsled, and I took a good look at my employer for the next month.

She was small, with neat strong features and a deep-tanned skin that didn't look very smooth but on her looked right. Like a statue done in a rough-finished style, maybe. Her hair was et black except for two sweeps of silver, not grey, but pure silver, like magpie wings over her ears. Cut fairly short and curly. Small pearl earrings.

She wasn't hiding her age—she must've been fifty or near that—but she wasn't giving in to it, neither. To me she looked pretty good. I mean, she'd got class. She'd certainly got cash; everything except her face was wrapped up in a coat that must've left half the leopards in Africa shivering in the wind.

Carlos said: 'Dona Margarita—this is Mr Gilbert Kemp. Dona Margarita Umberto.'

She leant forward a little and so did I and we shook hands. Her hand was strong, a little rough, no rings. All those years of whanging a tennis racket around, maybe.

'Delighted to meet you, Senor Kemp.' Quiet, confident voice; just about no accent.

I said: 'Well, here I am. I've met the whatsit back at the hotel—the Cézanne, wasn't it? When d'you want me to haul it out?'

Carlos and Dona Margarita glanced at each other. Then he said: 'Any time ye've a mind to, Mr Kemp.'

'Well—anything else you want me to take as well?'

She said: 'I think no. The only other picture we have acquired in Paris is somewhat large. A rather fine battle scene by—' she turned to Miss Whitley, huddling into the other corner and looking a bit like a damp alley cat alongside that piece of fireside leopard.

Miss Whitley sighed. 'Vernet. Horace Vernet.'

'Of course. Perhaps you know him, Senor Kemp? Napoleonic times—many soldiers, much cannon smoke, the generals on horses.'

'I know the size you mean. You aren't trying to get *that* out of the country without a licence?'

Dona Margarita smiled: a quick vivid white flash, with a touch of gold at the corners. 'No—we assumed that a picture more than three metres by two metres might defeat even you. So we have applied for permission to export; Senorita Whitley believes there should be no problem. So you need worry only about the—the Cézanne.'

Miss Whitley sighed again.

'Fine,' I said. By now the car was turning on to the bridge across to the Place de la Concorde, the driver moving easily in smooth bursts of accleration. Paris driving isn't the best-tempered in the world at any time; with the cold wind and fairly empty streets everybody else seemed to be driving in a blind rage and I do mean blind. But our boy was good.

Dona M caught the thought, or the look on my face. 'When a French chauffeur is good he is the best in the world. In Italy I drive for myself. In Belgium I much prefer the trains.'

I grinned. 'So how's the team done so far? Been anywhere except London or Paris?'

'We bought some pleasant things in New York before going to London. Nothing that is much important—so Senorita Whitley tells me—but I admit I like them.'

'Van der Velde sailing-ships,' said Miss Whitley. From her lack of expression I got the idea she didn't go a bundle on sailing-ships.

I said: 'Nothing wrong with a touch of the old Hornblowers. So you've had no—er, export problems until now?'

Carlos said: 'The London and New York stuff's been shipped direct. We're only starting to build up in Zurich now.'

'Okay.' I looked out of the window. Now we were starting up the great cold sweep of the Champs Elysées, except that you don't get a sweep, you get a series of stops and starts at the traffic lights all the way. 'Who've you been dealing with?' I asked.

Carlos said: 'Everybody, anybody wherever Miss Whitley or Monsieur Bernard think there'll be something to look at.'

'Yes, but who? Specifically?'

Miss Whitley said: 'I thought you didn't know anything about art.'

'I'm not talking about art, I'm talking about dealers. I mean, some gab a lot more than others. If they spread the word about your mission then my job's going to get tougher.'

'Well—' she glanced at Dona Margarita '—well, in New York I saw Burroughs and Brague . . .'

I said: 'Oh God.'

She looked at me almost sympathetically and gave a slight nod. 'I know, but they do have a lot of stuff. They're big.'

'So's Hell, I hear.' Harry Burroughs and Mitchell Brague were the sort of dealers who'd steal the tattoo off your chest, sign it Rembrandt and sell it in Texas for a million dollars. There was a story that they'd got started in the art business when they were in the American Army at the end of the war and had liberated a lorry-load of stolen paintings.

But I didn't believe it. I mean, what happened to the lorry? B and B would have gone into the trucking business as well.

'Well, you certainly went in at the deep end.' Then I thought of something. 'Still, if Harry and Mitch know what's happening, they aren't going to spread it around. They wouldn't share a sucker with anybody else. They've got offices in Paris and Rome, too, so they could be hoping for a second bite at the caviare. You've actually got some of that two and a half million left?'

Dona Margarita smiled gently. 'We actually have. Despite a small purchase at Burroughs and Brague.'

We were almost at the Arc de Triomphe itself. Carlos leant forward and opened the glass partition and said something fast and French. The driver gave a small polite nod.

Carlos sat back: 'When will ye be leaving for Zurich, Mr Kemp?'

'Are you through in Paris?'

'Aye, we're pressing on to Amsterdam tonight. Monsieur Bernard's there already.'

'All right. If there's nothing more to take, why don't I go today? I mean, there's usually a train about five o'clock. A Trans-European Express. I should get a seat, this time of year.'

Carlos and Dona Margarita looked at each other. Then she said: 'Indeed, why not? Carlos can arrange your hotel and the other things.'

'I may as well fix my own hotel. If we're staying separate, let's keep it that way. But I won't get in till nearly midnight. Can I get the thing into the bank then? I don't like the idea of sitting up in a hotel room with a picture that expensive all night.'

Carlos nodded slowly. 'Aye, I can arrange that.'

'Give me a ring at the hotel before I go. Before four-thirty. Tell me the arrangements. Oh—and taking a Cézanne out of France costs two hundred quid—right?'

Dona Margarita frowned and glanced at Carlos.

I said: 'He agreed on a rate for each job.'

Miss Whitley asked: 'And that's the rate laid down by the Institute of Art Smugglers?'

'Yes. I just happen to be the President.'

Dona Margarita said: 'Very well, Senor. But why are you not going by aeroplane?'

Because I don't bloody trust aeroplanes, that's why. 'Because they sling your baggage around on aeroplanes. Or send it to Hong Kong instead. On a train you can look after it yourself.'

'Ah yes.' She nodded, agreeing.

The car was circling the Arc itself, for the second time. Carlos asked quietly: 'Are you carrying a gun, Mr Kemp?'

Maybe I'd been half expecting the question, so I was half ready with the answer. 'Would you want me to?'

Dona Margarita smiled. 'That wasn't what Carlos asked.'

'So put it another way: if I was, would you want to know?'

'I think we had better. However separate we may be, in the end I am responsible.'

'No gun.'

Carlos said: 'Is that a question of principle, Mr Kemp?'

I shrugged. 'Of a sort. I've no basic objection to popping

off pistols at people, not if they seem to need it. But if you're in a hurry, and you usually are, there's always a chance you'll kill him. After that, things get complicated—particularly if you've got a Cézanne wrapped up in your last week's underwear.'

The women looked a little pained at the talk about underwear. Or maybe, come to think of it, at the idea I only changed my pants once a week.

Carlos glanced at Dona Margarita. 'Well, it's too late to do anything about it for this trip, Senora.'

'Yes. But perhaps we can think about it again, before next time.'

Well, perhaps. An unlicensed painting is one thing; an unlicensed pistol is something very much other. But that was next time. I just nodded.

They dropped me off on the corner by the metro station. The time was just on three-thirty.

FIVE

I TOLD THE DESK I'd be leaving without spending the night and they regretted it politely. They further regretted that I'd have to pay for the night anyhow. I regretted it, too, although I'd expected it and had been going to claim it off Carlos whatever.

I spent the next half-hour re-signing the Cézanne. Luckily he'd used a simple flat grey-brown in that corner, so once I'd mixed a poster colour to match, it was easy. Some of the older school write their signatures—when they write them at all—over fancy bits of leafery; that can be hell. I propped it up on the radiator to dry (you don't do that with an old master, neither) and sat back on the bed and admired it. The signature, I mean: a nice flowing Bert Kemp in a tasteful dark blue, rather more stylish than the original black P. Cézanne had used.

I still wasn't crazy about that picture.

By four o'clock I had packed everything else and was touching up the signature with a woman's hair-spray to match the sheen of the varnish. A beautiful job, even if I said so myself.

But still no message.

I took a nibble at the whisky while waiting for the spray to dry, then wrapped the thing in my pyjamas and packed it.

By twenty past four I was getting worried. I rang the desk: no message. So I rang the Prince de Galles and asked for Carlos. And the hotel much regretted but—the bastards had checked out.

After a moment of trying to swallow this, I asked: 'Amsterdam?' And they said yes, the Doelen Hotel.

I said thank you, rang off, and asked the desk downstairs to put me through to Miss Whitley. And they regretted but . . .

Sweet Jesus, what were these clowns trying to *do*? Rushing

27

off to Amsterdam leaving me to hump a £200,000 picture into Zurich at midnight and no idea of whether the bank was going to be there to meet me? By now I was beginning to work up a sweat. A Customs officer would only have to glance at me and I'd go white-faced and grey-haired. Hell, I was white-faced and pretty much grey-haired already. I was too old for all this —forty-four (or was it forty-five? Old enough to start forgetting anyway). I was slipping.

No, damn it, I *wasn't* slipping. I'd just never worked before for a silly bitch who didn't know her art from her tennis elbow. I ought to dump the Cézanne in the left-luggage and send her my resignation along with the ticket.

And go home and pay my own income tax?

I was going to Zurich. And it was time to start going.

The train wasn't crowded, but I hadn't expected it to be: I'd got my seat—a choice of seats—too easily for that. But it was family night, people going home from long Christmases or New Years in Paris, and with plenty of luggage. I wanted my case on the rack at the end of the coach; smugglers don't usually leave valuable goods out of sight, which is why I wanted to.

Twenty minutes before we pulled out, I was lucky to find luggage space; the family after me had to hump their goods and chattels down to their seats. It was a clean, bright green-and-cream coach with none of the flavour of the Great Trains. They're all gone, now, anyway. I walked into the dining car —just next door—and booked for the second sitting, at eight-fifteen. Then back to sit down with a small cigar and a copy of *The Times* and trying to look like an English milord.

The four-year-old girl with the family across the aisle didn't like my cigar, which showed remarkable taste in one so young. I thought of trying to explain—in four-year-old French—that by this time tomorrow I'd be in Amsterdam, where cigars really were cigars, but decided not. Let her suffer. She shouldn't be up this late anyway.

We pulled out at five-thirty on the dot, and started through the usual gangster-movie setting of half-demolished buildings and half-lit shunting yards you find behind any Paris station.

I wanted a drink. The jitters were back; I was committed. First stop was Basle—across the frontier. It was too late to change my mind now.

Damn it! I was an English milord travelling (first class) to see a chap about a spot of investment in Zurich. I turned to the business section and started reading why Britain suddenly was, or suddenly wasn't, in an economic crisis again. Then caught the eye of the four-year-old; *she* didn't believe in me. She thought I was a cheap crook smoking a roll of plastic oak leaves. That made two of us.

I needed a drink.

I managed to hold out until nearly seven, when we were slowing down through Troyes, then went forward to the dining car. If I'd wanted to make myself conspicuous, I'd done it now: I was the only one taking just a drink in among the six-thirty dinner.

But a big Scotch and the hell with the expense helped. The jumpy feeling began to fade. Not entirely: it was still a job with too many loose ends, but I was still a professional. I'd manage.

We rolled on. Through Chaumont at seven-forty, then at eight they decided to call the second sitting, so I just sat on. Why do they always give you four second-rate courses on trains instead of two good ones? Even French trains? Still, it all helped. Soon after nine I strolled back to my seat feeling far more milordly and smoking another cigar and the hell with my young friend, too. But she was asleep, of course.

After that, I must just about have fallen asleep myself. A small loudspeaker I hadn't noticed before announced we would reach Basle in *quelques minutes*, and I found it was five to ten. A moment later we stopped, and before I was properly awake the Customs were among us.

Two of them: one French, one Swiss, moving in that order. Neat, unobtrusive—you'd hardly notice them if they weren't part of your profession. You give your passport to the French one, he says: 'Rien à déclarer?' and you nod and say: 'Rien,' and he stamps it and hands it back. Two seconds later you give it to the Swiss, and declare a few cigars and a *demi-bouteille de*

Scotch. He nods at your airline bag, stamps your passport, hands it back.

It was that easy. Except that they were moving up towards the luggage racks. If they spotted anything there . . .

They didn't. It *was* that easy. We pulled into Basle station itself five minutes later. I was clear, and two hundred quid richer—almost. Now all I had to worry about was if the bank knew I was coming . . .

SIX

I DIDN'T WANT TO WAKE UP; I knew it would be worse when I did. I just wanted to lie there and let the little birds come and cover me up with leaves. And if they did it with earth and a tombstone, that suited me. Dead, I might have the same headache, but I could never be so cold.

After a time, I reached to pull up the blankets. And they felt gritty and crumbly and *Dear God, I've got the DT's!* That woke me—and it was worse, all right. I clenched my eyes to keep out the things that would be crawling up my stomach. But in the darkness they glowed even brighter. I opened my eyes; that hurt, too.

It was still dark. Slowly, very slowly, I lifted my hand up to my face and opened it. Gravel trickled out and spilled down my chin.

And that really woke me. I lifted my head.

For a moment I thought it had exploded. Then I realized I'd clouted it on something. Again. I made an effort and rolled sideways, and saw the stars above me.

I'd been lying under a wooden park bench. An area of gravel. A few bare spiky trees outlined against the sky. A few dim yellow street lamps. A low wall a few yards away.

On the feet—hup! Who, me? Yes, you, Kemp; something's wrong. Get on your feet, man. No, try somebody else, will you? You, Kemp, *you!* Well—could we start by just sitting, on the bench?

My head started a fireworks display and I suddenly remembered I had a stomach, too, but I got onto the bench. And then time passed, the way it does when you know you're going to be sick and you're trying to think of all the beautiful quiet cool things in life instead. Tall summer pines, and Christmas

31

card snow scenes, and the Brescian metalwork on Italian antique pistols and a yellow-green dry martini . . .

The martini did it. I reached the wall in three long steps and lost my Trans-European Express dinner down a forty-foot drop into long grass and dry trees below. But it cleared my head as well as my stomach. I now knew where I was: on top of the Lindenhof, one of those Walt Disney bits of the old town— steep, narrow cobbled streets and tall bent houses—that you find just a few yards off the modern main streets. I was staring out down to the river and the neon lights of the Limmat Quai beyond. Maybe ten minutes' walk from the station.

But what in hell had happened? Well, somebody had thumped me; that was clear enough. I did some careful exploring with my fingertips and found a sticky welt over my right ear and a bump like a burial mound just on my hairline in front.

Christ—the Cézanne.

I looked around—and there were my bags, stacked neatly at the end of the bench. The locks hadn't been forced. I found the key, opened the big case . . . And they'd found my key, too. I sat down and began to feel very old.

But ten minutes later I was down on the Urinanstrasse looking for a cruising taxi. It took me another ten minutes to find one, and then he didn't go a bundle on my condition: if he took me anywhere, he'd have preferred the police station. Damned law-abiding little city. But I kept mumbling 'Hotel Butterfly' and 'Doktor' and finally he gave in.

The hotel was a bit shook, too. But they got me a large Scotch and a doctor. The doctor was a neat, fussy little man with quick impersonal fingers and no belief at all that I'd been clouted by a passing car. He'd seen cosh wounds before, even in Zurich. But all he did was bandage my head, put a plaster on my cheek, and take cash payment. At least, that's all I thought he'd done.

When he'd gone I picked up the phone and asked them to get me the Doelen in Amsterdam. I'd better get the confession over and done with.

After some time—it was nearly one o'clock by now—I got through to Carlos.

'I'm in Zurich,' I said carefully, 'and I've had **an accident.**'
Pause.

Then: 'Just how serious d'ye mean?' On the phone he sounded even more Scottish.

'We've lost . . . the contract, I'm afraid. I'm sorry.'

'Aye, and so am I. How the devil did ye' manage it?'

'Look, I got a bit concussed. I just don't know. What about the police?'

'Have ye told them?'—sharply.

'No, but—'

'Ye'd better not, then.'

'They might know anyhow. I mean, there's several people know I've been in trouble. They could talk.'

'Then ye'll say nothing.'

'I can't give . . . our employer's name as a reference?'

'Ye canna!'

'Thanks.' I was on my own. And how.

'Ye'll be here tomorrow and explain?'

'Yes, all right.' And back selling guns by tomorrow evening. Oh well. It had to happen sometime.

He'd rung off. I lay back on the bed and closed my eyes. My head was full of a dull pain like toothache in the brain, with sharp jabs every time I moved my head. And that bastard of a doctor had taken one look at my whisky and refused me any sleeping pills.

So the next thing had to be a knock on the door, a sharp double rap that means business.

I called: 'Yes?'

'Kriminalpolizei.'

I got carefully off the bed and opened up.

He was a middle-sized man with square shoulders, narrow hips, and a face cut in square planes like a bit of Swiss wood-carving. Neat dark hair, a grey double-breasted raincoat that he kept buttoned the whole time. And about my own age.

He waved a card that might have been a dog licence for all I could see, said: 'Polizeileutnant Lindemann,' and sat down without being asked. I lay back on the bed.

He took out a notebook, turned the pages, read something, glanced at me, back again to the notebook. 'Sprechen Sie Deutsch?'

'No.'

'So,' He started reading aloud. 'You have the . . . cut—over the right ear, yes? And the bruise on the front head, yes? With some concussion but no . . . breaking, and no permanent brain damage, yes?'

'How the hell do I know?' But I knew that doctor had reported me all right.

'And it was taking place in a car accident, yes?'

'I don't know.'

His eyebrows jerked up the regulation amount to express official surprise. 'You do not know?'

'I can't remember. I found myself lying in the street. I assume a car knocked me down.'

'You did not get the number?'

I just looked at him.

He coughed in his throat and looked back at his notebook. 'What time was this?'

'I don't know. I got here just after midnight.'

'But your train had arrived from Paris at eleven-fourteen— yes?'

'Yes.' I'd been out, or waking up, for just about half an hour.

He leant slightly forward, got slightly more serious. 'Had you thought it—you might have been assaulted?'

I waved a hand. 'For what? There's my luggage. Here's my wallet—' I tossed it to him '—for what?'

Whoever they were, they'd been professionals. It would have been easier to pinch the whole suitcase—but then I could never have spun a story about a car accident. They'd only taken the one thing I shouldn't have anyway. They'd given me a problem by dumping me on the Lindenhof, but they could hardly take the risk of dropping me on one of the main streets, could they? I might have been picked up before I woke, babbling of green fields and Cézannes.

They were professionals. I'd like to meet them again. With

a Colt .45 in my hand I'd like to meet them. It would be a pleasure.

He was giving me a piercing stare. 'Can you account for the difference in time? I do not think you lay unobserved in a main street for half an hour?'

I shrugged as best I could while lying flat on my back. 'Maybe I had a cup of coffee in the station. Or made a couple of phone calls. I just can't remember.'

He stared at my middle. 'If you were dead, we could prove the coffee by analysing your stomach content.'

'Hard luck.'

He nodded, agreeing. 'Herr Kemp—what did you come to Zurich for?'

'To see a man at the National Bank.'

That was the password, all right. He gave me a quick glance, and I could see him picking the next question carefully. You walk carefully on a Swiss bank, even if you're Kriminalpolizei.

'About what business?' he asked, a shade too casually.

'Ask the National Bank.' And they'll tell you to go jump off an Alp.

'I believe you made a telephone message to Amsterdam. It was to who?'

'The man whose business I was seeing the National Bank about.'

He took a deep breath. 'And you talked about what?'

'The business with the National Bank.'

He stood up, looked down at me. 'Herr Kemp, we are not progressing.'

'I didn't know we were supposed to be going anywhere. I didn't even know being knocked down by a car was a criminal offence in Zurich.'

'You do not know it was a car.'

'That's right. It might have been a taxi. Or a lorry. Or an avalanche. Or one of the bears escaped from the Berne zoo and hitched a ride over here and . . .' Careful, Kemp. Maybe there *was* some brain damage. Or maybe I was just feeling old and battered and tired of cops.

He said slowly and carefully: 'I do not think it was a car, or a bear. I think you were attacked. It troubles me that you were not also robbed. You understand me?'

I understood: he thought I was bringing a touch of personal vendetta, gang warfare, into his fair city. Maybe I ought to spring up and cry: 'No, no, Herr Polizeileutnant, I'm not that sort of crook—I'm a different sort of crook.'

I shut my eyes and gave a very small nod; even that hurt.

He said: 'You will be leaving Zurich tomorrow.' And it wasn't a question.

SEVEN

IT WAS A LONG, BAD NIGHT, full of pain and dreams like the chucked-away bits of a horror film stitched together in any old order. I was on a motor-bike and it bounced on a bump and flew and I knew I could keep it flying if I had faith, only I didn't, and . . . there was a long black car that became a train in the night . . . there was the man I'd once killed and whose face I could never remember or forget . . . and I was a diver fighting an octopus . . . it had bad breath . . .

Not a good night. But in the morning the pain was just an ache: I was ready to go and make my excuses in Amsterdam.

The hotel was polite enough, but when I suggested they might help book me a flight to Amsterdam they practically offered to carry me out there in their arms and make sure I got a seat. Anyway, by half past ten I was buying a magazine at the top of the steps down to the final departure lounge.

A gentle American voice said: 'Well, hello there, Gil.'

A slight, middle-aged man in a slim unbelted raincoat; greying hair swept back very neatly, rimless spectacles and an expression that was a permanent shy smile. Once you'd noticed him, he was very obviously not just an American but a New Yorker—but you'd hardly notice him. He was just one of the extras you'd hire for an airport scene.

Meet Harry Burroughs, fine art dealer and even finer crook.

I said: 'Hello, Harry. Stolen any good pictures lately?'

He smiled apologetically; he always did. 'Why, no. Have you lost any?'

'Few, here and there.'

'That's too bad.' We fell into step going down the stairs. 'Who are you working for?'

'Myself. I'm an antique-gun dealer—remember?'

'Oh yes. Now I recall. Have you bought any good guns lately?'

'Few, here and there. What are you doing in Zurich?'

'Why, Mitch or I always come over at this time, just to see how things are going.'

And see who's in tax trouble and having to sell off his collection cheap. *In Zurich?* In Zurich nobody has tax troubles.

'Where are you off to now?' I asked.

He stopped, felt in an inside pocket and took out an airline ticket, then consulted it. 'Amsterdam.'

'We can share a seat.'

His smile got even more apologetic. 'Are you going first class, then, Gil?'

He smiled a last time, then nodded in embarrassment, and sort of just drifted away.

A careful type, Harry. He knew that every word might be taken down and used in evidence, and he wasn't providing much evidence. But he'd made a mistake. It cheered me up a little.

Amsterdam was cold, with a dampness in the air like a drowned hand. I rang the Doelen from the town terminal and Carlos told me to get down to a restaurant on the Nieuwe Zijds Voorburgwal and not stop off to look at any tulip field en route.

When I got there I remembered it: the middle-class Amsterdam businessman's favourite lunch joint, where he can show how good business is by wrapping himself around enough calories to feed a starving antique-gun dealer for a week. For a secret meeting, it was good: a big, echoing place seating about three hundred, and all talking or eating at the top of their voices. You'd need a camera that could see through a fogbank of cigar smoke and a microphone planted in the soup itself before you could pick up anything.

It took me some time to find them; they'd managed a table in the far corner. And they'd assembled the full court-martial: Dona Margarita, Carlos, Miss Whitley and a small man with very black curly hair, just turning grey, a very serious pale face and thick lips and glasses.

I dumped my coat and called: 'Monsieur Henri Bernard, je crois?'

He looked up from a gallon-sized helping of pea soup and said: 'Oui.'

'Je suis Bert Kemp.'

'Oui.' And he went back to shovelling soup. Serious type. Or maybe he was just trying to finish his soup before closing-time.

I sat down next to Dona Margarita, who'd tactfully kept her back to the room, and smiled across at Miss Whitley. I got a long cold look by return.

Dona Margarita gave me a brief smile and said: 'We understand you had trouble?'

'Let's say it had me.'

'Will you explain what happened?'

I started to shake my head, winced, and said: 'No. Sorry. I can't remember.'

Even Henri paused to stare at me. I was definitely on the transfer list.

Perfectly polite, she said: 'I do not understand that.'

I tapped my bandaged head. 'Somebody thumped me I was out for maybe half an hour and can't remember for a while before that. I mean, I can't even remember getting out of the train.'

Carlos said thoughtfully. 'Ye're claiming amnesia, are ye? What did the doctor say?'

I shrugged. 'I didn't ask him that. I mean, I *know* I can't remember. He couldn't tell me anything more.'

He looked dour. 'Did ye get in touch with the bank?'

'No, of course I didn't. But did you?'

'I warned them to expect ye, just before midnight. They'd be waiting.'

'At the bank? They should've been at the station. I mean . . .'

Just then a waiter arrived and I yelled an order for *russiche eieren*—Russian eggs. It doesn't sound much, but it comes

39

up a salad the size of the Garden of Eden. Could even be a snake in it, for all I know.

Dona Margarita said: 'You were saying, Senor?'

'Yes—oh hell. I should have told you what I wanted. What to fix. Next time I will.'

Carlos said heavily: 'If there is a next time.'

'Well—is there?'

Dona Margarita said: 'That is Managua's decision.'

I still didn't get this 'Managua' angle, but let it lay.

Miss Whitley asked: 'What will happen now, d'you think?'

'They'll be in touch—whoever *they* are. I mean they're not going to try and sell a picture like that, or just keep it. It'll be a ransom job. Cost you about another twenty per cent.'

Carlos asked calmly: 'Ye couldna have arranged the whole thing yeself?'

I kicked back my chair and stood up, getting a twinge in my head. 'And bashed my own bloody head in, I suppose?' Well, yes, actually. I mean, for twenty per cent of two hundred thousand pounds, it'd be worth it, wouldn't it?

Just then the waiter arrived with my plate and stood there, looking at me with impatient patience. So I sat down again and he slammed the salad in front of me.

Miss Whitley said: 'You didn't answer the question.'

Dear little girl. Bitch. 'I wish I'd thought of it.' I ate a Russian egg, or something, then said with my mouth full: 'But you had a security leak anyway, you know? I mean they didn't just thump me on the chance I was carrying a good picture. That'd be just too lucky. And I'll tell you another thing: Harry Burroughs was in Zurich. And he came here on the same flight as me.'

That stirred them up a bit. Henri jerked his head and almost shoved a spoonful of Erwtensoep up his nose.

'Ye met him?' Carlos asked.

'At the airport there. He didn't say much.'

Miss Whitley said: 'He's always in Europe, him or Mitch.'

'I know. But he made a mistake: he didn't ask what happened to my head.'

It took a moment, but they got the point in the end: I was

wearing a bandage like an apprentice turban and a wide strip of sticking plaster on my cheek.

'Implying,' Miss Whitley said slowly, 'that he already knew. But Harry doesn't go around assaulting people. He doesn't have to.'

Henri said flatly: '*Illogique*. Arri Burroughs could do anything that is possible.'

I said: 'He could hire people.'

Carlos said: 'So could yeself.'

'And has your mother found out who your father was, yet?'

His face went very white under his copper hair. Well, it was about time *I* hurt somebody. 'We have to consider the possibility.'

'Well, start considering the possibility I'll kick your arse through your—'

'Ye mind your language in front of Dona Margarita!' he shouted.

But she didn't seem bothered; she just said soothingly: 'Please—this is not the time for becoming angry.'

But by then I'd had enough—of them, Russian eggs, everything. I stood up again. 'All right—do I book a plane or a hotel?'

Carlos went slowly off the boil. 'Park Hotel,' he muttered. 'It's up by the Rijksmuseum, on—'

'I know,' I said, just for the pleasure of interrupting him. The taxi driver would know, anyway. 'Do I have the court's permission to leave the box?'

They all just looked at me. So I picked up my overcoat and got the hell out. Bastards, one and all. Anyway, now they'd have to pay for my lunch.

EIGHT

THE PARK IS—as Carlos said—up near the Rijksmuseum, the big public gallery of old masters, about half a mile from what I reckon is the centre of Amsterdam. A good quiet hotel, nothing flashy, no popular singers signing autographs on your shirt.

I booked in, and flopped onto the bed in a small old-fashioned room and tried to sleep. But no. My head still hurt whenever I wasn't thinking hard, and the sort of thinking I was doing hurt just as much.

After half an hour I sat up, reached for the phone, and asked for the Hilton Hotel.

And it was that simple. I asked for Mr Burroughs, waited until I heard the room phone ring, then cut off. Now I knew where he was. I'd been ready to ask for him in a dozen hotels in Amsterdam—but I hadn't expected to need to, not unless Harry was living well below his income.

Just knowing where he was didn't mean a thing, of course. Probably he'd've told me at the airport, if I'd asked him. Still, it made me feel that little bit better.

And then what? Amsterdam's one of my favourite cities, but it wasn't the time of the year to stroll along the canals watching them haul out the cars that have slid in. Forty florins a time, it costs you. You have to park carefully in Amsterdam.

In the end I went downstairs, drank the beer that I'd forgotten to order at lunch, and then walked quickly across to the Rijksmuseum. It doesn't have anything in my line, just paintings and Delft pottery and stuff, but art galleries have to be kept warm or all the pictures would get frostbite or something.

The inside layout is a one-way system leading up to their pride and joy: Rembrandt. There was hardly anybody else around, so I just strolled, stopping off to stare at an occasional landscape or seascape that nobody but a Dutchman would have thought worth painting at all, let alone so carefully.

And finally I got to the holy place itself: a big room with plenty of concealed lighting and just three huge pictures. But the four benches are arranged so that you sit and stare at just one: Rembrandt's 'Night Watch.' By then you want to rest your feet anyhow, so I sat down and gave it a spot of devotion. Actually, I quite like it; at least something's happening in it, even if I can't make out what.

I'd almost dozed off when somebody plumped down beside me. I gave whoever a nasty look—there were two other benches quite empty—and found it was Miss Elizabeth Whitley, art expert.

'I didn't know you had a secret passion for Rembrandt,' she said. 'Or are you just working out how you'd get *that* into a suitcase?'

The thing's only about eleven feet by thirteen.

'Just resting my feet,' I said.

'I'll bet they have all sorts of statistics about how popular that picture is—all because it's the only place you can sit down.'

'You don't like it?' I asked.

'It's all right. Not his best, but it's got something. Heck, it's got everything; that's its trouble.'

It's a dark picture of a mob of characters in cavalier dress barging out of an archway and waving pikes and a flag and a couple of guns and a chap beating a drum and a dog and a small girl in party dress . . . I saw what she meant.

'I suppose it's a bit Cecil B. de Mille,' I said. 'But I like the guns.'

'The . . . ? Oh, I suppose you would.'

'They're matchlocks, see that?'

'What?'

I pointed. 'See the loop of cord hanging down by the trigger? That's the match. Slow fuse. You lit it, stuck the burning end into . . . well, what we'd call the hammer these days, then pulled the trigger and it slammed down into the firing pan. Like sticking a . . . well, a match into your charge.'

43

'Really? Did it work?'

'Well, if you chose a fine day for the battle. And remembered to light your match first. It was the first type of hand-gun ever made; that's the interesting thing. When was this painted?'

'Sixteen-forty-something.'

'Yes. They'd had wheel-locks—the first flint guns—more than a hundred years by then. And the Dutch themselves had invented a better version, the snaphaunce, before 1600. Anyway, who'd go out on a night watch carrying a burning match to give 'em away?'

She gave me a small sideways smile, losing her chin in her collar. 'D'you know why it was called the "Nachtwacht"? Rembrandt didn't call it that. It was because it got so dark from tobacco smoke hanging in some officers' club all those years. He was hired to do a portrait of some regiment—all the officers chipped in money to have their faces in it. Then he did this. They hated it. But they owned it, so they hung it.'

I nodded—carefully. 'If it's military I see why they've got out-of-date weapons. I thought they were town burghers or something.'

For a while we just sat and looked at Amsterdam's officer class plus the little girl (the Colonel's daughter?). Then I remembered: 'D'you know what's all this Managua stuff they keep talking about?'

She seemed surprised. 'Managua's the capital of Nicaragua. That's where the collection will go.'

'I know, but why keep referring things back there?'

'They control the money. The Nicaragua government does.'

'They . . . ? But I thought it was the old girl's own cash.'

'Well, it is, but . . . I thought you knew all this.'

'Nobody tells me anything.' And *that* was the truth.

She frowned. 'Well—how much do you know about Nicaragua?'

'Damn little. Looked it up in an encyclopedia just before I came away. Sounds a sort of barefoot peasant sort of place. Not quite a swinging joint. I mean, it sounds like it could use a lot of things before an art gallery.'

She nodded. 'Well, that's what it's getting. Dona Margarita's

44

husband was a big landowner, an old-time family. They didn't have any children and he was the last of the line, so when he died she should have inherited the lot. Well, it seems that he was a Conservative and the government are Liberals—though I don't know what those labels mean down there. Anyway, they stepped in and sort of nationalized the land. That's where all the money comes from.'

'They paid her compensation?'

'Yes, in a way. She can spend it how she likes—as long as she spends it in Nicaragua. That's why she hasn't left the place in ten years.'

I sat and admired the scheme. There wouldn't be much to lash out your money on in Nicaragua, not once you'd got a couple of fancy houses and a new car and a few servants. And meanwhile they'd got your lands *and* the use of most of your cash. And all probably as legal as breathing. Hell, British governments have done as much.

I asked: 'So, what happened?'

'She finally talked them into letting her spend most of it on this collection—provided she presents it to the nation. She told me privately—' then she stopped and looked at me. 'Can you keep this to yourself?'

I gave her the winning smile. 'Crooks can keep secrets better than anyone.'

She frowned, but decided to press on anyway. 'Well, she really wants to go into politics and—probably, I suppose—win back the lands. She thinks presenting an art collection to the people will give her a good start.'

I stared. 'She's *crazy*. An art gallery wouldn't give you a single vote in Europe, let alone some place where half the voters probably don't wear shoes. Why not build a power station or a sewage farm?—I'll bet they need them.'

She nodded. 'Maybe the government wouldn't let her do anything that'd be really effective politically. Anyway, *they* aren't crazy. They get the collection, and if it's good things at the right prices, it's a very good investment. After all, you couldn't sell off a power station or sewage plant if you wanted to raise a bit of capital, could you?' After a moment, she added:

'Perhaps an art museum's better than nothing. Anything's better than nothing, for a politician. In America we've elected people for getting wounded in the war—not winning it, just getting wounded. One politician got busted when it turned out his war wound had been getting hit in the face with a pop bottle.'

I grinned. 'Well, she must be mad keen on politics.'

'Perhaps you'd be—in a country where you can nationalize land worth seven million dollars.'

'Hey, that's an idea. Maybe I'll stick with her and then I can go in as Minister of Defence or something.'

She looked thoughtfully at Rembrandt. 'I wouldn't have thought your record of defending Nicaraguan property was exactly one hundred per cent. At least, not the right way round.'

I rallied bravely. 'At least I got wounded, didn't I?' I touched the bandage.

She looked at me—just looked. Not blankly, but not with any particular expression, either. Just her normal face, rather round, rather young, her eyes maybe a little older and wiser. I mean, it was rather disconcerting.

After a time, she said: '*Did* you steal that Cézanne?'

'I'm beginning to wish I had.'

'But you *are* a crook, aren't you?'

'Well, maybe yes—but not *that* sort of crook.'

'I'm sorry: I don't know the differences between different sorts of crooks.'

When I didn't explain the differences, she just nodded slightly and stood up. I trailed after; down to the lobby through a long, high gallery with pictures set around alcoves off it.

She stopped from time to time to look at a painting. She just looked, the same way she'd looked at me. Not going up and peering at the brush strokes and nodding her head wisely or smiling secretly, the way people look at paintings when they think people are looking at them. She just stood back and looked.

As we got near the end, I said: 'What are you doing in here? I thought you'd be looking at the stuff that's up for sale.'

'I dropped a hint at a few dealers this morning; I'll do the rest tomorrow. It takes a few days for the word to get around.

46

So I'm just getting my eye in; a refresher course in the Dutch school, you might say.'

That made sense. 'I suppose Managua insisted on you coming along to see they didn't get landed with a load of old toad?'

'I think they'd have needed Henri and me—or somebody—in any case.'

Another thought struck—a long time late, but perhaps I could blame that on my head, at least for today. 'I suppose Managua must've approved me, too.'

'I'd guess so.'

'So if I go or stay doesn't depend on the boss anyway.'

'I'd guess not.'

'I wonder how they'll take it.'

This time her voice got a little dry. 'I wonder.'

As we got outside it was about four o'clock, just beginning to get dark, and still with the damp, creepy wind. She hadn't heard of the Dutch tradition of drinking genever at that time of a winter afternoon, perhaps because I'd only just invented it, so we stood on the wide Stadhouderskade waiting for a taxi.

After a time, I said: 'Is he having it off with her, d'you think?'

'What?'

'Carlos and Dona Margarita. Are they having it off?'

She stared. 'I don't get—'

'Well, I mean he could be banging her like a big bass drum and I wouldn't know. But is he?'

She finally got what I meant just at the time that I realized she hadn't got it. But even she should have *heard* of it.

She went on staring. 'You sure have a way of putting things. I don't know—I doubt it. But it isn't our affair.'

'Well, she looks pretty normal to me. Not *that* old. I wouldn't mind a bit of a game, set and match with her myself. But I wanted to know what happens if I think it's time to call Carlos an anus-faced twit. I mean, do I get fired?'

She winced and started looking for taxis again. 'I should think Carlos could handle that sort of problem on his own.

47

And right now, that isn't the most likely reason for you getting fired.'

I nodded, a bit gloomily. 'I suppose so.'

After a couple more minutes of not getting a taxi, she asked: 'Why would you want to call him . . . an insult?'

'Well the man *is* a twit. I mean, he banjaxed that Zurich trip, whatever else I did.'

'I don't suppose he's very experienced about art smuggling.'

'I know damn well he isn't. But he came to me; I didn't ask for the job.'

She gave a small nod. 'Yes. Frankly, I'd rather the whole thing was done legally.'

'Managua, maybe. I mean maybe they're trying to save a dollar.'

She nodded again. 'Maybe.' Just then a taxi unloaded at the museum. I thought about sharing it, then decided she'd probably had enough Kemp for one day and left her to discover bargain old masters by herself.

NINE

WHICH LEFT ME standing in the wind in an area notoriously uncrowded with bars. So maybe it was time to go dragon-hunting. The Hilton was only a shortish walk, anyhow.

I hadn't been there before; partly because it's pretty new, partly because I don't drink at Hilton prices on my own funds. It's planted in a suburb of big houses such as belonged to the types we'd been lunching with or even richer. You walk in through a lobby and past a row of shops—I stopped to buy some serious small cigars—and then into the bar.

It's mostly brass and thick yellow leather; probably they got the idea from Van Gogh or Vermeer or somebody—Dutch painters use a lot of yellow, as I recall. But comfortable. Big curved sofas and a whacking great plate-glass window overlooking a quiet canal and the big houses on the other side.

Just after four was the quiet time before the tourists got back from buying brand-new antiques along the Nieuwe Spiegel-straat; the only other customers were one big well-dressed man drinking quietly and professionally at the bar and a couple of large flowery local ladies knocking it back in a corner by the window. I settled myself on a sofa.

A waiter wandered across and gave my bandage a thought-ful look.

I ordered a beer.

He shuffled an ashtray around and asked: 'You have had an accident, sir?'

'I got into a fight—' his face froze '—with a Volkswagen.'

He smiled quickly and went away reassured. I suppose you have to check. Snoopy bastard.

After that, I just sat and watched nothing happening on

the canal outside. Funny how long you can watch nothing happening on cold water when you're in a nice warm bar. Anyway, I was prepared to go on watching a lot longer than I was allowed to.

The first I knew was a soft American voice saying: 'You'll pardon me, sir, but I wondered if you'd care to do a little drinking in company?'

The answer was No, but I didn't make it to this one: it was the professional boozer from the bar—and I'd been right about him being big; he was built like a Russian war memorial. And topped with one of the ugliest faces I've ever seen; it looked as if it had been in the middle of a three-car crash, except it had obviously been born that way.

I said: 'Sit down,' and he landed on the sofa like a crashing airliner.

'My name,' he said slowly, 'is Edwin Harper, probably related to Harper's Ferry.' He shoved out a hand like a bull-dozer claw.

'Bert Kemp.' We shook hands. He was surprisingly gentle, or maybe not so surprising. Big men, and particularly big Southern Gentlemen, and most particularly big drunk Southern Gentlemen, can be very gentle. They can also pick you up in one hand and throw you through the plate glass into the cold, cold canal.

He said: 'I would believe you're English, Bert, so possibly you didn't get that remark of mine about Harper's Ferry.'

'John Brown's Body. They captured Harper's Ferry, him and all his something crew.'

'Quite right. Perhaps you'll take another beer, or maybe something stronger?'

'I'll stick on beer.'

He lifted an arm and cracked his fingers like a .45. 'Boy! —or whatever you call 'em in this country.' He turned back to me. 'You would appear to have had an accident, Bert.'

Here we went again. 'Lost an argument with a car.'

He shook his big head gravely. 'European driving scares me close to death, Bert. I'm in the trucking business myself, and I'll tell you any of my drivers who behaved like you see here everyday, why, they'd be finished with Edwin Harper right then.'

I just nodded. The waiter zoomed up with my beer and a big tumbler just about full of what looked like neat whisky and ice.

Harper lifted his glass. 'To your returned health, Bert,' and took a rather bigger mouthful than I took of my beer. 'And you'd be in what line of business yourself?'

'I deal in antiques. Mostly old pistols.'

'That is most interesting, sir. I have one or two on the wall of my little den, back home.'

'Really?' Probably a pair of 1930s horse-pistols. Though he might have a good early Colt, of course.

'You should meet my little lady. I reckon she's spent just about my whole year's profit on antiques this trip. And I'd guess she's working on next year's right now.' He chuckled, drained his glass, and waved at the waiter.

'For your sake, maybe I'd better not meet her, then.'

He laughed outright, then turned suddenly thoughtful. 'Yes —I find that small men make good dealers—you'll pardon me saying that, I'm sure. Small men can push—people expect them to push and they don't take it badly. I'll make a deal with a man my own size—when I can find one—but the rest I leave to my wife's brother Charlie. He stands about knee-high to a gopher in a hole and he screws out contracts I'd be ashamed to dream about.'

He shook his head wonderingly. The waiter appeared with another round, gave me a sympathetic glance and hurried off. The bar was beginning to fill up, now.

Harper took a sip that would have floated a nuclear submarine and said, as if he'd just thought of it for himself: 'I guess the Good Lord made us and gave us each our special talents.'

Oh my God we were on to God. I agreed quickly and gulped my beer.

And then I saw Harry. He came into the bar slowly, diffidently, looking around with his shy, hopeful smile. When he saw me, the smile flickered a moment. Then he came across.

51

I stood up. 'Mr Harper. I'd like you to meet a very old, dear and crooked friend of mine. Harry Burroughs.'

Harper got to his feet surprisingly easily. 'I guess you must be real friends for Bert to introduce you that way. My very great pleasure, Harry.'

Harry's smile deepened. 'Bert likes his little joke.'

We all sat down again and the waiter appeared almost before Harper had time to crack his fingers again. Only almost. Harry ordered a martini. 'Are you staying here, too, Bert?'

I shook my head. 'Just a drinking visit.'

Harry nodded and started inspecting Harper out of the corner of his eye. With that casual but well-cut steel-blue suit, the conservative black shoes, the general air of owning the ground for ten yards around—even in a Hilton—our Edwin certainly reeked of money. And Harry could smell a penny in a garlic patch at fifty paces.

He said slowly: 'You aren't thinking of buying one of Bert's very old, dear and crooked antiques, are you, Mr Harper?'

'Just drinking,' I said quickly.

Harper asked: 'Are you in the same line of business as Bert, Harry?'

Harry glanced at me, and said carefully: 'Our interests coincide, at times.'

But Harper wasn't noticing any undertones. 'I'd guess,' he said, 'That with things like art and antiques, they're worth just what anybody's ready to pay for them. It must be a difficult business.'

Harry said gravely: 'You've gone straight to the root of the whole thing, Mr Harper.'

I said: 'Always assuming you're getting what you think you're getting.'

Harper considered this. 'But if a man thinks he owns, say—what's the name of an artist?'

'Cézanne,' I said.

'All righty, a See-zan. Say he thinks he owns it, but it's truly only a fake. Now, has that man been cheated? Would he get more pleasure out of owning the real thing? Personally, sir, I'd doubt it.'

I left that to Harry. He said: 'Does a man get the same pleasure out of his wife if he doesn't *know* she's cheating on him?'

'That's a most interesting comparison, sir. The Bible, of course says that the sin is in the mind of the man who does it, even if nobody knows. I guess maybe it's the Good Lord's way of compensating: that not all sins cause trouble. But I guess you gentlemen must have to consider this philosophy almost every day in your business.'

Harry and I looked at each other.

'Speaking of which,' I said, 'd'you know who fakes Cézannes these days? I know who does Utrillos and a couple of Picasso boys, but who does Cézanne?'

You could almost see the wheels going round. He blinked, lowered his glasses for a better look at me, took out a big cigar, finally said: 'Cézanne's pretty well catalogued by now.'

'I wouldn't know. Just who fakes them?'

Harper asked: 'You think you've bought one, sir?'

'Not me; I can't afford 'em. Let's say I'm asking on behalf of a client. I may want to go and kick in somebody's head— just on a business basis.'

Harry was taking his time with the cigar: stripping off the band, sniffing it, checking it over for Cuban affiliations. At last he said: 'I haven't heard of anybody. It could be an old one.'

'Come off it. Cézanne hasn't been in the First Division that long. It'd have to be recent.'

He shrugged, smiled, and started waving matches at the cigar. 'I still haven't heard anything.'

Harper said: 'Quite a fascinating conversation, gentlemen. I see that Bert prefers the short direct method of business.'

He wasn't seeing half of it, but I gave him a quick, ashamed smile. And now I wanted to get out. I'd put all five in the ten-ring, as far as I could judge, and it was time to lay down the gun and rest on the laurels.

I looked at my watch. 'My God. Sorry—I've got to scoot. What do I owe?'

Harper, of course, wouldn't hear of it. I argued just long enough to sound genuine (I hoped)—but I wasn't really

53

interested in what Harper thought. Anyway, I was out of the hotel by half past five.

And asleep in the Park by six.

The phone woke me. It was Carlos telling me to get my skates on and down to the Doelen plenty chop-chop.

I was having trouble remembering who, where and why I was, the way you do after just a couple of hours sleep, but I remembered enough to object. 'What about a bit of security for once? If we all meet in a big hotel . . .'

'Aye, but it's urgent. I'll give ye the room number and ye come straight up without asking the desk.'

'Well, it's your problem. But it was my head last time.'

'Ye'll come right away, then?'

I would. I found bits of clothing I'd scattered, rang the desk to get a taxi, and was on the way by half past eight.

It was a nice busy time at the Doelen, so I slid past and upstairs without any questions asked. But the damn head bandage wasn't exactly helping; it was difficult to look inconspicuous —although it has the advantage of making you indescribable. They forget all but the bonce-binding.

The room—probably Dona Margarita's—was the lounge of a suite; big, comfortable and old-fashioned, with a lot of soft lighting, frilly lampshades, squashy velvet-covered chairs and sofas. Not grand—the Dutch are bad at being grand. But they're good at being comfortable; they spend the money where your backside can feel it.

Miss Whitley and Henri Bernard had already arrived, and were sitting with drinks in hand.

I said. 'Sorry I'm late. Scotch if it's going, please.'

Carlos said: 'Help yeself,' rather coolly, so I did. There was a small table loaded with bottles in one corner.

Dona Margarita was draped over one end of a sofa, wearing a long high-necked housecoat in blue, embroidered with silver dragons, sipping a glass of champagne and looking every penny a millionairess.

She smiled briefly at me and opened the meeting. 'I must apologize to all for bringing you here at dinner time, but Carlos took a most interesting telephone message just an hour ago. If you please . . . ?'

Carlos turned to a small cassette recorder planted on a table beside the telephone and clicked it on. 'I dinna start recording right away, I'm afraid.'

We got a few moments of humming, then a strange voice: '. . . *you may be interested.*'

Then Carlos: '*What sort of picture?*'

'*Post-Impressionist French school but signed by a very rare artist: Bert Kemp.*'

Long pause. Then Carlos: '*And ye want to sell this picture? For how much?*'

'*One hundred and fifty thousand dollars U.S.*'

'*I canna make a decision myself.*'

'*If you want to buy, you will pay cash in Swiss francs. You will put it in a packet addressed to H. S. Jonah at the Poste-Restante at the central post office in the Voorburgwal. The picture will then be delivered to the National Bank in Zurich. You understand?*'

'*Aye. I get it.*'

'*I will not call again. Mr Jonah will wait to hear from you. He will not wait long.*'

You could hear the phone click; Carlos turned off the recorder.

Dona Margarita said: 'So, Senor Kemp, your prediction has come true. What do you advise?'

'Go home to Nicaragua.'

That jolted them. She sat up straight. 'I beg your pardon?'

'It proves he didn't pick on me just because I *might* have been carrying a picture; he knew it was yours. He knows where you are. He even knows your bank. I mean, security's just pointless with this bloke.'

Carlos said: 'Ye knew all those things yeself.'

'Yes. That's why I wouldn't have been bloody fool enough to put all that into the phone call. He didn't need to mention the bank, did he? He could've asked you where to leave it.'

Henri said: 'That is logical. But this is also most fast. Less than one day from the stealing to the offer.'

I shrugged. 'Why not? Anyway, I might have speeded things

up a bit. I bumped into Harry Burroughs out at the Hilton today and dropped a hint that we thought the Cézanne might be a phoney after all.'

Henri bristled. 'It was *not* a fake!'

'Harry wouldn't know. But he might just speed things up in case we decided to cut our losses.'

Dona Margarita frowned. 'It seems perhaps you talked about our mission, Senor?'

'It was just a hint—no names. It wouldn't have taken with anybody who wasn't involved already. And I thought Harry knew quite a bit anyhow.'

Carlos said: 'Ye wouldna have speeded things up yeself before ye got dismissed?'

'Oh, *shut up*, you—' I saw Miss Whitley stiffen '—you twit.'

'Please,' Dona Margarita held up a hand. 'You have not yet said what you advise, Senor Kemp.'

'Hundred and fifty thousand; it's a bit high—about twenty-five per cent, isn't it? But you'll get the picture back. I mean, if they could've sold it at face value they'd obviously be doing that instead.'

Dona Margarita asked: 'Why should they not just throw it in the river when they have the money?'

'Reputation. Stealing and ransoming art's an accepted business these days. If somebody shoves a Cézanne down the plughole instead of giving it back, the word'll get around. Nobody'll pay ransom any more. And somebody'd give them— Harry—a working-over for rocking the boat. You'll get it back.'

Miss Whitley leant forward and said tentatively: 'But couldn't you try to fool them? Like watch for the man who collects the packet?'

I shook my head. 'They've worked this out. That name— Jonah. That means it goes in the pigeon-hole for the De Jongs, maybe the Jansens as well. I mean they're like Smith and Brown in Holland. Lots of letters in that hole. And they could wait days to pick it up; I can't hang around the post office all that time. Anyway, they *know* me, damn it. Pay up.'

Henri said gloomily. 'You know much about this business.'

'That's what I was hired for.'

Dona Margarita lit a cigarette and looked around. 'Now—thank you, Senor—we have an expert opinion. Shall we then pay?'

I said: 'I thought that depended on Managua anyway.'

Carlos frowned. 'How did ye know that?'

Miss Whitley was pale, but her head was up. 'I told him. I didn't see why he should be kept in the dark.'

Dona Margarita considered, then nodded. 'I am sure you are right. I am sorry, Senor Kemp. So, what do we advise Managua?—to pay?'

I said: 'There's just one thing we could try first.'

'I thought ye said there was no hope?' Carlos said suspiciously.

'Not fooling them on the deal—but we might bypass the deal entirely. Suppose I went and had another word with Harry—'

Henri said: 'I think you do not know this Harry so well, Monsieur.'

Miss Whitley nodded.

I said: 'Suppose I told him he might walk round a dark corner one night and come back with a smashed kneecap.'

There was a shocked hush from the sofa-full of art expertise. Dona M seemed to take it more calmly. 'You are very sure it *was* Senor Burroughs.'

'I'm sure enough.'

Miss Whitley found her voice; but not a very big one. 'Would you really do something like that?'

I touched my bandage. 'He risked fracturing my skull. I'd do it.'

She went on staring as if I was something that had been dredged out of the canal. 'And what if this form of gentle persuasion didn't work?'

'He's got another kneecap.'

'My *God*!'

'But anyway, we're playing deterrents. We're betting Harry can be scared into handing the picture back free.'

Miss Whitley said: 'D'you think he'd believe you'd do something like that?'

Henri turned to her on the sofa. 'Mademoiselle—*you* believed it. I find Monsieur Kemp most convincing on such matters.' Then he turned to me. 'But if Harry did *not* believe, or called your bluffing, then we have the problem of all deterrents: would you progress with your threat?—or abandon the matter and pay the money?'

After a long time, I said. 'I said I'll do him. I'll do him.'

'Ahhh.' He gave a long satisfied noise and leant back. 'But possibly he also has a deterrent, a button to press. Had you thought that he will, of course, know who has done this thing to him? That he will then hire more men to . . . alter your knee also? Or perhaps truly to fracture your skull? And then it will progress, like two doctors operating on each other, cutting off one piece, cutting off another, until . . . *futt.*' He smiled. '*Mon ami*—you are a romantic. Like, perhaps because you deal with guns, like the old Western gunfighters. But forgetting that because you shoot a man, then another man will want to shoot you. Until the last scene in the Main Street—or perhaps the Piccadilly—when you meet the last one . . .' his hands waved delicately '. . . and *pan, pan, pan*, you are dying in the dust with, perhaps, Mam'selle Whitley crying the tears all over you.'

Mam'selle Whitley said: 'You really think so?' But she couldn't help smiling. Neither could anybody else; Dona Margarita laughed out loud.

I didn't. So maybe it hadn't been the subtlest idea I'd had, but still . . . ah, the hell with it. I stood up and barged past Carlos and filled up my glass again. 'All right, go ahead and pay up. It's your money.'

Dona Margarita said: 'Senor—I wish that were entirely true. But perhaps it is easier that it is not. I do not wish you to die in Main Street—or Piccadilly—just for my Government. We will tell Managua; they will probably pay. A hundred and fifty thousand dollars is a very small part of our expenditure.'

Carlos said: 'About two per cent.'

'Thank you. And our collection will increase in value by that much in how long?' She looked at Miss Whitley.

'Three months, maybe.'

'So we have the money back before the collection is even shown. We will remind Managua of that, also.'

I said: 'So where do I stand?'

'But yes.' She considered. 'I believe, Senor, that you have shown you did not steal the picture. So we will recommend to Managua that you stay.'

'Thanks,' I growled.

But Carlos couldn't leave it alone, of course. 'Ye still did let the picture get stolen, remember.'

'Thanks for reminding me. And you fouled up the arrangements with the bank. Next time we'll do it my way.'

'And ye'll have a gun.'

There was a quiet time. I put my glass down slowly and said: 'Look—I've just been talked out of the rough stuff. But now you want me to start carrying a gun?' I looked at Dona Margarita.

She was taking it calmly, as always. 'I would accept a difference, Senor, between attacking a man and defending some property.'

Well—maybe, though the end result can look a lot the same. And maybe if I'd had a gun in Zurich, then . . . if only I could *remember*.

So I said carefully: 'I've said my piece about carrying a gun, and I'd rather break only one law at a time. But okay—if you want it, I'll carry it. Just on the job, though; not all the time.'

I finished my drink. 'I can fly back to London and pick one up tomorrow. Won't take a day.'

Carlos said: 'Canna ye get one here?'

'Not without a lot of questions asked—specially if you're just a tourist. They've tightened up gun laws a lot on the Continent the past few years.'

Dona Margarita said: 'I am sure it can be arranged. Perhaps Carlos can do it for you?'

You bet he could. I'd far prefer his name on any pieces of paper to my own.

Carlos seemed to accept it. 'What sort of pistol d'ye recommend?'

I chewed it over. What I'd most like was a Walther PPK chambered for .22, or a small Mauser or Browning Baby in the same calibre. But . . . 'You'd better try for a target gun in .22. Go for a thing called the Browning Target—costs about thirty-something quid—they make them in Belgium so they should be around. And get a spare barrel—long as you like.'

'It doesna sound verra powerful.'

'It's either that or a thirty-eight or nine mill. And I'm not carrying a Luger or something around. I might just bluff my way through with a target gun if it gets found. Looks nice and innocent—until you stop one. I mean, it does a lot more to you than a jacketed .25 or .32.'

Carlos nodded without necessarily being convinced—or that's the way I read it, anyway. 'Ye are the expert.'

Miss Whitley said: 'Do we *have* to have all this, really?'

That got me, a bit. I said: 'Look, if you weren't hired to cook, then stay out of the kitchen.'

She blew up. Well, not much; she didn't have the face or the style for it. She just went pale and petulant. 'I came on this . . . this trip just to help buy paintings. Now we seem to be down to discussing gunfighting and what bullets cause the nastiest wounds. I'm sorry, but I don't see the connection.'

I said: 'Get your weight back on your bottom.'

'What?'

Henri said, with that world-weariness the French do better than anybody: 'Monsier Kemp, with his superb English tactfulness, was just saying that you always knew this . . . this buying was not always to be on the normal lines. Please to sit down again.'

She sat, slowly and rather dazedly.

I said to Carlos: 'I'll need a box of fifty Western Super-X hollow points, too. Can you remember that? Must be hollow points.' He nodded.

Nobody said anything for a time. Then Miss Whitley stood up again and said in a small cold voice: 'If that's everything, may I go and have dinner, please?'

Dona Margarita: 'But my dear—naturally. I am so sorry to call you in at this time.'

I said: 'Wait a minute. One more thing. I don't want anybody picking up a picture by themselves. I want to be right there the moment the thing becomes ours. I mean Dona Margarita's. That's the only way. All right?'

She didn't look madly excited by the idea, but just shrugged and then nodded.

I looked at Henri. 'All right? Have you got any prospects?'

'There is perhaps something. We do not know yet. But soon.'

Miss Whitley said good-night to everybody except me and went out.

Dona Margarita stretched and sat up straight. 'I have a meeting at ten, so perhaps you will excuse me?'

Carlos whipped to his feet, his face expressionless. Henri and I got up slower. At the door—to her bedroom, I suppose—she turned and said: 'Perhaps, if Managua approves the payment, Senor Kemp should make the delivery to the post office? He is our guard after all.'

Carlos glanced quickly at me, then agreed. They were certainly going flat out to trust me again. A packet of money—raw cash—that's being paid as part of an illegal deal is the easiest thing in the world to skip out with. I mean, it's hardly likely to have a lot of signatures and forms and things attached.

Then I caught Dona Margarita's eye and she was having the same thought. She smiled quickly, said good-night, and went out.

Carlos said: 'I think ye'd best not go downstairs together. Leave one at a time.'

I said: 'I'll stay a while. You don't keep a bad Scotch here.'

TEN

THAT NIGHT I slept late and deep. So naturally I felt terrible in the morning, or what there was left of it. Still, there was that much less time before you can decently be seen in the bar.

When I got downstairs I got the desk to find me a doctor, and went round to have my bandage changed. So of course I had to tell my little story about a car accident again and he didn't believe it, either. I assured him it had happened in Zurich, not in his fair law-abiding city. (Come to that, since it really *had* happened in Zurich, why the hell didn't I tell him the truth? Habit, probably.)

Anyway, he said I didn't need a bandage; a sticking plaster would do. But I told him I was a coward about yanking off sticking-plaster, so he put a new bandage on anyhow. The sticking-plaster bit was true, but also I had my own idea about when I stopped being The Bandaged Man.

I was back in the Park in time for the first beer of the day. But then what? It was still January outside and still working at it. I'd been to the Rijksmuseum; I wasn't interested in Rembrandt's house; I wasn't going on any sight-seeing trip on the canals; it wasn't tulip-time and anyway the hell with tulips.

I had another beer. About half past noon Miss Whitley came in from the cold wearing red cheeks and her black coat. She saw me, but that was all.

I had a third beer. It was turning into one of those grey flat days like when you were a boy and went to stay with grandma and she turned in for a kip in the afternoon and you weren't allowed to touch anything because you'd break it and that applied to the radio too and the whole day was as exciting as the view inside a coffin. I used to spend those afternoons reading the dictionary, it didn't matter if she caught you at that—she thought I was increasing my word power or something. You know you can find something dirty or sexy on nearly every page of a good dictionary?

The Park Hotel probably even didn't have a good English dictionary.

Soon after one I took a taxi down to Cook's and spent half an hour checking through every route and timing from Amsterdam to Zurich—planes, trains, the lot. That woke me up enough to feel like lunch and that made me brave enough for a stroll down the Nieuwe Spielgelstraat to see if the dealers had any antique hand-guns they'd undervalued. They hadn't, of course.

And that put me back in the Park just after three. The message at the desk said simply: 'Please call H. Bernard.'

He was in the Schiller, in the Rembrandtsplein, just round a couple of corners from the Doelen and more central than the Park. So, just for something to do, I didn't ring; I went along and beat on his door.

He'd been there several days and hadn't wasted a minute creating a good solid French fug: a heat around seventy-five degrees and a rich smell of Gauloises. Despite that, he'd only taken off his jacket. He still wore a waistcoat and tie.

'It is kind of you to come, Mr Kemp.'

'You think you've got something?' I shut the door behind me and loosened my tie.

'I think, I think . . . it is most possible.' The light was dim, but there was a glint behind his spectacles and an excitement behind his careful tone.

'What is it?'

'A Van Gogh—I think. Uncatalogued.'

I'd opened my mouth to say that if it was uncatalogued it was probably phoney, but then shut it again. He must have thought of that already, and anyway, I couldn't tell even a real Van Gogh from my sister's kids' paintings. In fact, sometimes I think . . . never mind.

Instead, I asked: 'What's the price?'

He did a little currency conversion in his head. 'It is just over a hundred thousand of your pounds. A good price.'

63

'Where is it?'

'A private house, near to l'Haye. The Hague.'

'Who else knows about it?'

'One dealer—that is all. The owner discovered the picture himself. Now he wishes to sell privately. Not the publicity of an auction.'

I got the point. It would make a bigger price in an auction —especially in London, where auctioneers take a smaller cut than on the Continent—but if the current owner really had discovered the thing himself, just about all that hundred thousand pounds was profit anyway. There's no 'school of Van Gogh' selling at a quarter the price of the master himself and later discovered to be a real Van G. So he'd probably bought it for two florins and a dirty postcard.

And Holland has a capital tax. If he hadn't publicized the buying, he needn't publicize the selling. The government would swipe all the extra profit he'd get in going to an auction-room. And more.

I said: 'And he'd like to be paid in used notes, small denominations—right?'

Henri grinned; he knew all I'd been thinking better than I did myself. 'He is very happy for the money to be paid in Switzerland. That is easy for us anyway.' Nothing passing through a Dutch bank to alert the tax men; that added up, too.

But there was a snag, of course. I had to say it now, and the hell with his feelings.

I said: 'If it's only been spotted by this owner and this dealer —and you—then there's no authentication. I mean nothing scientific. No spectograms, no X-rays.'

He smiled confidently. 'But this I can arrange easily. There are many experts in Amsterdam for these things.'

I stared at him. 'Like hell you can. Hand it in for X-ray and you'll blow the whole thing. A Dutch expert isn't going to keep quiet about a Van Gogh discovery.'

The smile fell off his face so hard you could hear the thud. He wasn't so damn clever about the sharp end of the art biz as he'd believed. 'This I had not quite thought about,' he said slowly.

'Well, let's sit down and think about it.' I stripped off my jacket and pulled my tie even looser. 'Is that a bottle I see over there?'

'Of course—please to help yourself.' It was a bottle of tepid white wine with a smokey taste. I poured a glass and sat down with it; he just went on standing there staring at the floor and making small nibbling movements with his lips.

Then he said: 'The X-ray is not possible. In Paris, yes—I know a doctor . . . he could arrange to do it most secretly at a clinic.'

I nodded. I could fix the same thing in London, unless my contact had been slung off the medical register by now. I said: 'Spectrogram of a paint scraping? I mean, you could just take in a fingernail-full of paint; they wouldn't know what picture it's off.'

'For the Impressionists, the spectrogram is not so good. The paints have not changed so much since then, like with the old masters.'

So we settled down to a little more gloom. Finally I said: 'Look—it's being sold as a Vincent Van Gogh, isn't it? I mean, the owner says so?'

He looked up, a little surprised that I knew the right term for a 'guaranteed' picture: the artist's full name. But hell, did he think him and Elizabeth Whitley were the first art experts I'd met?

He nodded. 'Yes, but—'

'So, if you're happy, then buy it and we can get an X-ray done in Zurich. Then if it's no good, we give it back.'

'*But*,' he said firmly, 'the selling is most secret. The owner could say he never sold it to us.'

'Then we say we'll tell the Dutch authorities about him stacking away all that capital in Switzerland. That'll scare him. And *we* won't have committed any offence, remember. I mean, Dona Margarita isn't under Dutch tax laws.'

It took a little time for him to catch up; then he nodded and smiled slowly. 'And this is the man who knows nothing about the art.'

'I'm talking about law, not art.'

'Ah yes.' He got up and refilled his glass.

I asked: 'Anything else in the wind?'

'You mean to buy? Nothing to concern you. I may recommend one or two minor paintings, post-Impressionist. *Papier peint*—how do you call that?'

'Wallpaper?'

'Yes. Every museum must have walls, it must have wallpaper. It leaves room for change. And always somebody likes them. In Nicaragua, they may be the stars of the show.' He shuddered slightly. 'It is a pity one must go so far to see what we have collected. The Cézanne, my Van Gogh . . .'

My Van Gogh. Already he'd discovered it, bought it, hung it. I hoped to hell the X-ray turned out right; it would be a black day if it didn't.

I shifted the subject slightly. 'I thought Holland was full of good paintings?'

'Yes, but not to sell. You know why? It is the story of two wars. You recall that in 1914 the Dutch did not fight, did not even become invaded. They were the neutral ground between England and Germany. They did business with both sides; from this, they made money, much money. After the war, with money and stocks in much confusion, many men of business invested in art. It was wise. So one had the great private collections.'

He wriggled in his chair and undid a single waistcoat button; maybe the heat had jumped a few degrees. My shirt felt like a dirty dishcloth.

He went on: 'But in 1940 the invasion *did* come. And behind the tanks, the art collectors. For Hitler, for Goering, even for Himmler. And unfortunately, for the Hollandais, they were most honest—in their way. They said—"We wish to buy that Vermeer on your wall. We believe it is worth four hundred thousand guilders. Here is four hundred thousand guilders in Wehrmacht occupancy notes. Perhaps you wish to sell?" And the owner said "Yes, *naturellement*" and so they put their Lugers back in their holsters and paid the money and removed the picture.'

'The war giveth and the war taketh away,' I murmured. He gave me a sharp look, then grinned. '*Précisement*. But comes the Liberation—the V-day. The businessmen wish their pictures back—no? Again there will be trouble with money, with stocks. But not with art. But the Hollandais government is more wise: it says: "But you sold these pictures, no? You were paid. They are not yours any more. They will come back from Germany, yes—but they come back to us: to the museums." It was very simple. It worked very well. The museums now have many good things—but thank you to the collectors of Hitler and Goering. And those paintings are not for sale to such as us.'

'Nice story. Does it have a moral?'

He shrugged and spread his hands. 'The moral? Perhaps Van Meegeren found one—when he forged the Vermeers and sold them to the Germans. But then the government of the Hollandais charged him with collaboration and he had to reveal himself as a forger to disprove the charge. So they put him in prison for that, instead. No, perhaps the true moral is that governments always win.'

I finished my drink. 'Van Meegeren would have painted Vermeers anyway, wouldn't he? Whether Holland was occupied or not.'

'That is true. He had started before the war. It was a strange business. My friends who know Vermeers better, they say they are very bad pictures. They say that now, of course.' He smiled quickly.

'Still, I suppose Van Meegeren was really the last of the old masters, wasn't he? I mean, nobody's going to fake the old stuff now, not with spectrograms and X-rays and whatever they think up next. But the moderns—Picasso and Miró and so on —I mean, you walk into the same shops and buy the same paints and canvases they did. Like you say, spectrograms are no use there. And they didn't rework their stuff enough to show patterns on the X-rays, did they?'

He was looking at me fairly intently. 'I am following you. Please go on.'

I leant forward and slopped some more wine into my glass. 'Well—with Picasso and Miró you can check back because they're still alive. But the rest, the ones that are dead, you got to depend on an expert. If he says it's okay, then it's okay: you buy it. It isn't worth taking a second opinion. This is only the ten thousand pound, twenty thousand—maybe up to fifty, that sort of prices. It ain't the Vermeer and Michaelangelo prices. But if you got an expert, I mean a man with a real name, really trusted, then his cut on just a few pictures could really be worth something. I mean it's silly, he's giving the okay on pictures worth fifty thousand quid and what the hell's he get out of it? You ever meet a poor stockbroker or insurance agent? Why should an art expert be different?

'Just take you—just for an example. I'd bet that inside a year you could make more money than you've seen in your life. You could retire down to Cap d'Antibes and in a big house and you'd have enough left over to buy some of the real art to look at. For a man like you, I'd say that would only be fair, wouldn't you?'

Now he was really looking at me; steadily and carefully and with no more expression than the dull glint in his thick glasses. 'Are you making a—how do you say it?—an indecent proposal to me?'

I winced. 'Christ, no; I'm not trying to jump into bed with you. I'm just saying it would be logical for a man like you to pick up an opportunity like this. I mean if somebody put him in touch with the right people.'

'The—right—people,' he said slowly. Then nodded. 'I see. Like perhaps Harry Burroughs?'

'Harry's just one example. And he's suspicious: he might think you was an agent provocateur unless you had somebody to introduce you properly. And you wouldn't—I mean the man we're talking about wouldn't—want to work for just one dealer. That'd look bad in itself. You'd need a whole lot of dealers—but you'd need somebody to tell you the right ones, wouldn't you?'

The look went on. 'And that somebody would—perhaps—take ten per cent for being an agent?'

I waved my glass. 'Most of the work would be on the Continent. Let's say fifteen per cent.'

'I knew you were a crook,' he said carefully. 'I did not know you were this kind of crook.'

'So make it twelve and a half per cent.'

'I did not mean that!'

He was getting worked up. I finished my drink and stood up; excitable types can do sudden things. I wanted to be on my feet if he got sudden.

'Well, it's not really so different from what you're doing now,' I said soothingly. 'I mean, you're only giving an opinion. That's all that any expert does, in any case; that's normal. I'll bet there's people who say the Sistine Chapel wasn't by Michelangelo or Titian or whoever it was. And if it came on the market I'm damn sure I could find them for you. And look at the boys who said those Van Meegerens were Vermeers. They were just wrong. But the poor slobs didn't even make any money out of it. It could happen to anybody. I mean you don't *know* a Miró's a Miró unless you stood behind him when he painted it, do you? Just an opinion. So look on it like an insurance: one of these days you could be wrong, honestly wrong. It would still screw up your reputation. So why not make a bit of money on it while you still got it?'

He stood up himself, moving like a badly handled puppet. He was boiling inside and only just keeping the lid on. 'Foutez le camp!' he fizzed. 'Et ne—I do not wish to meet you ever again. Not again, not ever. Allez!'

'If you say so . . . But I'm afraid you're stuck with me, chummie. Until this job's over. Keep in touch as arranged. I'll promise not to make any more indecent proposals; okay?'

'Foutez!'

So I foutezed.

ELEVEN

BACK IN MY OWN ROOM I poured a drop of Scotch to wash out the taste of the wine and considered the progress made. In the last twenty-four hours I'd convinced Miss Whitley that I was a blood-hungry gunman and Henri that I was pimping for every forger in Europe. Well, as long as it didn't stop them co-operating professionally, it needn't rock Dona Margarita's boat.

Which reminded me: I rang Carlos at the Doelen. He wasn't overjoyed to hear from me.

'When there's a need to communicate,' he said, 'then we will contact ye.'

'Just thought you might have something for me, by now.'

'Tomorrow. Then I'll tell ye.'

'Okay. By the way, you haven't heard from Henri in the last few minutes?'

'No—we're meeting soon to discuss the painting. Have ye seen him?'

'Just finished a chat with him. We got talking about modern forgeries. He got the idea I was trying to seduce him into being the sort of expert who gives the okay on duff stuff. I mean, he got it all wrong. We were just talking. He gets excited easily, though. I didn't want you to take him too seriously, that's all.'

Pause; then: 'I see, Mr Kemp. I'll remember that. Thank ye.'

He rang off.

At least now I'd got my shot in before Henri. On the whole, not a bad day; anyhow, another day, another dollar—and that reminded me, too. I spread out my money and counted it; it wasn't all gone, but it was going. And I couldn't very well ask for the two hundred pounds we agreed for my escorting the Cézanne to Zurich. And a Van Gogh out of Holland would

70

only rate fifty pounds. Hell. But maybe Miss Whitley would turn up something really pricey . . . but not if Henri was right about the scarcity of good paintings for sale here. Damn.

And it wouldn't be exactly tactful to ask Carlos for another spot of pay and expenses until they'd heard from Managua.

Still, not too bad a day. I bought myself a quiet dinner in the hotel and went to bed early.

I got the word at about eleven-thirty in the morning: Carlos had a couple of parcels for me. Where could we meet?

I thought of a few clever places like the middle of the Vondel Park or down at the main station, then named a small bar just off the Rokin. Carlos agreed—it was just around the corner from him—but he didn't know what he was letting himself in for.

He found out about twenty minutes later. It had what the guidebooks call 'atmosphere'—a mixture of smoke, sweat, spilt beer and bad breath. It was like a crooks' dive out of some Victorian novel. But it was warm and cosy.

I'd got a table fairly near the door and was sipping at a glass of genever when he shoved his way in, looking a bit stunned and defeated and clutching his parcels to his chest as if they were newborn twins.

'Why on earth did ye choose a place like this?'

'It's warm. And if anybody's following us, he'll look as conspicuous as we do.' The rest of the customers looked like—well, they *looked* like crooks, but they were probably porters, labourers, local layabouts. I may have been the only pro villain in the place.

Carlos wiped two fingers across the seat of the chair, stared at his hand, then sat down carefully and put his parcels on the piece of old, stained carpet they used as a table-cloth. He leant across and whispered in a sort of shout: 'I've got—the thing ye asked for. Browning Target.'

'Two barrels? And the hollow points?'

He nodded. 'And we heard from Managua: they say pay up.' He tapped the smaller parcel. 'The address is on the inside. Just take off the top wrapping and hand it in.'

I stared at the parcel. A hundred and fifty thousand dollars in Swiss francs. Christ.

'You've started to trust me again.' Suddenly I wasn't too keen on the atmosphere in that place myself.

He shrugged a pair of expensive camel-hair shoulders, maybe cut a little wider than you'd choose in Europe. 'Managua said ye can stay—*if* ye carry that thing.' He touched the bigger parcel.

Just then a waiter fought his way across and Carlos ordered beer—which showed some common sense. My genever tasted like paraffin.

I asked: 'Any more from Henri?'

He gave me a look. 'Aye. Ye were right—he *did* get certain ideas about your little chat yesterday. He's worried about ye.'

I shrugged. 'I was just checking up on him. I mean, if he doesn't know anything about forgery then he's no use to you, is he?'

'He's got a verra distinguished name.'

'I wouldn't know.'

The waiter banged down the beer and got paid. This was a strictly cash-on-delivery joint.

Carlos took a cautious sip and didn't spit. 'We've contacted Managua about Mr Bernard's picture, and we should hear by tonight. We'll meet then. Dona Margarita has a friend with a boat so we'll take a wee cruise on the canals.'

'Doesn't sound very secret.'

'I'd say it was no worse than a car—better, perhaps. Nobody'll overhear us and they can't exactly follow us.' Well, that was a point. 'We'll pick ye and Miss Whitley up on the Amstel, by the Amstel station, same side. At seven-thirty. There'll be dinner on board.' It didn't sound like an open rowing-boat, then. But I was beginning to trust Dona Margarita's taste in personal comforts anyhow.

He took two quick swigs of beer and stood up, tapped the parcels. 'Ye'll take good care, then?'

I nodded. He went out.

I sat and watched the parcels grow bigger and more obvious

and felt the crowd turning to stare at them . . . . I was on the street about thirty seconds after Carlos.

I didn't try anything fancy at the post office. In the taxi I stripped off the outer wrapping, checked that the label said H. S. Jonah, and handed it in at the Post Restante. Then I went and looked up a dental supply shop in the classified directory. After that I walked out; there just wasn't any point looking for anybody looking for me or suchlike.

The dental place was a little wary when I asked for enough cold-cured acrylis stuff to make a dozen sets of bridgework; maybe they thought I was practising tooth-picking without a licence. But it wasn't a dangerous drug or anything like, so in the end they took my money.

Next stop was a handyman shop. I got a small hacksaw and some spare blades, a little can of oil and a thin, round file. And so back to the Park.

By now it was well into lunchtime, but I was too interested in finding out if Carlos had picked the right gun. I ordered a bottle of beer and some ham sandwiches to be sent up, then opened his second parcel.

And he'd got it right. It was a Browning Target .22—a size-able gun, maybe a shade smaller than most military automatics, with a long barrel that made it nearly a foot overall and a fat, comfortable one-piece butt-plate in chequered wood. Actually, I'd never handled one before; it's a fairly new design and I still prefer my pre-war Colt Woodsman. But it was a nice piece of workmanship.

It wasn't quite new, but not much worn, and the previous owner had lightened the trigger pull to just about what I wanted. The spare barrel was brand new; it was four and a half inches, which counts as short—but not short enough for me.

Then I had to shove the whole lot under the pillow in a hurry as my beer and sandwiches arrived.

When we were alone together again, I switched the barrels. All you needed was to loosen one screw, pull back the slide, and the whole thing, including breech and back-sight, lifted off. I

73

reckoned I could change barrels in under fifteen seconds. I sprinkled oil on the hacksaw and started cutting.

It took time and two busted blades and a lot of oil dribbled onto my pyjamas, but in the end I had the short barrel sawn off just at the point where it started to thicken out into the breech. I'd lopped off about two inches, along with the big blade foresight which would have caught on any pocket. Far as I could judge, the bullet would only have two inches of travel inside what remained; I wasn't going to win any 25-metre shoots like that, but I wasn't planning to try, neither.

The butt-plate came off by undoing just one screw, leaving a straight sharp-edged frame around the magazine. I walked about the room trying it out like that, but the edges were too sharp and my thumb had no place to rest. Time to start a little dentistry.

I used my sandwich plate, and mixed up most of the powder with most of the hardener until I had shiny soft pink wax, with a surface tension that stopped it cracking or crumbling. I wiped a little oil onto the butt frame, rolled out my mixture into a thick pancake, and wrapped it around the butt. It skidded a little on the oil. I held it, shaping it to my fingers. I cut a bit off here and there, held it again, cut off some more.

Serious target men build huge, shaped grips this way; I didn't want anything like that. A grip fully shaped to your hand makes a gun rock steady—but it takes far too long to get a hold of it. I wanted something simple and a lot less bulky than the wooden affair I'd taken off.

Finally I bodged a hole for the fixing screw and pushed it through, then lit a cigar and poured the rest of my beer while the stuff hardened. Just in time I remembered the plate and scraped it clean before it set.

I made myself wait about fifteen minutes, then took out the screw. The whole new butt slid cleanly off backwards: a thin, odd-shaped shell with a faint pearly glow. I wiped the rest of the oil off, fitted the new butt back on, then roughened it up with the file so it wouldn't slip in my hand. I reamed out the barrel a bit, too.

And I had a gun.

I stood and pointed it at things around the room. It seemed to be aiming where I was. Yes, I'd got a gun. And I'd got the feeling of having a gun. You can get the best materials in the world and the best craftsmen and engrave pretty pictures on the barrel and then inlay it with gold and make the cock like an eagle's head and the butt of ivory carved like a Roman warrior with jewels for eyes—but in the end what you've got is a gun. And you stand there pointing it and you feel just a little bit like God.

A nice piece of work, Kemp, *bloody* nice. The people back at the Fabrique Nationale would have taken one look and screamed with rage and pain at what I'd done to their lovely pistol. Then they'd have taken a second look and screamed for the gendarmerie; there was only one target you'd be shooting at with that flat stubby gun.

But it took just half a minute—I timed it—to change it back so that I had a fat-butted, long-barrelled job with foresight and backsight that you couldn't have carried hidden even under the Sheikh of Araby's cast-offs. No pro gunman would hump around a pistol like that, would they, officer? Just a keen 25-metre target man, that's all.

I toasted myself in a shot of Scotch; the bottle was beginning to run dry. Well, I should be on my way past a duty-free shop soon.

And this time, Harry, try it again. The man with the pink-pearl pistol will be waiting.

TWELVE

I RANG MISS WHITLEY in her room just before seven to ask
if she felt like sharing a cab, and she couldn't think of a reason
why not just then, so we met downstairs at about a quarter
past.

Finding the boat was no trouble: the choice was between
a couple of barges, half a dozen dinghies and a cabin cruiser
about fifty foot long, glowing a gentle white in the lamplight.
We climbed down a steep flight of stone steps and on board.

It wasn't new, I'd guess, but it had that solid well-kept feel
of old Rolls-Royces and Pullman carriages. There was a bridge
or control cabin or whatever raised up in the middle, probably
some cabins up front, and a long lounge or saloon at the back.
The party was down there. At first glance, it was like a discreet
little dining-room from the top floor of a Paris restaurant:
soft orange wall-lights along between the portholes, long leather
benches and a narrow teak table down the middle, loaded with
silver and napkins and salads and bottles.

Dona Margarita had a deep leather chair right at the back,
Carlos a folding canvas job, and Henri was parked on the end
of one of the benches.

Carlos got up. 'What will ye be drinking, Miss Whitley?'
Then, to me: 'Would ye tell the helmsman we're ready to
start?'

I put my head back into the control-room. There was a
bloke in a thick blue pea-jacket standing looking at a faintly-lit
panel of instruments.

I said: 'Belay the anchor, old cock. We're all aboard.'

He turned and looked down at me—well down, since he was
standing a good two foot higher to start with. 'Pardon?'

'Hoist the mainbrace. Splice the jib.'

'You wish me to cast off?' he asked, in perfectly good English.

'That's right. I knew there was a word for it.' It always gives me the giggles the way boat-type people actually say these things. Still, I suppose I call parts of guns by their right names.

I shut the solid wooden door behind me, and went back to dig out a Scotch and soda. The lights suddenly dimmed and a diesel engine rumbled. Then another.

I sat down on the opposite bench to Henri, who didn't seem in a hurry to catch my eye. 'Nice little job you've got here. Whose is it?'

Dona Margarita smiled. 'A Dutch friend who once played tennis with me.'

'He must have turned pro early.'

'Ah no. The professionals did not make this sort of money in those days. His family was in the shipping work.'

She was looking a bit of all right, that night. A simple black dress that made her high-breasted and thin-waisted; a high neck with a single lump of modern-sculptured gold for a brooch. And a nice lot of nice leg showing below the waterline. If Carlos *was* getting in any overtime, he was on to a good thing.

The boat started to move gently. Carlos looked at Miss Whitley. 'Would ye like to eat now, or wait a while?'

She shrugged her blue tweed shoulders—yes, she was back in that rig. So it looked as if we were going to have a bit of a chatter first.

I asked: 'How's the Van G?'

Henri stayed not looking at me. 'Good. It is right.'

'Right age and all that? Are we buying it?'

Carlos said: 'Aye. Managua agreed if Henri approved it, and released the money this afternoon.'

'I'll pick it up tomorrow, then. All right?'

Henri said: 'I will collect it.'

There was a silence.

Then I said: 'Okay—long as you take it to Zurich, too. I mean, I don't mind anybody doing my job, just as long as I get paid anyway. Fifty pounds for this trip, by the way—all right?'

Carlos glanced at Dona Margarita and they had a moment of telepathy. Then he nodded.

Henri said stubbornly: 'I have discovered that picture. When I last bought a picture, Mr Kemp achieved to lose it.'

'You didn't buy that picture,' I said nastily. 'You haven't got the money. Anyhow, the last time you chose a picture, I got it far too late and somebody knew all about it.' I touched the bandage still around my head. 'This time I do it all myself. But you can come along and vouch for me.'

Dona Margarita said: 'My friends, there is no need of this. It is Senor Kemp's special work to carry the paintings. So perhaps he should collect them also. After that, if something happens, then we shall know only who to blame.' And she gave me a little amused smile.

Henri finally looked across at me. He liked the idea of blaming me, anyway. 'And how will you take the picture to Zurich, Monsieur?'

'I haven't decided yet. And when I do, I won't tell anybody.'

More silence. Miss Whitley was also looking at me—almost approvingly, for once.

Carlos made a long bagpipes noise. 'Wee-eel, we'll certainly know who to blame.'

'That's my job.'

Henri wasn't so sure, but he couldn't argue with the boss class. He went back to biting on an imaginary lemon.

I asked generally: 'Apart from this one, how's it all going?'

Miss Whitley said: 'A couple of items. A seascape and a landscape. Nothing great—but good.'

'D'you want me to take them as well?'

'No, there'll be no trouble there. I'm arranging it myself.'

I nodded and reached across the table and took a cracked lobster claw out of a bowl of ice. 'Tell me—how d'you contact Managua on these deals?'

Carlos said: 'Through the consulate laddies in Bern. Miss Whitley or Mr Bernard can write to them—telephone if it's a rush job like an auction—and Bern cables Managua and Managua cables the bank in Zurich. It's not so slow if ye're a wee bit lucky.'

I'd guessed it must be something like that. I mean, you can't exactly send your own cable saying HAVE VAN GOGH PLEASE SEND HUNDRED THOUSAND QUID AND APPROVE SMUGGLING OUT TUESDAY WEATHER LOUSY LOVE UMBERTO. And you can't code it, neither. The cable companies won't accept cables they can't read—except from the diplomatics.

Dona Margarita added: 'Bern can approve minor purchases itself—up to a certain figure. That assists the speed.' Then her face went still and serious. 'I do not *like* to have my money spent only on the whim of some peasant in Bern.' Then she smiled again. 'But if it is the decision of my government—I must be democratic.'

I said: 'For the time being.'

She looked at me quickly. 'Do you suspect me of political ambition, Senor Kemp?'

I took another piece of lobster. 'Since you mention it—yes.'

Carlos said testily: 'Don't eat the whole lot yeself, man. Pass it around.'

I handed the bowl over, plus a silver sauce-boat of mayonnaise, and avoided Miss Whitley's eye. It had been her had told me about the political angle.

Dona Margarita nibbled at a claw. 'You will understand, Senor Kemp, that it may not be wise to boast too much of such an ambition. That I would much appreciate if you kept this secret.'

'Sure, it's no business of mine if you think you can collect votes with an art gallery.'

'The effective voters in Nicaragua may not be quite as many —I am talking in proportions—as perhaps in many other countries with a longer history of the voting system.'

Miss Whitley said thoughtfully: 'I'd say you needed a pretty big middle class before you got one of them inside a museum. Just look where the art museums are: Europe, the States, Russia, and a few cities like Rio, Buenos Aires, Mexico, Sydney, Melbourne. Not Africa, not Asia, not the rest of South America. You don't get Arab oil sheikhs buying up art, not even just to impress their friends. Their friends don't impress with art.'

Henri grumped: 'Arab sheikhs do not have friends.'

I said: 'Isn't art a European idea? I mean, the sort of art you hang on a wall. So naturally you'd get the museums in places which are Europeanised. Other places, art means carving on a temple, or the architecture itself. I mean, you can't hang that on a wall.'

Everybody was looking at me, a little surprised.

Then Dona Margarita said: 'But this is all my point: that the Umberto collection will make Nicaragua *different*, more civilized. That is why it must start complete; why we cannot buy for quantity and then do the exchanging with other museums that you talk of. We must start with one of the truly best small collections in the world. Not one bad thing, not one dull thing, so that the total is more than the parts added together.'

'And then?' Miss Whitley asked.

'Ah, then—then perhaps for the opening day, we have a Festival of the Arts. Some music—not the big orchestras but the soloists, the pianos, Casals, the string quartets—not too expensive but good, very good. The dancers from Spain, perhaps. And so on.'

'Just exactly,' Miss Whitley asked slowly, 'whose middle class are you trying to impress?'

Dona Margarita smiled appreciatively. 'Possibly not that of Nicaragua. Possibly that from further north.'

Miss Whitley frowned. 'But tourist dollars—they don't usually go to the people who really need them, the peasants.'

I said: 'She just told us: peasants don't vote.'

Dona Margarita smiled again, this time sadly. 'Alas, I am afraid that is—so far—very true. The money I attract to the country will go almost entirely to those who can . . . show their gratitude.'

I said softly: 'Viva Senora Presidente.'

She looked at me. 'It is most doubtful, Senor. But—just possible.'

Just, maybe. Spanish blood tends to rather narrow ideas

about a woman's place, as I recall, but if they bought anyone, they'd buy this one. She had the age, but still the looks, and she'd married into a fine old political family. And maybe they were still proud of her as an international tennis player, too.

Carlos said: 'Ye'll understand that all of this goes no further. No talking to the newspapers.'

'Please, Carlos.' She held up a royal—or maybe I mean duly elected—hand. 'These are our friends. But—my friends—now you see why this collection must be perfect, to get itself talked about.'

'Giving proper credit to your "friends", of course,' I said, not showing my normal suave tact for once.

She just smiled again. 'But of course—to Senorita Whitley and Senor Bernard. Politically, it is better for me to be thought of as a tennis player than a connoisseur of the arts. In Nicaragua, that is. And for yourself, you wish a little plate on the wall saying "This collection was smuggled by Senor Gilbert Kemp"? It is an idea, perhaps. It would most certainly get talked about.'

That got a laugh all round. Even Henri looked happy, and it gave him a chance to say: 'If Monsieur Kemp is successful in smuggling anything, it will deserve to be talked about.'

Dona Margarita gave him a warning frown. 'Please. But one more thing, my friends. I believe my collection—*our* collection —should have something that is most special; unique. A collection inside a collection, or just one picture that the true experts will come, *must* come, thousands of miles to see. Like perhaps the Mona Lisa in Paris, or . . .' and right there, she ran out of examples.

Miss Whitley said: 'Botticelli in the Uffizi. Rembrandt right here.'

Henri said: 'Van Gogh at l'Haye. The Impressionists of Chicago.'

Madam Presidente nodded. 'Exactly. Now, my friends— shall we eat properly?'

We ate. I'll say one thing for the next Presidente of Nicaragua, when she wanted to eat she had a banquet-sized appetite. Or hollow legs. She was picking it up and shoving it away—not rudely, I mean, but as if food had only just been invented. Miss Whitley was doing a quiet job on a piece of chicken with some sort of chopped-up jelly; Henri just fed.

And the boat purred along. By the time we'd finished, the cabin was a little stuffy and I didn't think my cigar would help, so I stepped up into the control cabin and watched the view go by.

We'd obviously been heading back into town, with plenty of buildings and lights all round. I asked the driver where, and he said we were just coming out into the Oosterdok—down by the main station, where the real shipping started.

So I just stood and smoked for a while and looked around the cabin. If you were born stupid enough to want to go messing about in boats, this was definitely the boat. There was a small brass steering-wheel, a panel of engine instruments and controls, a lit-up map table, some sort of depth finder and even a radar set. She obviously wasn't built just for the canals.

Just as we came out into wide water and saw our first lit-up cargo boat, Carlos stepped up beside us and lit a .50-calibre cigar. He asked the same questions, then he turned to me.

'When d'ye plan on going to Zurich?'

'Soon. If Henri's doing the paying, how soon can he get the money?'

'He's got it already; a bank draft on Zurich.'

'Good. I'll ring you to make arrangements with the bank then. And this time, I'll tell you what to arrange—okay?'

He looked at me, his face serious in the dim instrument lighting. 'Aye, I'll do that.'

We went under the railway bridge and out into even wider water, with a line of anchored ships stretching off to the right. We turned down alongside them.

I asked: 'Are we finished in Amsterdam now?'

'I'd think so. Ye can stay on in Zurich awhile if ye like. As long as ye keep in touch.'

'Where's the next stop?'

'Venice. D'ye know it?'

'I've been there. Rome and Florence too?'

82

'Mayhap. Depends on how we get along.'

Italy—ummm. Oh well, we'd see when we got there.

After a time, I asked: 'How did you get a name like Carlos MacGregor?'

His cigar glowed and he puffed a small thundercloud out of a side window. 'Around Central America ye'll find a lot of Fernando Murphys and Luiz Smiths. Most of them went out there after the Napoleonic wars—mercenaries fighting for Bolivar. It's likely my ancestor did the same; I havena been able to trace him all the way back. But a lot of them married, got land grants, settled down out there. My family happened to keep in touch with Scotland—I was at school and university there. But I'm a Nicaraguan citizen.'

That accounted for his accent, then.

I finished my cigar and decided I was getting a bit cold. As I started down, Carlos put a hand on my shoulder and asked quietly: 'Are ye carrying the gun?'

'Yes.' I was, too. I wouldn't have done normally, but I was just practising to see how easy it was to carry concealed. He looked me up and down; it was in my inside left breast pocket, with a piece of stiff card behind it to stop the shape showing through. I wouldn't get the fastest draw in the world, but I was assuming the other side wouldn't expect any draw at all.

Then he nodded. 'Good, Verra good. Good luck with Zurich.'

I went down to the saloon.

THIRTEEN

THE ALARM WENT OFF with a noise like a mother calling her child for the third time. I fumbled around, turned it upside down and banged it until it stopped.

My first idea of the day was that it was a lousy idea. It was six o'clock and Christ but I felt terrible. Still, it had been my own idea; I was stuck with it.

I didn't even crawl out of bed; I'd've been sick if I had. I just picked up the phone and, when somebody got around to answering it, asked for the Schiller.

They took their time, too, and they also thought it was a lousy idea. But I finally convinced them it was a matter of life or death, family crisis, million-florin deals and anyway Henri *liked* being woken at ten past six.

Like hell he did. He croaked: 'Qui est la? Il n'y a pas que six heures—'

'On your feet, Henri. We've work to do.'

'It is *you*. What is this stupidity?'

'We're taking off for The Hague in three-quarters of an hour. Slap it about a bit.'

'Mon Dieu! I did not agree that this—'

'Just do it now and agree later. If you're surprised, somebody else may be, too. You've got a hire car, haven't you? So pick me up at a quarter to seven.'

He made a long grumbling noise that ended as agreement.

'And don't forget the money.' I put the phone down.

Five minutes later I got up cautiously and started to dress without bending down too much. Then washed, shaved, packed —all at the speed of a tortoise sleepwalking. But by twenty to seven I was downstairs with my bags.

The night porter frowned at them. 'You are not leaving?'

'Yes I am.'

'But I do not have the bill.'

'That's not my fault.'

Just then Henri thumped on the door. The porter let him in. He was dressed as if his clothes were marching out of step with his legs, and he looked at me through his thick glasses with pure, simple hatred.

'This is most stupid,' he said.

'Call it tactical surprise.' I dealt the porter three hundred florins. 'Look, it can't come to as much as that. My friend'll pick up the change when he gets back.'

The porter still didn't like it. 'I do not know—'

'There's no law says I can't leave when I want to, is there? Not if I pay my bill. If you haven't *got* the bill, that's your problem, mate, not mine. Right? Right.'

I picked up my bags and walked out into the street.

After a moment, Henri followed. 'You were very rude,' he said.

'Well, how do *you* feel, this time of the morning?'

'It is your own idea, this.'

'I know, I know. Where's the car?'

It was parked under a light just up the street; a fawn Volkswagen with a long rusty scratch along the right rear wing. I dumped the cases on the back seat. 'All right: The Hague, let's go.'

Henri fumbled the key into the starter, then took off his glasses and rubbed his eyes. 'I must have coffee.'

'We'll get some on the road. Now—get started.'

The streets were almost empty, the lighted lamps hanging like forgotten overripe fruit. Just a few cyclists, moving briskly in that cold; a few cars and vegetable lorries. In ten minutes we were clear of the town and out on the airport road past the artificial rowing-lake.

Neither of us said anything until I tried lighting a cigar. Henri said flatly: 'I will be ill.' I ground the cigar out again.

Schiphol Airport was brightly lit but with nothing moving. Henri pointed out that their snack-bar might be open. I said:

'Later.' The Volkswagen chattered on and made the turn for The Hague fast. Henri knew the route, all right.

It's less than fifty miles to The Hague, and on good roads. We'd make it in little over an hour unless we hit bad traffic at that end.

But at half past seven, and past the halfway mark, I reckoned we had time for coffee at a lorry-drivers' café. That took twenty minutes, into which we crowded about ten seconds of conversation. But maybe we felt a bit more human after it. Anyway, Henri didn't object when I relit the cigar.

Before we started up again, I opened my case and did a conversion job on the Browning: short barrel and pink grips. Henri watched sourly in the thin yellow glow from the interior light.

'I do not think you will need that.'

'When I'm carrying a picture I'm carrying a gun. Them's my orders. You know that.'

He grunted and crunched the car into gear.

After a few minutes, he said: 'I will not find the real gem, the picture to talk about. With the Impressionists, the moderns, there are not such pictures.'

'I don't suppose the girl will find a new Mona Lisa, neither.'

'But for her, such pictures exist. For the Impressionists, it is the whole collection that is important. If they had give me *all* the money, I would have found them the best Impressionists collection not in Europe or America.'

'If they'd given *me* all the money, they'd've got the best antique arms collection in the world. They won't get that in any part of art.'

'They do not want old pistols.'

I sighed. 'So they told me. Anyhow, you've got 'em a Matisse or Manet or what-was-it? . . .'

'Cézanne!' he spat.

'Yes. *And* a Van Gogh discovery. That'll get talked about.'

He just grunted and frowned, not much soothed. The hell with him, then. I hadn't been hired to hold his hand.

We belted along in silence except for the Volkswagen.

It was still dark—sun-up wasn't due much before nine

86

o'clock—when we ran into the first Hague traffic. But Henri didn't turn off for the city; he kept straight on through Voorburg in the general direction of Delft.

I started to ask questions, then decided he must know the route anyway. We took the left turn towards Delft, then almost immediately a right onto a smaller road. We ran about two miles, then turned into the drive of one of a wide-spaced row of big suburban villas.

I couldn't see much, but I could feel it: it was one of those big, fancy red-brick houses about a hundred years old. Dutch Victorian, with a pointlessly tall roof and an over-complicated curly parapet in front. Several lights were on, but most just leaks from heavily curtained windows. Privacy, you know.

Henri switched off the engine. The silence was very sudden, and he started in a whisper: 'It is still stupid. We are too early. He may be not yet awake.'

'Somebody's awake. Anyway, that bank draft'll get him out of bed.'

'He could be most angry!' Suddenly, he could see his great discovery slipping out of his hands just because I'd made him bust in on the seller before his cornflakes or whatever the Dutch have for breakfast.

'A hundred thousand quid never got anybody angry at any time,' I said soothingly. 'Come on. Let's wheel and deal.'

He followed me reluctantly up the front steps and let me press the bell.

The door was opened by a middle-aged woman—probably a housekeeper—in a long, dull black dress. She gave me a suspicious look, then saw Henri and recognized him.

He said quickly: 'Madame—je suis desolé que . . .' And a long spiel about how sorry he was that we were there so early, but circumstances forced it, and—

I said: 'Let's get into the warm,' and took a step up.

She let us in.

It was a tall, warm hall, parquet-floored with a narrow strip of carpet down the middle. A few pieces of heavy, dark old furniture, a vase or two, a couple of pictures.

'Why didn't you buy *them*, too?' I asked.

Henri glanced at them, wrinkled his nose. 'It is not my period, but anyway . . .'

There were a couple of dark, dull landscapes, and even I could see that's all they were. The army might just have used them to teach aiming orders—'right of arc, bushy-topped tree; at five o'clock from that . . .' But they were probably too dull for even that.

Funny thing; art must've been a hell of an important and popular thing, hundred and more years ago, for so many people to have churned out so much bad stuff. Now it's television and books. Funny.

Just then the owner came out. He was fat, and I mean gross; a huge stomach, wrapped in a red silk dressing-gown, that waggled as he walked. With four chins, and three of them went on up the sides of his face past his ears, so that his features were framed in horseshoes of fat. He had small eyes, rimless glasses, and he held out a hand like a blown-up rubber glove.

'Shentlemens,' he said. Some of his teeth were gold, the rest just yellow.

Henri started off to apologize in French, then introduced me. I stayed back and just nodded; shaking that hand would be like milking a cow.

The owner—he seemed to be called Hooft—didn't seem bothered at our early call. He swung around, his belly just missing a side table, and waved us after him. We went into a back room that was obviously his study.

It was big, but crowded. There were several bookcases full of what looked like law books; a huge desk with telephones, a tape recorder and other gadgets; some lockable filing cabinets, and a vast safe. Hooft went to the safe and started twiddling. I just stood and gazed at a couple of naked negresses who were holding up standard lamps and looking madly pleased with the job.

Hooft turned around with a picture in his hands. Henri took a fast step forward and practically tore it away from him, then held it across the back of a chair under one of the lights and gazed at it.

It was really love.

Hooft just stood, looking impassively over his shoulder; after a while I edged in and looked over the other. It was one of those wild landscapes, trees and cornfield and sky all in big whirling strokes that look as if there's a big wind blowing, but somehow still at the same time. You know, it looks frozen. Or maybe I mean just unreal.

Finally Henri nodded very slowly. 'C'est vrai. Yes. Now—' He fumbled in an inside pocket, took out an envelope and passed it over.

Now it was Hooft's turn, and it was true love again. He studied that bank draft as if it was a free ticket to Heaven, Pullman class. He peered at it, held it up to the light, felt its surface with delicate fingers. More delicate than I'd thought he could manage.

He didn't even bother to apologize. Well, how *do* you accept a draft for a hundred thousand pounds? I don't know. I'd like to.

Anyhow, it didn't seem to bother Henri. He had his toy, and his knuckles were white in the lamplight as he gripped it.

Then Hooft was finished. He turned and smiled at us. 'Shentlemens—you will like the coffee, now?'

I said: 'Sure, there's no hurry.'

Henri looked at me, a little puzzled. Hooft pressed an intercom on his desk and gave an order.

'Please be sitting, shentlemens.' So we sat, Henri still clutching the Van G.

'You have hurt the head?' said Hooft. Observant, since I was still wearing the turban of bandages.

'Car accident.'

He squashed his chins up and down. 'Is bad, the cars.'

'S'right. We aren't keeping you from the office?'

He chuckled and waved the bank draft. 'Today I think I have earned enough already.'

The housekeeper knocked and came in with the coffee. Big cups all round. And good stuff.

Hooft loaded his cup with sugar, and asked: 'You are guarding the painting, yes?'

'Yes.'

'You are not like a guard—big.' Another chuckle.

'It isn't a big picture.'

That killed him. That was the joke of the year. He rolled in his seat, slopping coffee into his saucer. 'Herr Kemp—I like you much. Is very good.'

I gave him a sickly smile and sipped my coffee.

Henri chipped in, in French, asking if Hooft knew any other pictures along this line. Hooft spoke French better than I did, so I couldn't follow too much, but I guessed Henri was really trying to find out where the Van One-ear had come from. Still, as I wasn't getting the details, I got up and strolled round the room, seemingly peering at the books. Round behind the desk, past the windows—with heavy curtains drawn, blue curtains that jarred a little with the pink of what wall-space showed behind the bookcases and cabinets—and finally back to the centre of conversation.

I'd looked at my watch when nobody was looking at me. Just past nine o'clock.

'Well,' I said, 'maybe we'll wander along. Better get back to Amsterdam and store this masterpiece in the vaults.'

For a moment, Hooft looked worried. 'Herr Kemp—I do not wish this painting having any questions asked. Where it came from.'

I shook my head. 'No questions. No problems. Nobody knows nothing.'

He shrugged, a big quivering movement like patting a jelly. 'It is your work.'

He levered himself onto his feet and escorted us to the front door.

FOURTEEN

THE SKY was solid blue-grey cloud: behind it, the sun might just be up by now. Around us, the houses and trees were just shapes in various tones of grey. Henri went carefully down the steps, clutching the picture in front of himself like a shield.

Hooft smiled benignly and called: 'Bon voyage. Haf a good travel.'

I nodded, waved, climbed into the car.

Henri said: 'Now we put it in the case.'

'Not yet. Just dump it in the back until we're round the corner.'

'But it might become damaged.'

'Not in a couple of minutes. Drive slow.'

He didn't like it, but he drove—and slow. We crawled out onto the road, turned back towards the main auto-route. He stayed in second gear.

After about half a mile we found a driveway that didn't seem to lead anywhere, and pulled in. Henri held the picture while I opened my bag, then he wrapped it in my dirty shirts —*and* clean ones—and slipped it in. He hated to see it go.

When my case was carefully wedged flat on the back seat, he said sombrely: 'You have forgotten to sign this one.'

I grinned. 'So did Van Gogh. By the way—is that normal?'

'Yes. Many of his paintings have no signing. Now—we go to Amsterdam as we told Herr Hooft?'

'Not likely. We're not doing any bloody thing we've told anybody. Utrecht.'

'Utrecht? But why?'

'There's a train at ten fifty-nine. One change at Basle and I'm in Zurich before midnight.'

'But I do not understand Utrecht.'

I grinned. 'Illogical—I know. So nobody else can logic it out, neither. Just head for Utrecht. It's only sixty kilometres.'

He switched on. 'You have a ticket?' he asked dubiously.

'No. *Nobody* knows what I'm doing.'

We crawled back onto the road, Henri making his gear changes as smooth as possible, and frowning at my ideas.

'You have not told M'sieu MacGregor about this?'

'Not yet.'

'The bank at Zurich will not be open.'

'I'll ring Carlos from Utrecht and arrange to get myself met.' With a proper password and all, this time. I fingered the pistol in my side trouser pocket.

We reached the main road, turned right. Henri speeded up —but only a bit.

'Snap it up,' I said. 'We've got time, but we look bloody obvious if we crawl on a road like this.'

It was a modern road, not as wide as it should be, but flat and straight. Reluctantly, Henri speeded up to seventy kilometres.

After ten minutes I was pretty sure nobody was tailing us. But you can never be quite sure on a road like that, with half the cars keeping the same speed and position for miles at a time.

I asked: 'How did that fat crook Hooft get a Van Gogh?'

Henri gave a small shrug. 'He discovered it.'

'The hell he did. Look at those pictures in his hall. And his study: the colours, and those lamps. He doesn't know a Van Gogh from kiss-my-arse.'

He said coldly: 'But you know very much about art, Mr Kemp?'

'No, but I know a bit more than he does. And I couldn't discover a Van Gogh if I fell over it.'

'I accept you saying that. But also we know another rich person who is buying paintings but does not know about them.'

'The Boss Lady? Yes—but she's got you and the Whitley bird to help out.'

'Not to forget yourself. Perhaps Herr Hooft also had advisers.'

'That's what I mean, mate.'

He frowned, thoughtfully. After a time, he said: 'I must accept that also.'

'So I mean—you're not going to keep quiet when that picture goes up in Managua, are you? I mean you're going to accept the roars of applause, aren't you? And the poor bastard what discovered it first is going to be doing his tiny twisted nut about it.'

He said sourly: 'Why does it matter to you?'

'No reason. But I don't see why a bloke like Hooft would have that sort of picture.'

'And I do not see why the Umberto Museum of Managua should have it, either.'

I grinned again. This trip hadn't been exactly one long laugh, but making Henri miserable seemed to help. He hunched gloomily over the wheel, grinding out the kilometres to Utrecht.

By ten o'clock we were halfway there. I unpinned my head bandage and unwound it carefully. The last bit turned nasty, and I ended up spitting on my fingers and wetting the piece of lint to peel it off the crusted blood. But finally it was off.

I twisted the driving mirror to take a look. There was a sizeable scab there, but a bit of work with a spitty end of bandage and combing my hair down put it out of sight unless you were really looking.

Any description of me as the Man With the Bandaged Head were outdated as of now. We reached Utrecht station around ten-forty.

I hauled my bags out with Henri flapping around me like a young bird on its first flying lesson. I put the luggage firmly down by the ticket counter and said: 'You get me a ticket to Basle, first class. I'll ring Amsterdam.'

'You are going to Zurich,' he fluttered.

'Make it Basle. I'll buy the second half there. There'll be time.' A small point, but why leave any trace you don't have to? Somebody might just check on who'd bought tickets for Zurich.

It didn't take long to get through to the Doelen, but it took a little time to raise Carlos. I made it fast and businesslike. Or at least I tried.

'It's Kemp. I'm on my way. I want to be met at the station at a quarter to midnight. Right?'

He havered for a moment. 'We weren't expecting this, ye know.'

'So let's hope nobody else is—except the bank. You've got over twelve hours to fix it, all right?'

'Aye—I expect so.'

'Bloody well better be so. I want a driver holding up a card with the name CONRAD. Got that?'

'Why that name?'

'I don't know. Doesn't matter. Then I go up to him and say: 'I'm Conrad—what's the weather like here?' And he says: "The same as yesterday." Got it? Then we drive to the bank.'

Long pause. Then: 'Aye—I reckon I can arrange that. Will Mr Bernard still be with you?'

'At that end? Of course not.'

'Well—I think ye'll find he wants to go.'

'I'll push him under the bloody train first. Have you got that password?'

'Aye—I'll fix it. Quarter to midnight. He'll be there.'

'Good. See you in jolly old Venezia.'

When I got back to the ticket window, Henri was standing beside the luggage, looking both slightly sheepish and defiant.

'Well?' I said.

'I am coming also.'

'The hell you are.' But Carlos had known something, after all.

'You cannot stop me.' When you came right down to it, I couldn't really push him under the train. Nor shoot him. But the last thing I wanted was some bloody amateur tramping around at my side turning white at the Customs and peering over my shoulder to see if we were followed.

'What about your car?'

'It can wait there.'

'Got your passport?' I wasn't very hopeful, though; the French are so used to carrying identification papers that he'd hardly have forgotten it.

Anyway, he just nodded.

What looked like our train pulled in.

'*All* right, then. Get on board. But from now on, just don't know me. Don't talk to me. See you in Basle.'

He hurried through onto the platform.

It was just a normal express, not as swank as the T.E.E. trains, and without a proper dining car. But at least you could get a drink and a sandwich. I dumped the big case at the end of the carriage, and took a seat halfway along. I could feel Henri giving a horrified look at the back of my head, and I knew he'd sit as close to that end as he could. And he did, silly bastard. He was going to sit there staring at that case like some kid at a party watching the conjuror's hands.

We rolled out on time, heading for Eindhoven, an hour away. The train was planned to run through as many countries as it could: Belgium, Luxembourg, France, and finally Switzerland. Why they didn't plan to slip across a bit of Germany while they were at it, I don't know. It all meant three Customs checks (with Luxembourg they don't really bother), but only the first one mattered: I wasn't illegal once I was out of Holland.

I read a paperback until after Eindhoven, then strolled along to the buffet car, with Henri's shocked glare following me like a north wind. Did he think anybody was going to pinch a case in broad daylight? And if they were, it wouldn't be until they were getting out—and Maastricht was over an hour ahead.

So I had coffee with a genever chaser and a couple of rather travel-stained rolls. Outside, the weather was clearing to a hard, bright cold day, with little puffs of white cloud alone in a blue sky, just like Van Gogh painted them. Funny. I remember my parents had a reproduction of one of his Dutch landscapes on the parlour wall, and I always thought that little thick lump of cloud was bloody stupid. But you actually get them over Holland. Something to do with it being flat, I suppose.

I had another coffee, another genever, lit a cigar. A quarter of an hour before Maastricht, I went back to my seat. Henri was still watching my case as if he expected white rabbits to jump out of it.

While we were standing in Maastricht, Customs officials —Dutch and Belgian—came along the carriage. And they started on Henri. I kept half an eye on them, and they seemed to be taking more time than they should. He'd got a ticket for Basle and no luggage, of course. That'd get anybody suspicious.

Then the Belgian official went back and picked up a case: *my* case.

He showed it to Henri, then came a few steps down the carriage and called something in Dutch. After a moment, I got up. 'That's my case. What's the trouble?'

He took a few seconds to shift gear into English. 'This is your case?'

'Yes.'

The Dutch one came up behind him. In straight protocol, he asked: 'Do you have anything to declare?'

I frowned, thought, shook my head. 'I don't think so. There's some whisky in my bag—' I pointed to my airline bag under the seat. 'But anyway, I'm going to Basle.'

They waited. I showed my ticket and passport. Then—then they both looked down at my case.

This was the crunch. But this was why you hired yourself a pro.

I took out my keys. 'Shall I open it?' And while they were finding the picture I was going to be losing the pistol, down behind the seat-cushions or somewhere. 'But what's the trouble, anyway?'

They glanced at each other, then the Belgian one leant forward and whispered loudly: 'The man—there—he was looking at your case. He has not his own luggage.'

I looked suitably shocked, then peered past them down at Henri. He was as white as if he'd been painted for the general's inspection. 'That man? With the glasses?'

He nodded gravely. 'Please be careful with the cases. There is much stealing these times.'

'My God, I will. Thanks very much.' Then they helped me fit the case up beside the window, assured me it wouldn't trouble anybody because this train never got very full, gave me half-salutes and went back to complete the round.

I sat down again.

When the train pulled out a few minutes later, I lit a cigar. I still had a picture, and a pistol. I was still a professional. Of course, I might just kill Henri when we got to Basle.

It was a dull, grinding journey. I had two more lots of coffee, genever, and sandwiches and dozed as much as I could. We crawled into Basle about on time, just before nine-thirty.

I headed straight for the cafeteria, dumped the bags by a table and got myself a plate of cold meat and salad. Henri sat down beside me a couple of minutes later. He hadn't done any dozing, and as far as I could judge, he hadn't left his seat the whole trip.

'What happened with the Customs?' he asked hoarsely.

'They thought you were going to steal the case. You were just sitting there watching it like a bloody hawk.'

'Mon Dieu.' He rubbed his forehead. 'I almost . . . I am very sorry.'

'I don't tell you how to price pictures; why not stop telling me how to smuggle them?'

He nodded nervously. 'Yes . . . but when I said to Carlos, they were happy for me to come also.'

'You'd *planned* this already? With them? They *knew* you were coming?'

He nodded again.

Well, I suppose Carlos had half said that on the phone. But it was nice to know they still didn't trust me. I watched the picture while Henri watched me. Cosy.

'I'm working for a right bunch of nutters, aren't I? Christ, it's bad enough carrying a gun without you nits trying to put the finger on me all the time. Another trip like this, and—' But I was just getting loud and pointless. I'd taken on a job with amateurs; I could always quit. Why the hell wasn't I working for pros like Burroughs and Brague, though?

I cooled down. 'All right. *All* right. Now go and buy us two tickets for Zurich. We'll stay together on this one. *You* carry the case and *I'll* watch. Then we'll both be happy.'

FIFTEEN

THE CONNECTION TO ZURICH was a cold, bright empty
train smelling of antiseptic and wet ashtrays. Henri and I sat
side by side, him still staring at my big case, and nobody saying
much for most of the time.

After twenty minutes it began to snow outside.

Henri asked: 'Have you arranged the hotel?'

'No.'

'But we will stay at a hotel?'

'No, we'll kip down in the nearest snowdrift. What do *you*
think?'

'And you will go on to Venice? When?'

'Tomorrow.'

I wasn't going to sit around until the cops had checked the
hotel registers.

He nodded. 'And I go back to Amsterdam.'

'Utrecht. You left a car there.'

'Of course.'

And that was about all we said until Zurich. We were late,
but only a few minutes. Everybody else in the coach—only half
a dozen—charged out to get into the taxi queue. We took our
time.

I said: 'You carry the case. I'll be behind you.' I took my
bag in my left hand, stuck my right on the butt of the Browning
in my coat pocket, followed him out.

It was cold; the really vicious dry inland cold, like stepping
into a cold-storage vault.

But was it familiar? It must have been like this a few days
ago. Same time of night. Maybe the same platform? Anyway,
just like this. The dim yellow lights, the high roof over the
coffee stalls and cafés and left-luggage places beyond the

98

buffers. People hurrying, muffled up, or waiting, stamping their feet. Like this. Just like this. *Could I remember?*

I was a few yards behind Henri, to his right. He'd turn right at the end of the platform. Then I'd pull across to the left, my left side close to the wall. Would they come at him from behind? Or be bunched in front—just a small group that opened to absorb him, a gun rammed in his ribs, a fast order and a waiting car? *How had they done it to me?*

We were off the platform. Turn right. A man folded up a newspaper with a sudden movement and walked briskly forwards, between us—and I had the gun most way out of my pocket before he'd finished one step. But he just walked on, not noticing.

Jesus, I was strung up tight as a banjo. But no bad thing. Now two men walking in towards us. I closed up to the wall, ready to slam my back against it. They passed, hunched, not talking.

(Hell, they'd recognize me anyway, wouldn't they? Or maybe they'd recognize the suitcase Henri was carrying? They'd done me once. The whole thing was so damn . . . Never mind. Just stay strung up. Watch, Watch!)

Then, incredibly, a notice saying CONRAD. Held up by a man in dark uniform, peaked cap, short dark overcoat. Henri had already stopped.

I walked up. 'I'm Conrad. How's the weather here?'

'It is like yesterday.' How any man could get so little expression into so few words. He sounded like a computer. Anybody who'd overheard would have thought 'password' immediately. But at least he was here.

(Had he been here last time? Or somebody like him? Had they put in a phoney driver—waited until I was in a phoney car? Why couldn't I *remember*?)

'Vous êtes de la banque?' Henri asked.

'Non, M'sieu, je suis un . . . chauffeur.' Just a hired car. Well, maybe to the bank a hundred thousand pound painting was peanuts.

'You done this job before? I mean a few days ago?' I asked.

'No, I am not doing it . . . not before.'

All right. 'Let's go then. Bank Nazionale.'

He made to scoop in the big case. Henri, of course, wasn't having any. For a moment they just stood there, each pulling on the case, Henri glaring and the driver looking surprised.

I said: 'For God's sake let him have it. Have to go in the boot anyway.'

Reluctantly, Henri let go. (But had the same thing happened to me? I wouldn't have made a fuss, of course. Just made damn sure—casually—that the thing got in the boot. Then climbed in the car and . . . And?)

The car was a black Mercedes parked behind the taxi rank and its queue. I shoved Henri in, went round to add my small bag to the boot—and make sure the suitcase got there. It did.

It was snowing, lightly but confidently, as if it expected to stay. The street was speckled in the lamplight, with tyre tracks showing in long curves. We pulled away smoothly and turned right, towards the Lindenhof. The natural way to the bank, down by the lake. (But was that how they'd got me? Turn up by the Lindenhof with a remark about a street blocked by repairs, stop at the kerb a moment, maybe two more men jump in . . .)

If anything like that happened this time, somebody was going to get shot first and questioned later. I was holding the Browning in my lap.

But nothing happened. Nothing. We pulled up at the bank five minutes later.

It took just another minute for the driver to press a bell, the door to open, us to get the cases inside, the door shut. And suddenly I was very tired. Nothing was going to happen here, nothing had happened before. I'd never got this far.

It was a big, empty room, cold neon lights on cream walls. There were just us, an elderly character in some bank uniform, and a banker. Young—maybe thirty—with short, smooth fair hair and rimless glasses, but certainly a banker. You can't learn to play that sort of part in five minutes. Neatly, rather than smartly, dressed; polite rather than friendly; more careful than helpful.

He sat behind a big desk and wrote and said: 'One oil painting . . . colours blue, yellow, green . . . of trees in a field.'

Henri bristled his fur indignantly. 'A Vincent Van Gogh.'

Our banker smiled cautiously. 'I cannot vouch for that. Now—the size?' He measured it carefully with a heavy desk ruler. 'Fifty-three by eight-seven centimetres.'

I said: 'You missed a couple of millimetres in there somewhere.'

He looked up sharply, then smiled again. 'It is good enough. For the collection of Dona Margarita Umberto, government of Nicaragua. Delivered by . . . ?'

Neither of us said anything. He looked up again.

I said: 'Does it matter?'

'It is on the form.' The pale eyes looked at me steadily. He must have guessed roughly what my job was. It didn't bother him, and it didn't interest him, neither. It was just on the form.

'Gilbert Kemp.'

He wrote it down. 'You will sign, please?'

I signed. He carefully tore off a receipt and passed it over, then nodded to the uniform. The painting was carted off through a small wooden gate and down a flight of stairs. Henri watched it go.

I pointed to one of the desk phones. 'Is that working? We haven't got a hotel yet.'

He nodded, opened a desk drawer and took out a guide to Zurich, then politely got out of earshot. I thought about the Butterfly, unthought, then found the number of the Central rang it, and got a room. Then passed the guide over to Henri. He got in at the Continental.

And that was that. Our banker opened the front door for us—the uniform was still messing about down in the dungeons —and shoved us into the cold cold snow. By now it was coming down in big, slow flakes. Already the street was covered.

Henri asked: 'Shall we find the taxi?'

'Don't expect so. I'm going to walk it.' By now I was so tired that it was somehow easier just to walk than to start making decisions about whether I'd more likely find a taxi on this corner or that one.

'Will you telephone to Carlos?'

'No. Tomorrow.'

He hesitated, then: 'I will, then. We will meet in Venice. I am—your pardon for being stupid. You did things well.'

I just nodded and picked up my airline bag and started walking.

I told them to let me sleep and they left me to it, but my part wasn't so easy. I was back in the dim light of the Zurich Bahnhof, peering about among the muffled, hunched, hurrying figures, trying to recognize, trying to remember. By three in the morning I was meeting the banker disguised as a hire-car driver . . . I wrenched myself properly awake. If I went on like this I didn't stand a damn chance of recognizing a real memory.

So I walked the floor for five minutes and drank a glass of water and ate three aspirins and wished it had been Scotch and sleeping pills. But it worked. When I lay down again I went under like a crash dive. And stayed there until past nine o'clock.

I lay in bed and drank coffee (why the hell doesn't a hotel bring you one big pot of coffee when you ask for it? Because they then have to bring you a second small one and get tipped again, that's why) and stared at the sky beyond the window. It had cleared to a hard sunny blue, and the reflections on the ceiling showed there was snow lying outside. Perfect winter-sport weather for those who wouldn't prefer to stay home and break a leg in comfort and privacy.

About ten I got out of bed, found my Cook's Continental rail timetable, got back in and started looking up trains to Venice. I could get one just after noon, which seemed about right. Fine. I was beginning to feel good. A job well done the day before, nice weather outside, an easy jaunt down to Italy this afternoon.

I got up for keeps and started looking for a clean shirt—and of course I'd let Henri walk off with my case. The big one, the smuggling one. I'd been too damn tired even to notice. Ber-last. Now what? Now make the silly bastard bring it round here. I picked up the phone and asked for the Continental.

I asked for Henri and a voice looked something up and muttered *zwei, drei und zwanzig*, then told me that Herr Bernard had left instructions not to be disturbed.

Oh hellfire. Silly *sleeping* bastard. But at least I was in the habit of using my small bag as an overnight job, for sleeper trains and one-night trips, so I could shave. I wished I'd remembered to put in a clean shirt. Normally I don't much care, but this morning I actually felt like wearing a clean one.

By half past ten I was tramping along the lakeside feeling worse than I should have felt, mainly because I felt I should have felt better. The Continental was less than half a mile, back towards the National Bank and the end of the lake; a modern job with a lot of brass-framed plate-glass and marble-chipping floors. The lobby was jammed with what looked like a coach party—anyway a lot of people talking too loud and falling over each other's luggage—so I just ploughed through and walked up to room 223.

At the last moment I decided to play it careful: if we weren't to be noticed together, then that's the way it should be. So I waited until I was sure the corridor was clear, then tapped on the door.

Not a squeak. So I tried the door: locked. So I looked up and down before giving a good thump—and there was something sticking out from under it. The key-tag and, of course, behind it the key.

So I unlocked the door and walked in.

SIXTEEN

AFTER A FEW SECONDS I said: 'Jesus God Almighty.' Then I turned around very quickly and locked the door again. Then I took a second look.

When I go, I don't want it to be that way. Not with a pillow rammed down over my face to stop the screams and then a knife working—and I mean working—in under the ribs. The bed looked as if somebody had thrown a bucket of blood on it. Well, you can bleed a bucket if the bastard killing you doesn't know how to use a knife properly.

I suddenly seemed to want to sit down and take off my coat and—no, I couldn't afford to be sick. I took the gun out of my pocket and held it and pointed it and began to feel a little better. Or angry, perhaps.

Then it occurred to me that the gun wasn't a bad idea anyway. I moved across to the bathroom door and pushed it open and dropped into a fighting crouch. But nobody, of course. They'd locked the door behind them, hadn't they?— and shoved the key back under the door, except the big fat tag on it had jammed.

I turned back and looked around the room. A mess. They'd ripped open my big case—really ripped it, with one zip torn loose, although I hadn't locked it—and scattered about my second suit, shirts, pants, vests, shoes, socks, handkerchiefs, ties. Everything. Anger at not finding anything, maybe; you couldn't hide a Van Gogh in a shoe. The wardrobe door was open and Henri's suit had been slung down, too. The dressing-table drawers pulled open. Bedside cupboard door. One corner of the carpet turned back. They'd given the room a real going-over.

And now?

Now pick up the phone and call the cops and sit and wait. And then start answering questions—in triplicate. Once to give them the general outline, again to fill in the details, a third time to see if you remember what you said the first time. Questions about who we were working for, what work, and do you have a licence for that gun in your pocket, Mein Herr? Oh? And why not? You understand we must take a serious view of this, *nicht war*?

Or run. The Central for my bag and to pay my bill, then the Bahnhof and the first train for Venice. No reason for them to be watching me. They might not even find him before the train went.

And *my* suitcase?—*my* clothes scattered all over the room?

I sat down and looked at the bed and said quietly: 'Christ, can't you do *anything* right?'

All right, but now let's think how the cops are going to tackle this. First off, they want to know who he is. Well, that's no problem; he'll have registered under his real name, they'll find his passport and *carte d'identité* . . . or would they? So I went and rummaged in his suit jacket—and they'd left the lot, even including his wallet. I skimmed through it, turning up about two hundred French francs, nearly three hundred florins and an English five pound note.

Well, if a sneak thief panics enough to kill, he can panic enough to run out so fast he forgets to do any thieving. But I didn't want to leave the cops any other theory to play with.

I wiped the wallet and dropped it. Now came the real problem. If my suitcase hadn't been torn up, I might have packed up my stuff and walked out . . . no I wouldn't. They might not notice me just strolling through the lobby, but a man with a suitcase is a man walking out on his bill. I was going to have to leave most of it. I started searching through the scattered clothing, his and mine.

Henri and I were about the same build, so the clothing all *might* be his. Of course, if you tried it on him, you might notice a difference—but why should you try? What would you expect to learn? No police force in the world has the time, men or money to question the obvious.

I hoped.

One snag was that a lot of my stuff was British. Not all; I travelled around and got stuck in places without a clean shirt and put it on the expenses as a taxi ride and a plate of pizza. But Henri travelled, too; he could have picked up a couple of shirts in London.

My second suit was British—but bought ready-made and paid for in cash. No name in it nor back at the shop. Still, I searched it carefully for scraps of paper I might have forgotten. And just as a real artistic touch, I shoved a couple of Henri's papers in one of the pockets.

The suitcase was British, and good. The one part of my luggage I pay real money for is the luggage. But British cases are better than French ones, so maybe Henri had . . . Anyway, no initials on it anywhere. Not for a pro smuggler.

Shoes? I stuck one alongside Henri's and there was nearly an inch difference. I shoved my spare pair of shoes in my overcoat pockets. Pity, because they were actually French, and it would have been another artistic touch.

Christ, Kemp, stop standing around gloating about how clever you're being and remember how damn long you're being!

That left my second pair of pyjamas. Henri had slept raw— so now I either had to put them on him or take them away. Well, I wasn't going to put them on him, because the blood was drying and the stains might be in the wrong places or not enough—and also for another reason. But pyjamas don't go in pockets that are already stuffed with shoes and guns. I started to undress.

Halfway through, somebody knocked on the door.

I went as cold and stiff as the Matterhorn, my trousers in my hand. If somebody walked in now, no explanation I could think of, up to and including the truth, was going to do any damn good. No police force in the world has the time, men or money to question the obvious.

Then I remembered I'd locked the door.

Another knock. 'Mein Herr?'

I could have done a sleepy French voice well enough to fool a Zurich chambermaid through a locked door—but in the long run that would start questions being asked. The cops would know Henri had died much earlier than this.

She tried the handle. I stood there, breathing quick and shallow through my mouth.

Then, after about another hundred years, she gave a Germanic grumble and her trolley squeaked on down the corridor.

But now I really moved. I dragged my pyjamas over my underclothes, tucked the trousers into my socks, slung the rest of my clothes back on top. Then I wiped over everything I might have touched. Finally, I went back to the bed.

I didn't shift the pillow; I didn't want to know how he'd felt about dying. But I wanted some idea about when. You can't tell, of course, not unless you're a proper pathologist with a thermometer and a lot of maths, and even then you're half guessing. But from the way the blood was drying, I made my own guess at several hours. Maybe soon after the hotel had opened that morning.

Which meant . . .? It meant it was long past time for me to be out and gone.

The chambermaid's trolley was parked outside a room a couple of doors down the corridor. She might have heard the sonic bang of my passing, but she didn't see a thing; the quickness of the Kemp deceives the eye. And the lobby—God bless lazy bus drivers—was still jammed with tourists.

When I looked at my watch, I'd been in the hotel less than fifteen minutes. I caught the eleven forty-six for Milan.

SEVENTEEN

YOU GET INTO VENICE LATE, nearly ten o'clock, and the station is cold, bright, modern, empty. Just a few porters, who don't bother you when you're just carrying an airline bag, and a hotel tout who wakes up and asks: 'Hey, you wanna good cheap 'otel?'

So you say: 'No. A good expensive one.' You've earned that, at least. And it really shuts him up.

But the Grand's closed in winter, and you'd best stay clear of the Gritti and the Bauer Grunwald and the Danieli; the big she-chief will be booked into one of those.

So I rang the Luna and got a room, then took a water-taxi from the steps outside. That really *is* living. What those motor-boats cost for a fifteen-minute ride is up in the old masters class.

For all of being five or six hundred miles south of Amsterdam, Venice wasn't any warmer. There was a faint scum of mist on the Grand Canal and the air was like a cold damp bedsheet. Just a few vaporettos charging up and down, a few lonely lights outside the old palazzos, and not a gondola in sight. They take the winter off to count their summer money.

Or maybe I was just feeling a bit low.

So the first thing I did at the hotel was get them to ring the Doelen. I should have been in I Corps, or some sort of espionage, so I could have said something like 'I'm afraid our sales-man's caught a bad cold' and Carlos would know straight off Henri was dead. I mean, if he'd been in I Corps or espionage as well, of course.

Anyway, the first thing he said: 'And where are ye?'

'Venice. I just got in.'

'And where's Henri? Did he say he'd be back here today?'

'Look—er, Henri's had an accident. That's what I'm calling about. I mean a bad one. The goods are okay but . . . Look, just get a Zurich paper tomorrow.'

After a bit of thought, he said: 'Aye, I'll do that.'

'I'll come back there if you like, or I'll stay here.'

A bit more thought. 'Ye stay on there. We'll be doon . . . tomorrow probably. Where are ye staying?'

I told him. Then I added: 'Look, I know Henri didn't check out of his hotel there; didn't pay his bill. *Don't you do it*. I mean just forget it.'

'Ayyyye . . .' a long thoughtful sound.

'I'll see you down here.'

He said Aye again and rang off. I found I was sweating, and I'd got out of the pyjamas back at the Central in Zurich. Though I used to be able to wear pyjamas over my underclothes a solid week, back that first winter in the army. And I mean a solid week, day and night apart from the lavatory, and anyway the state they were in and the food you got you'd be constipated for a week and no matter. Baths?—you mean when some bastard's nicked the bath-plugs and the light-bulbs and anyway there's no hot water?

Jesus, but I was living posh these days. So I had a bath just to prove it.

Halfway through the night I woke up sweating, back in Henri's Zurich room and this time I'd forgotten to lock the door . . . It took me a few moments to get full awake, and those moments weren't funny.

But I hadn't forgotten, had I? I hadn't forgotten a thing. In fact, I'd handled that pretty well, considering the mess the silly bugger had landed me in. I mean, imagine getting yourself killed like that; opening the door to just anybody, so early. Stupid twit. He might've been planning to land me in it. But he hadn't managed to.

I was clean. I was clear. I turned my pillows over to the cool side, and the rest of the night was a good one.

But the day wasn't so good: grey, cold and drizzling. I drank a lot of coffee, then went out and wandered the alleyways west and north of San Marco, buying shirts, socks, underclothes and a pair of trousers; a different item in each shop. I still needed a big suitcase, but I was going to take time choosing that.

Then I checked the newspaper stands behind San Marco, but they hadn't got any foreign newspapers in yet. So I went and drank more coffee in Florian's and stared out across the cold piazza. The pigeons had just been fed, and the stones were covered with a crawling grey mass of them. Then a small boy walked across through them, kicking at them with every step and them fluttering up around him like autumn leaves. I grinned; pigeons make me feel like that, too.

Then he was gone and the pigeons had taken over again, a squirming carpet of big insects. And just a few empty tables, a few lit shop windows under the arcades. Somebody with a fancy mind once called the Piazza San Marco the 'finest drawing-room in Europe'. Well, I'll tell you, mate: in winter the roof leaks and they forget to turn on the heating.

It was well past noon and I'd switched to a Scotch and soda before I got a *Neue Zuericher Zeitung* from one of the news-stands.

And Henri had got famous, all right; he took up two full columns on the front. They hadn't found a photo of him, though, so they'd made do with a shot of a lot of police cars and ambulances outside the hotel. I don't read German, bar a few words, but I settled down with another Scotch and started to pick through the story. After all, I knew it already.

They mentioned Paris: that would be Henri's home town. The Louvre: maybe he'd advised them in the past. Britain, the U.S.A., Italy—all places Henri must have travelled.

My God!—had he got a wife?—I mean widow? I hadn't thought of her. If she took a look at that luggage and clothing the story would blow wide open. In fact, she'd probably know about Dona Margarita and she'd blow that straight off. I went back through the story looking for *Frau* and *Kinder* and couldn't find them, thank God.

And there was no Dona Margarita or Nicaragua or Gilbert Kemp and not even an Amsterdam, so the newspaper hadn't back-tracked him very far. Though that didn't mean the police hadn't. And there was always that bloke at the bank . . .

I picked up my parcels and hurried back through the rain to the hotel.

I had a late lunch, then spent most of the afternoon lying on my bed rereading what I could of the *Zeitung*, counting my money and working out my expenses. As far as I could make it, Carlos owed me fifty pounds for the Van Gogh, a week's pay, which was thirty-five pounds and another twenty in expenses. The five pounds a day for shop overheads were being paid directly to my bank in London.

Well, I wasn't getting rich. Not surprising, staying at a place like the Luna. But I was getting too old for some fleabag *pension* in the middle of winter.

I lay and brooded about it until it was dark outside, then did the thing you usually do when you're worried about money: went out to a really expensive bar for a really stiff drink.

There's a Harry's Bar in every big city in Europe, even if they aren't all called that. Comfortable, clean, pricey as hell and the best hamburgers and club sandwiches in town. The right thing is to despise them as not being 'typical', of course, but be blowed to that. I mean, what the hell are all those Italian and Chinese restaurants in London so typical of?

Custom was pretty thin that afternoon, but as usual it was almost all American. Some brand of non-Catholic priest was chatting to a big man with that sandpaper type of skin that usually means an outdoor job; oil, maybe. And a couple of young men with hair so short and sports jackets so bright they could only have been officers out of uniform.

And Mr. Edwin Harper, probably related to Harper's Ferry.

I turned quickly to the bar and kept my back to him. He was at a corner table, with a thin, elegant woman in a black dress and a sun-tan that she couldn't have got anywhere except the Bahamas or the ski slopes.

I quietly ordered a Scotch. Well, he might not even remember me, the state he'd been in when we last met. And if he was in anything like that state again I wasn't so sure I wanted to meet him; big drunken men scare me. If they suddenly decide to thump you and you aren't big enough to thump back, you've got to do something not in the book of rules to get out of it in one piece. Use your knee, or your fingers in his eyes or something. Then you're a vicious little rat and nobody loves you. And he's just a big fun-loving boy.

Screw big fun-loving boys.

I sipped my Scotch and listened over my shoulder. It isn't a very big room; just the length of the bar and about room for one row of tables. I couldn't actually hear what was being said, but it seemed quiet and calm enough. And maybe he'd get angry if he thought I was ignoring him. So in the end I turned around and waited until he looked up and caught my eye.

He stood up immediately. 'Well, I believe it's Bert Kemp! How very pleasant to meet you here.'

We shook hands. He waved at the table. 'Will you join us?—or are you waiting for someone?'

At Harry's Bar prices free drinks are always welcome. You vicious little rat. Oh well. I went over.

He introduced us—or tried. 'Mr. Bert Kemp of London, England, I'd like you to meet the Contessa di—ah hell, I just can't get my tongue around it.'

She smiled and held out a lean, firm brown hand. 'Castiglioncello. How d'you do, Mr. Kemp. Call me Kate.'

I'd *thought* she wasn't likely to be Mrs. Harper. Not just that she seemed all that European—I mean plenty of American women can do that—but she didn't seem quite the same style as our Edwin. We sat down, Harper muttering: 'Cas-*tigl*-ioncello. I'll get it soon.'

The Contessa asked politely: 'Have you been in Venice long, Mr. Kemp?'

'Just yesterday. I don't suppose I'll be here more than a week.'

'I like Venice in the winter. It has a nice sort of melancholy —and no gondoliers, of course. Also you can change your mind and get up to Cortina so easily. Are you here on business or pleasure?'

She had a slight accent I couldn't place. (Later I found she was Greek by birth, and successively English, French and Italian by marriage. What makes politicans think they invented the Common Market?)

Harper said: 'Bert collects old guns.'

'I deal in them,' I corrected. 'I can't afford to keep them.'

'Do you find many in Venice?' she asked.

I shrugged. 'There's a chance. It's an excuse to get out of Britain for a while. And there's always the naval museum here; that's quite fun.'

Harper finished his drink, assumed we'd have the same again, and whistled up a waiter. 'Two dry Martinis and a Scotch and I mean *dry*. I want them to *hurt*.' The waiter smiled and went away.

I asked: 'Are you just touring around, Mr. Harper?'

'Call me Edwin, Bert. Well, Venezia's actually business. They got a conference of trucking business on here, so I give 'em a little talk on how we do things in the States and then I report back to my association how they do things in Europe and well, sir, it all looks very legitimate on the tax returns.' His big ugly face cracked into a cheerful grin.

The Contessa shook her head. 'They come to Venice, of all places, to talk about road transport.'

'Well, Contessa, the manufacturers don't mind it one bit. They just can't get stuck with the expense of bringing their trucks over to show off, and they know their opposition can't either, so it only costs them a lot of fancy paperwork. So everybody just has one big good time.'

The waiter brought our drinks. Harper said: 'Your health, Contessa, Bert,' and refuelled himself. Then: 'Say, Bert, have you seen any more of your old friend Harry Burroughs?'

After a moment I said: 'No. Why?'

'After you'd left us that evening—I'm afraid I was really tying one on that time; I do really owe you an apology for that —well, after you'd gone, we got talking and when I said I'd be coming down to Venezia, he said maybe he'd see me here.'

'I see,' I said slowly. 'Well, it's always nice to meet Harry again. Tell me more.'

EIGHTEEN

WHEN I GOT BACK to the hotel again there was a note half an hour old: get round to the Gritti Palace at the speed of light only inconspicuously. Hell's teeth, Carlos was really busting security like Christmas balloons, what with hotel-room meetings and leaving messages like that for me. He'd even given the flaming room number.

It was a nice room—of course—on a corner overlooking the Grand Canal—of course. And the gang was all there, with a *Zeitung* and a Geneva paper spread over a coffee table. They looked at me with the same sombre expression all round.

Dona Margarita said: 'Zurich does not seem to be your most lucky town, Senor Kemp.'

'That's right.' I sat down in a high-backed chair. 'Well—let's get one question over and done with. Hands up everybody who thinks I killed him.'

Miss Whitley looked quickly down at the newspaper. Carlos sighed and nodded. 'Aye—it's a question maybe somebody'll ask if we don't. Ye'd best tell us the answer.'

I held up a finger. 'I carry a gun, not a knife.'

'Ye wouldna use a gun in a hotel room in the early morning.'

'True 'nough. But even if I'd used a knife, I'd have used it a sight better than that. I mean, he was really cut up.'

They stared. Dona Margarita asked incredulously: 'You *saw* him?'

'Yes, I saw him. Walked in on him about half past ten.' I turned to Miss Whitley. 'D'you read German? Does it say when he was found?'

'Some.' She didn't look back at me. 'About midday.'

'Does it say anything about his luggage?'

She ran a finger down the column. 'It had been opened, Robbed. Thrown about.'

'Yes. Well, it wasn't his luggage, it was mine. He hadn't taken any. But he'd been carrying that case before, so maybe he just picked it up by instinct. The one the picture'd been in. And I was just too bushed to notice that night. Anyway, does *that* answer your question? I mean, like I'd chop up my own luggage and then leave it lying around?'

Now they were all looking at me, Miss Whitley included.

Dona Margarita said: ' I did not think you had killed him, Senor Kemp. But for the police—perhaps the evidence works the other way about. Why did you not report it then?'

'I was carrying a gun, remember. They'd have searched me, just as routine. That's half of it. The other half's that I'd've had to say *why* we were in Zurich. And that blows the whole thing: your name, the pictures, the whole trip. The cops'd never promise to keep that quiet.'

After a moment, Dona Margarita said quietly: 'Thank you, Senor. I value that.'

Carlos said: 'Aye, but what happens now? They'll be on to ye by now, Mr. Kemp.'

I shook my head slowly. 'I don't know about that. Once they think of me, yes. Bert Kemp's in it up to his dandruff. But there's no direct link to me. There's nothing in my luggage to say it's mine. If they want to run sweat tests on the clothes then they can prove it ain't Henri's, but that won't tell them who it *does* belong to. One weak point's the bank, but I don't think the bank knows who Henri was. It was my signature they got. And they don't seem to have dug up any picture of Henri, so the bank may not recognize him; nobody gets a man from just a description. And anyway, why should the cops check all the banks about an art expert?'

Everybody went right on looking worried, in their own ways.

So I said: 'They can track Henri back to Amsterdam, probably. And if they check all the hotel registers they'll find I was in town the same time. Me and a few thousand others. And the same thing in Zurich. It's still me and a few thousand others. But I mean—why *should* they do that? A man gets knifed and robbed in a hotel room; why d'you go checking hotel registers all over Europe? It takes time, money. The cops have got other things to do as well."

Miss Whitley said carefully: 'Do you mean that you are *not* going to go back and tell the police anything? You're not going back at all?"

I spread my hands. 'Well, if I tell them anything, it's the truth, the whole truth and nothing but. The whole story comes out then. And like I said, the cops won't keep it to themselves. The whole expedition's kaput.'

'Henri has been *killed*. Murdered.' She glared at me as fiercely as her face allowed. 'Doesn't that mean more than this—shopping trip?'

Carlos looked a little shocked.

I said: 'If we tell them the whole story it'll probably just muddle them anyway. He was knocked off by some sneak-thief. Nothing to do with art.'

'How d'you know?' she snapped.

Well, I didn't, of course, but: 'Art thieves don't kill people. I mean, you can't ransom a picture back once you've killed a man and got the story stuck all over the front pages. You give him a quiet thump in a quiet alley—like they did with me—and leave him the chance of keeping quiet about it all.'

'You seem rather good at keeping quiet about crimes.'

'Too bloody right. I'm a professional crook, remember? Oh hell,' I growled, 'I need a drink.'

Carlos waved a hand at a row of bottles and glasses on a corner table. He certainly got organised fast. Well, I suppose it was a standing order everywhere they went: two bedrooms with baths and a living-room, full load of bottles in the corner. All you need is money.

There was silence except for me clinking and gurgling in the corner. Then Dona Margarita said: 'Do you believe the connection—with myself—*can* be concealed?'

I shrugged and spilt whisky on my new trousers. 'You'd know better than me. You've been keeping pretty separate everywhere you've been. But d'you think Henri told anybody? His family, somebody he worked with, something like that?

You write him any letters, anything he could have left in his files?'

Carlos shook his head. 'It was all on a personal basis, same as yeself, Mr. Kemp.'

'Then you stand a damn good chance. Are you going to try it?'

Dona Margarita looked quickly, rather warily, at Miss W. 'I cannot decide immediately, Senor Kemp.'

I took a deep breath of Scotch and soda. 'Well, just make it as immediate as you can. And it's got to be unanimous, too. I mean, either we all stay quiet or we have one big ugly rush to the Zurich cop-shop. I'm not being left out in the cold while somebody else is doing the confessing.'

Miss Whitley said coldly: 'I suppose you mean me.'

'I suppose I do.'

She glanced back at the papers spread over the table. 'I suppose . . . I suppose it really wasn't anything to do with art?'

'Ye mean Harry Burroughs?' Carlos asked bluntly.

There was a hush. It was one thing to think—assume, rather —that Harry had arranged me getting thumped and the Cézanne getting nicked. Murder was a big step beyond that.

I said slowly: 'Harry got some pretty good professionals that first time. I mean, they managed not to kill me. And if he'd known we were there at all, he should have known we'd already dumped the picture.'

Miss Whitley asked: 'You saw the room—had they been looking for anything?'

'They'd really torn it apart. More than they'd need for a picture or anything.'

'And they say he *was* robbed.' She was looking back at the newspaper.

Now we'd got to the delicate part. 'Well, no, not really. That was me.'

Her eyes were popping and she was leaning forward like a jockey at the last furlong post. 'You . . . did . . . WHAT? *You* took his money?'

'Well—yes, on the whole. I mean, I thought it would help

the sneak-thief theory along a bit. Sort of distract them from the art side.'

'My God.' She sat back and upright, like a schoolteacher finding I'd brought a sun-bathing magazine into Shakespeare class. 'So you weren't just concealing evidence, you were actively messing it up. I don't suppose they'll ever find out who killed him now. What did you do with the money?— buy a new suitcase?'

I shook my head wearily. 'Not yet. Look—I didn't do this for fun. I mean, if I'd been working on my own I'd've gone to the cops right away.' (Well, I'd've been more *likely* to go to them, anyway.) 'But I'm on a job. I mean, part of the contract's that I keep this . . . shopping expedition quiet. Secret. That's all I was trying to do.'

She looked at me for a long time, without any expression. None at all; that was still the one expression she was good at. Then finally she said: 'Just how *would* you kill a man with a knife? You said you could do it better than they did.'

'You mean a naked man lying on a bed and I'm holding him down with a pillow over his face with one hand?' She went white, then nodded faintly. 'One push *upwards*, in among the ribs, then sort of screw the knife around—' I moved my hand in the air '—until I was sure I'd got his heart. Not a lot of stabbing around and bouncing off the ribs downwards. They're like a venetian blind, you know, arranged—'

Dona Margarita said firmly: 'That is *quite* enough, Senor.'

By now, Miss Whitley was looking really grey. But she'd asked. She'd hinted I *might* have been the killer after all.

After a time, she asked in a small voice: 'Was that—that other way—the way it was done?'

'I saw him.'

'Yes.' And after a pause: 'I'm sorry.'

Carlos said: 'Just where did ye learn to use a knife, Mr. Kemp?'

'Army.'

'Ye were a commando?'

'Christ, no. Do I *look* brave? I was an armourer sergeant. Small-arms stuff. But I picked up a bit from the types who were keen about small-arms. They seemed to be keen on knives, too.'

Meaningless chat. We were both watching Miss Whitley. Gradually her face was looking less like the newspaper you wrapped the fresh fish in.

'Were ye in action?' Carlos asked softly.

'No. Base Depot. I invented a new change-button for a sub-machine gun. They didn't adopt it. Silly buggers.'

Carlos frowned. 'I've mentioned your language before, Mr. Kemp . . .'

'Sorry.'

Miss Whitley looked up, then down at the papers, then around at the rest of us. 'Well—what have we decided?'

I said: 'It's your decision. If you talk to Zurich, we all do.'

She said thoughtfully: 'I suppose nothing we can do will bring Henri back to life . . .'

Life's just a bowl of clichés, as somebody said. But I knew we were all right now. She was talking herself out of being a solid civic citizen. All we had to worry about now was the Zurich *polizei*, and how much they were worrying.

'While we happen to be met together, I've got my expenses and things worked out.' I handed over the paper.

Carlos read it slowly and carefully. Then: 'How much did ye take from Mr. Bernard?'

'About thirty quid.'

'Aye.' He crossed out a couple of items. 'Well, that leaves a balance of—'

Elizabeth said sharply: 'But aren't you going to send that back? To his family?'

'How?' I asked. 'Anything like that would be as suspicious as hell. We can't even do it anonymously. Hotel thieves don't send back money.'

Carlos nodded. 'So we owe ye just a hundred and twenty-five pounds.' He gave me a bunch of lira. 'Ye'll get the rest next time we meet.'

'Thanks. You don't feel like contributing to my lost luggage, do you?'

119

He looked up, surprised and almost shocked. 'It wasna our fault, was it? Ye'll get the insurance.'

'Of course,' I said grimly. 'I can just see the claim form. Where lost: at the scene of a murder. Anyway, I forgot to insure it.'

He shrugged. 'That still doesna make it our fault.' Christ, but six generations of the tropics hadn't thinned down his Scottish blood much. Dona M had known what she was doing when she hired him as Keeper of the Royal Pesos.

But then she stuck in her oar. 'I think we can be generous. Senor Kemp has been very sensible about the affair. We will pay half.'

She called that generous, did she? The mingy old bag probably spent half my luggage on meals for a day, let alone the rate for that suite.

But it was obviously the best I'd get. 'Thanks. Just put back that thirty quid, then.'

Out of the corner of my eye I caught her quick smile. Naturally, it hadn't occurred to her that one big suitcase and my gear wouldn't cost more than sixty pounds. Maybe she really had been prepared to be generous. But it was too late now.

I turned for the door, then turned back. 'Oh, we mentioned Harry Burroughs. Well, he's probably in town—or soon will be.'

Carlos frowned. 'How d'ye know?'

'Met a man. Harry had told him he'd be down here about now. Seems some rich old lady kicked off recently and he thinks her collection might be up for sale. I mean, that's what he's supposed to have *said*. It *could* be just a coincidence. I'll find out where he's staying, anyway.'

'I dinna want ye going talking to that man.'

'I won't.' Although I'd certainly talk to Harry if I wanted to —and if I thought it would help. 'I'll just ring a few hotels and ask if Mr. Burroughs has arrived yet. I needn't leave a name. But remember—he can do exactly the same thing. *If* he doesn't know already.'

NINETEEN

NEXT MORNING I finished off my shopping with a sports jacket in a nifty sort of grey with bits of blue and brown in it, another shirt and a smuggling-size suitcase. The case cost a bit, of course, but it was a better job than I'd expected. I'd forgotten the Italians knew about leather.

I dumped the stuff back at the Luna and went out for an early lunch at a small trattoria nearby. Then round to San Marco for the first Swiss papers. And Henri had faded away to a half column on page three—still with no picture, thank God—so either the police weren't making much progress or weren't talking about it.

After that I did my round of telephoning and tracked Harry down at the Danieli, over the other side of San Marco, beyond the Doges' palace.

So I rang Carlos and told him.

I added: 'It's really beginning to look like he's following you around. I mean, now we've got Zurich, Amsterdam and here. You don't know if he was in Paris the same time as you?'

'No, I'm afraid not. It couldna be the truth that he's here for the reason your friend gave?'

'To look at the art in some estate somebody's just left? Well, it might be. I could try and check that, too, if you like. I've got nothing else to do. Or have I, yet?'

'No, not yet. But dinna concern yeself—ye stay out of Mr. Burroughs's way.'

'You're the boss. Or nearly.'

We rang off. Still, I *hadn't* got anything else to do . . .

I started with Paulus Boemack. He was German and an artist, though you wouldn't necessarily guess the second. He was tall, slim, looked about ten years younger than he was, with a handsome hatchet face and fine blond hair. I mean, any film producer would have snapped him up as the noble young Wehrmacht officer who gets shocked by what the S.S. is up to but soldiers loyally on until he stops a burst from a tommy-gun in the stomach—it's always the stomach—and dies nastily. Very moral. And maybe it really would have happened to Paulus if he hadn't missed the war by a good ten years.

What he actually did was forge Utrillos.

He lived in a small flat over by the San Rocco where if you leaned out of the window and didn't fall two stories into the stinking water, you could just see the Grand Canal. I puffed up the narrow stairs and thumped on his door.

'Ja? Was ist?'

'The art police. Open up.'

There was a pause, then a scuffling noise, then the sound of the door being unlocked and unbolted. He peered out, a bit pale, then said severely: 'That was not funny.'

I grinned. 'It's all right, mate; I'm here on business.'

He went on looking suspicious but unhooked the door-chain and let me in. Well, maybe he had a right to be cagey; the last time we'd met he'd been handing back a large lump of money that one of my clients had been stupid enough to let go. I seem to remember I'd been holding a gun at the time.

He shut and locked the door carefully behind me. 'I have not been selling any pictures in Italy since—since that time.'

'That's a good boy.' If he'd stuck to his usual routine of forging a French artist in Italy and selling the results through a dealer in Germany, he wouldn't have had any trouble. I mean, a few international complications and a couple of extra middle-men can confuse the issue nicely. But middle-men cost money and he'd got greedy. Once.

'What do you want?'

'Just a little help. That's nice.' *That* was a big canvas with sea-shells, a bit of old rope, some sand, a crumpled beer-can and a fish skeleton all over it. Oh, there was some paint, too.

'It is not *nice*,' he snapped.

'Sorry. How're you and Maurice getting on?'

He took the canvas off the easel and rested it in a corner. Then lifted the false top of a big table and took out a smaller, still-wet canvas and looked it over. 'You nearly have made me spoil it.'

'Sorry,' I said again. Even I could see it was Utrillo. I mean, it was the usual corner site in a dull Paris suburb with a big triangular piece of road filling up the foreground. I suppose, once a year, he went round with a colour camera snapping likely scenes, then painted them up leaving out the Citroëns and Vive de Gaulles.

He dabbed at the picture. 'It is not so good. There is another —in Warsaw—who does Utrillos. They are horrible. You can know them with the eyes shut. Is making the business bad.'

'Hard luck. Why don't you try a few Mirós or Modiglianis then?'

He glared at me. 'It is not possible to change the style like you change the shirt! This is art!'

Well, come to think of it, I suppose it was. So I said 'Sorry' for the third time.

Then: 'Look, mate, did anybody with a big collection— an old lady, I think—go dead recently? In the last few weeks?'

He frowned thoughtfully. 'They die all the time, the rich old ladies. They come to live in Venezia, beautiful Venezia, and they rent the big palazzo and sit on the balcony breathing the canal air and *fuff*—they are dead like the plague. Every Christmas they are dying. And never they buy modern paintings first.' He went on thinking.

Finally he said: 'The English one. The Lady, Lady—' he snapped his fingers and flicked a spot of paint on the picture, and swore. 'Lady Witherford. She is dead at Christmas. They say she had much art but . . .' he tapped his head. 'She is crazy. Nobody goes to her palazzo.'

'Was she on the phone?—or d'you know where the palazzo was?'

'Why do you want to know?'

I shrugged. 'I might have a client, that's all.'

'But of course, your client does not want modern pictures.'

123

'You mean the Spirit of Modern Venice?' I nodded at the sea-shells and old rope in the corner. 'I'll put in a good word for you. But I should stick to Utrillo.'

'It is getting difficult, with the horrible stuff from Warsaw. Now they are becoming suspicious; they want the authentication. Papers. Proofs.'

'Have you tried smuggling them in?'

'What? Why is that good? They want proof, not secrets.'

'No, I mean you try smuggling them into Germany and you tip off the Customs first and they catch you, see? And you pay import duty on it and they give you a whole heap of forms valuing the thing and showing you've paid real money on it— I mean, that's pretty good proof it's genuine, ain't it?'

He said slowly: 'I did not think of that . . . Yes, perhaps it is good. Thank you.'

'Be my guest.'

He put down his palette. 'I will look in the telephone for you.'

A minute later I had the address of Lady Witherford, crazy, deceased.

TWENTY

WHAT I SHOULD HAVE DONE, of course, was ring Elizabeth Whitley and tell her to get her skates on and we'd see if we could con our way into the palazzo and maybe make a bid, if there was anything worth bidding for. But I had a doubt or two. One was that if the old lady hadn't been cool for a month even, the will certainly wouldn't have been proven or probated or whatever. And the other was that Miss W rather struck me as an upright young lady.

Anyway, the next morning I snuck off to try and do a little art valuation on my own.

Either Lady Witherford had come late on the Venetian scene or His Lordship—I assumed she'd been a widow—hadn't left her enough to keep her in the style to which she wanted to become accustomed. The palazzo was up towards the wrong end of the Canal Grande, past the Rialto and damn near opposite the fish market. I took a vaporetto up to the Ca' d'Oro and then walked around several corners, talked a little sign language, and finally got to home.

The gate in the garden wall opened at a push—a hefty push. I walked through the garden itself, about the size of a billiard table, through an arch and out into the open central courtyard. Suddenly, it seemed very quiet.

As palazzos go, it wasn't a very big one, and even as Venetian palazzos go, this had gone a long way down. The orange-red walls staggered upwards on all four sides, streaked and with the plaster coming off in big scabs to show the crumbling brickwork beneath. The narrow windows were all shuttered, but the paintwork was flaked and faded to the same grey as the wood. An old gondola was drawn up just inside the watergate, its planks sprung, the brass sea-horses crusted with green. And there was a skirting board of green slime running around all four walls.

It was like being inside a skull that had been dredged up from the canal bottom. Smelt like it, too. I shivered.

Then a vaporetto gave a gurgling cough beyond the water-gate and I was grateful for the noise. I walked up to the main door and pressed a bell.

After a long time a shutter above the door creaked open and an old crone stuck out her head and told me to go away, in Italian. Well, I suppose that's what she said; it was certainly what she meant.

I bowed up at her—not easy, that—and said: 'I have come from London to see the paintings,' just as if I really had. Hell, if the old toad had been working for an Englishwoman, she should speak English.

She did, too. 'The Lady is dead. Go away.'

'I know she is dead. That is why I have been sent to see the paintings.'

She glared at me. Then somebody appeared behind her and she gave way and Harry Burroughs looked out and said: 'Well, hi, Bert. Didn't know you were turning art dealer. Come on up.'

He was waiting for me at the top of the wide marble stairs, none of them quite level. Nor was the floor, and the walls weren't vertical and there couldn't have been a true right-angle in the place.

We shook hands and I said: 'You must feel right at home in a place as crooked as this,' and he chuckled shyly.

Then: 'What are you looking for Bert?'

'Bargain-hunting. Any arms or armour about?'

'There's nothing for sale, you know. The estate won't be probated for months.'

I just nodded and looked around.

It was dark—just a few well-shaded bulbs round the walls—and the air was thick, damp, and smelt of old ladies as well as the canal. The room was furnished like a junk shop. Just about every foot of floor had a small table or davenport or desk on it, and every inch of tabletop had a clock or a vase or something on it. The walls were more picture than wall-paper.

I said: 'Jesus.'

Harry waved a hand. 'Go ahead and look. I've been doing a little kind of cataloguing myself.' He walked over to one big, dim, dirty picture. 'I'd say that's Tiepolo—or was.'

I saw what he meant. The canvas was sagging almost in folds. I touched it and it was damp. Hell, it was *wet*. Below, the plaster on the wall was a gritty paste.

Harry moved on. 'And that's Gainsborough—once.'

We walked around. He said a few more names, but over half the paintings were the sort you'd find hung in the halls of country hotels. You know—Highland cattle or a still life of a dead rabbit and a lobster and a bunch of wet grapes, that sort of thing. The old bird had obviously just wanted something to cover the walls and hadn't counted the difference between Tiepolo and your sister's kids.

Harry stopped by a door and looked back. For once, his face was set and sombre. 'A million dollars. A million dollars' value's been just rotted out of those pictures.' He shook his head. 'Why in hell do they do it? Why do they buy pictures if they can't look after them? I'd hate to have been one of her children.'

I nodded again. I'd been trying to work out what Harry was after in that art cemetery. And I thought I'd got it: he was going to be the Resurrection and the Light. Buy at a knock-down price because of their condition—then get a bunch of restorers, toucher-uppers and whatnot to bring them up to mint condition again. Maybe one or two of the most damaged (but simplest) would go quietly down the drain—after they'd been carefully copied and the copy aged a bit. He'd have a proper bill of sale to prove he'd bought the genuine job.

Nice work if you've got the capital to finance it.

'This isn't half of it,' he said, and led the way down a long gloomy corridor lined mostly with prints, engravings, etchings, maps—all black-and-white stuff. Some of it was propped on tables or just against the walls; the paper was bulging and drooping, but it was all behind glass so it wasn't as bad as the paintings.

He stopped. 'That's about the only one you could sell straight off.'

It was an engraving. Smallish, about nine inches by eleven, and neatly framed so the weather hadn't got into it yet. It seemed vaguely familiar: a knight in armour on a horse, with his lance at the slope and a bit of fuzz at the point, and alongside him an old boy with a skull face and a helmet full of snakes, and behind him a character with a wild-boar's face and various horns thrown in. Dead symbolic, you know?

Harry said: 'Dürer.'

I might even have guessed it myself, especially with the little AD monogram on a milestone down in the left-hand corner.

I just nodded and we walked on.

We went through two more rooms, smaller but just as crammed and rotting as the first. And by then I'd had enough. I sat down on a green plush sofa, then got up again. It was like sitting on a bank of seaweed.

'I'll leave you to it mate. There's nothing here for me.'

'You're not going to bid for that suit of armour?'

I'd noticed it—but you can't fill up rust holes the way you can touch up a bit of flaked paint. I shook my head. 'It's all yours, Harry.'

He just smiled apologetically, and I left him there.

On the way back down the corridor I stopped for a second look at the Dürer engraving. Then I looked back, and Harry wasn't in sight, so I took it off the wall and shoved it behind a big map propped below. I found something else on the floor roughly the same size and hung it in the space; there wasn't any pattern in the hanging, anyway. Only Harry would notice, and maybe not even him. And he wouldn't bother to come looking, anyway; if he thought the same of me as I thought of him, he'd assume I'd just nicked it outright. Being a bit more honest struck me as a bit of a giggle.

Downstairs I snooped around until I found the old house-cleaner or cook or whoever she was, brewing up a big saucepan of soup-bones. Even that smell was an improvement.

'Signora, you have been most kind,' I said, all formal and

fine-old-English-gent. 'Molto grazie. Will you allow me to pay for your time?'

She gave me a bright suspicious look, but my two thousand lire vanished without a rustle somewhere into her clothes. I mean somewhere; you couldn't tell just where. Below her long Venetian face, she looked like a pudding dressed for boiling.

I took out my diary. 'Madam owned some fine paintings. My clients will be most interested. May I know the name of the lawyer who is handling the estate?'

Another suspicious stare, then she said: 'Signor Foscari.'

'You are most kind. He is a good lawyer?'

Her body wobbled, so maybe she was shrugging. 'He is a thief.'

Well, I certainly hoped so, but it seemed best not to say it. I just bowed and backed away. 'You are most kind.'

She watched me go. As I was almost out of the door, she said: 'He is at San Michele, arranging her Ladyship's tomb.' Then she brought her hand from behind her back and took a long slurping sip at a glass of clear liquid: grappa, I suppose. At ten in the morning.

Outside in the courtyard, I stopped and lit a small cigar. I wanted the smell of something burning, not just rotting.

TWENTY-ONE

I STILL HADN'T anything else to do, so I walked directly away from the Canal Grande, zigzagging through narrow alleys until I came out on the quay on the north side. You could see San Michele a few hundred yards off across the still water, faint and flat in the mist. Just a low, red-brick-walled island with the spires of cypress trees poking up behind.

There's a regular vaporetto service from the quay, but first I dropped into a café for a snifter—yes, I know: at ten-thirty in the morning—and a telephone call. It turned out I was lucky to catch Elizabeth Whitley.

'I'm going out; I've got an appointment,' she said briskly. 'What is it?'

'A Dürer engraving.'

'How would you know?'

'It's got the monogram—AD, and a date: 1513. But I mean, everybody knows Dürer.'

'That's why he gets faked so much.'

I could have said Harry shared my view, but she probably wouldn't have been impressed. Anyway, I'd been told to stay away from Signor Burroughs, hadn't I? So I said: 'Well, suppose it's real—what's it worth?'

'How can I tell? I haven't seen it.'

'Well, there's a knight on a horse and a chap with a skull face holding up a big egg-timer and behind them there's a sort of devil, I suppose . . . Sounds a bit like those Swedish movies, doesn't it?'

'Where d'you think Bergman gets his ideas from? It might be a "Knight, Death and the Devil"; there's a few around. If it *is*, then it's worth—oh, say seven thousand dollars.'

'D'you want it at that price?'

'Ye—es. We got another Dürer in New York; they'd make a nice pair. But not until I've seen it.'

'Course not. But can you get your hands on that money fast, without going through Managua?'

'I can go up to ten thousand. But—'

'Never mind, love. I'll ring you later. I've got an appointment.'

San Michele is a cemetery—and nothing else, bar the chapel and the offices and so on. A few acres of flat land crossed with neat gravel paths, walls, rows of cypresses, and the whole thing held together by the bones of fifty generations of Venetians. If they've left enough cash for it, mind. You get your first few years' lodging free, then you have to start paying rent—or they dig you up and dump you in a communal pit in one corner. A pricey place to die, Venice.

At the office they told me where Lady Witherford's new address was, and roughly how to get to it, and I plodded off into the cold. They didn't have much custom that morning: a workman with a wheelbarrow, a few cats slinking along in the shelter of the walls, and from somewhere the thonk-thonk-thonk of a stonemason cutting a new headstone. That apart, there was just me and the mist.

But there was nothing creepy or sad or even particularly impressive about it all. I mean, you could stand there and convince yourself you were alone with God-knows-how-many thousand dead, but there wasn't anything of the cornfield of death idea you get in the French war cemeteries. It was all too clean, too neat, modern—nothing like Venice itself—and a mess. No two graves were the same; there were family tombs like small chapels complete with courtyard, and everything right down to a wall of stone coffins, six high, like sideways-on filing cabinets. Well, I suppose the bloke upstairs wouldn't be likely to drop his boots or snore.

In the end I found Lady Witherford's last resting-place—I mean unless she defaulted on the rent and got slung on the community dump—by the group around it. A couple of workmen and a tall thin man in a black overcoat, black homburg and a blue nose, all having a barney about the grave itself. As far as it had gone, she seemed to be getting something about the size and shape of a double bed in white marble.

I hung back, waiting for them to finish and reading off the nearby tombstones. Funny how the Italians leave off the first figure of the date; it gives you a bit of a jolt to see a brand-new stone labelled n.912, m.967. And build a fancy piece of carving around a rather poor little photograph.

A deep voice said: 'Signor?'

I turned round; the workmen were trundling off. 'Signor Foscari?'

'Si.' His face was long and solemn, his eyes dark.

'Do you speak English?'

'Yes, I do.'

'My name's Gilbert Kemp.' We shook hands without him taking off his gloves. 'Er—I've been looking at some of Lady Witherford's pictures, I mean just a glance really, since you'd let Harry Burroughs have a look, well . . .' He just went on staring at me. I was beginning to sweat; if this one was a thief he was right out of my class.

But I staggered on. 'I—I mean my clients—well, I think they'd like to make an offer for just one item. A small one.'

'The estate has not been settled yet. Not even started on properly.'

'No, I suppose not. I mean, I don't suppose the pictures are even catalogued. Not even counted, probably. The way she collected, it doesn't sound like she'd keep a list.'

He stared a few more seconds, then slowly turned round to the half-finished tomb. 'She was a very great lady,' he said sonorously. Then he took off his hat. 'Requiescat in pace.' He put his hat on again. 'Which picture do you want?'

'A Dürer engraving. It's about the only one in the place that's in good condition.'

He thought for a moment. 'When the estate is settled I may —perhaps—get instructions to sell the art. Probably Signor Burroughs will make an offer.'

'Harry isn't interested in a market price. He wants to buy cheap and start restoring.'

He started a slow march away from the graveside. I went with him. 'Then,' he said, 'it will be my duty to put it all in the market openly.'

'Same problem: you've got to sell to some expert. An ordinary collector won't buy stuff in that condition.'

He stopped at the end of the gravel walk and looked back. 'A very great lady.'

And she must have left her affairs in such a tangle that he'd have a legal banquet picking it over with his long, gloved fingers. A very great lady—for a lawyer.

Suddenly, but just as solemnly, he said: 'How much?'

I'd thought of being out that evening, but then decided I'd better stay available. Dead right, too. I was sitting in my room trying to decipher the *Zuericher Zeitung*—still no progress on the Henri Bernard front, thank God—when something like the riot squad beat on the door. I opened it and something like the riot squad whizzed in, except that it was only Miss Whitley, art expert. Angry. Even her tomcat collar had all its fur standing up.

'What on earth are you doing?' she blazed.

'I dunno. What *have* I done?'

'Sending somebody round with that Dürer—he wanted four million lire in cash, no receipt, no questions.'

'Well, I left you a note saying he'd be coming. Was it genuine?'

She shook her head impatiently. 'It's genuine, all right. But it must be stolen, isn't it?'

I shrugged. 'Not by me, not by you, maybe not by anybody. I mean, if it was Foscari himself you saw—tall bloke? Long nose? Looks like an undertaker?' She nodded sharply. 'Well, he's the lawyer handling somebody's estate. He must have power of attorney. If he wants to turn some of the estate into money . . .' I shrugged again.

'In *cash*? And not giving a receipt? He's pocketing it!'

'Maybe he'll knock it off his bill at the end.'

She took a short walk around the room and arrived back still fuming. 'My God—it's still stolen!'

'Look,' I said soothingly, 'you got offered a real Dürer at a real price. And if we don't buy it, Harry Burroughs will—and he won't pay four million, even. Anyway, why not check with the Boss Lady and see what she says?—it's her decision, really.'

She suddenly stopped being angry and turned gloomy instead. 'I think I know what she'll say.'

'Buy.'

She nodded, then said miserably: 'Oh damn it—you *are* a crook.'

'Me? What have I got out of it all? I'm just a loyal employee.'

'All *right*. I'll ring her up.'

'Fine.' Then I remembered I'd been told not to go getting mixed up with Harry and his projects. 'Don't bother to mention where I found it, will you?'

She looked at me suspiciously. 'All right . . .'

I nodded at my bottle of Scotch. 'Like a drink?'

She shook her head. 'I'll get back.'

'While we're in these parts, are you going up to see Faggioni?'

'Yes. I've got an appointment tomorrow.'

'Ever met him before?'

'No. Please don't tell me he's a crook, too. I've heard about him.'

I nodded.

She hesitated, then said: 'I suppose you know him professionally?'

I nodded again. She asked: 'How good is his English?'

'It varies. Depends whether he wants any misunderstandings or not.'

After another pause, she said: 'I suppose you want to come, too?'

'Let's say I wouldn't mind renewing an old . . . friendship.'

'Oh, *all* right.' Just crazy for my company, she was. 'Ten-forty-six train tomorrow.'

TWENTY-TWO

FAGGIONI lived in Padua, but that apart it's quite a nice town. Under thirty miles directly inland from Venice, up a long canal.

In summer you can go by boat, if you've got the time and like stopping every half mile to look at another Palladian villa. We spent a non-conversational three-quarters of an hour on the train and arrived about half past eleven.

The old boy had a house in a back street so narrow you were standing right up against it before you saw it. So you couldn't tell the size, except that it was huge, nor the shape, except that the front was roughly square. It had a blank, blind look to it, without any mouldings, the windows barred and shuttered, the walls of old grey stone that would take a big cannon a long day to punch through. Well, it wouldn't surprise me if somebody took a cannon to Fajjy one of these days.

I pressed a bellpush beside a prison-type door, and after a time a young man let us in. He had long black hair, a white jacket, black tie and too-tight black trousers; Elizabeth dealt him a visiting card, and after that we stood and waited. The hall was tall, wide, and lit by lights that were probably never turned off, summer or winter; all lined with bits and pieces of classical statues. Just lined; they weren't arranged at all.

She snooped along the line, then looked at one piece closer. 'My God—d'you know who I think that's by?'

'You're probably right. He doesn't touch junk.'

The thing was a life-size stone job of some god or warrior who'd dressed in such a hurry he'd forgotten to.

I said: 'He probably hasn't got space upstairs with the real good stuff. I'll try sticking it in my pocket on the way out.'

She gave me a look. 'We're here on serious business, remember.'

'If I forget, Fajjy'll remember.'

She looked around again, and sounded a little awed. 'I knew he was big, but I didn't know he was *this* big.'

Which is probably just what the old bastard wanted her to think. Leave the customer waiting with some easily-recognized high-class stuff just lying around anyhow to show you haven't got time to be bothered with it, and the customer'll get the idea that you're big. And important, and rich. So maybe the customer won't push too hard on a bargain.

'By the way,' I asked, 'are we now the proud owners of a Dürer engraving?'

Her lips tightened. 'We are,' she muttered.

'Thought we would be. Bloody clever of me to spot it, don't you think?'

'Like you said: everybody knows Dürer.'

Just then the young man came back and said that the Master would see us now.

The Master's room was a smallish ground-floor study, a bit cluttered and mostly filled with bookcases. Just a rack of unframed pictures behind the huge old desk, a single framed picture on an easel in one corner. No daylight; dusty old dark-red curtains that stayed drawn the year round.

Faggioni was a small, old, fat man with a stoop, though how he managed to stoop with a stomach like that on him I don't know. His brown suit, his thin grey hair, even the cigarette sticking out through the stained straggly moustache, everything about him looked rumpled. He looked worth about five lire and a used bus ticket.

He hauled himself up from behind the desk and looked at us over his glasses, then consulted Elizabeth's calling-card Another bit of the old psychologics.

'You are Miss Whitley? I am most happy.' He held out a fat, pale hand. 'I once met your most famous father.' He took his hand back—she didn't seem to want to hang on to it too long—

and flapped it at a bookcase. .I have read everything of him. It was so sad to learn of his death.' Then he looked at me.

I said: 'Hello. Again.'

'Gilbert. I am more than most happy. We have not met since . . .'

'Not since I took that little state-financed holiday. Three years ago.'

He wobbled his head around. 'That was most terrible. I cannot think how—'

'I can.'

Elizabeth was giving me a curious look. But she decided not to make anything of it right then.

Fajjy turned back to her. 'You are buying pictures, signorina?'

'I'd be interested to have a look,' she said carefully.

'You are collecting for someone?'

'One or two people. In the States. It gives me a chance to look at the museums over here.'

He nodded as far as his chins let him; he hadn't shifted his cigarette from his face the whole time. 'I have some. Not much. I am not so interested now. I am dying.'

'Oh yes?' I said cheerfully.

He looked at me. Then took the cigarette out of his face, gave a long crackling wet cough, spat on the back of his hand, and stared at it. Then licked it off again.

I felt Elizabeth shudder beside me.

Faggioni went on looking at me. 'Dying,' he said firmly. 'My doctors tell me.'

'Get a doctor who says you aren't dying, then. You can afford it.'

'The money—it does not matter. I give it away. I am dying. My pictures—I give them away. Take what you like.' He flapped a hand at the padded racks behind the desk. 'Pay me what you want.' He looked at me reproachfully and gave another attempt to cough up his socks.

Elizabeth walked tentatively round the desk. 'Can I have a look, then?'

He yanked out a picture. 'Canaletto—a young one, of

137

course.' It was a fairly flat scene somewhere in Venice, a bit romanticked up.

She held it, tilting it slightly from side to side, said 'Yes,' and gave it back.

He pulled out another. 'Caravaggio.' A woman from the middle up, with a lot of fancy folds in her clothing, all done with heavy sharp shadows. She gave it a brisk look-over. 'Could be.'

They went on like that, taking no more time than if they'd been counting clean towels. The old swindler's psychology didn't seem to have had much effect; Elizabeth was quick, efficient, non-commital. Except when he handed her a square of old wood with a faint head of a woman on it.

He said: 'Raphael.'

She said: 'Never.'

He gave her a look, then shrugged and smiled sadly. 'You are the daughter of your father.' He put son of Raphael back in his cage. 'You would like to see the galleries?'

'If we may.'

He took a huge bunch of keys out of the desk and pressed a bell-push. After a few moments, the boy in the white jacket opened the door. Fajjy led the way out.

I'd done the tour before so I wasn't surprised, but I was still lost after a couple of minutes. It was like a house designed by a child, and not a hell of a clever one, neither. Rooms were just jammed in anywhere, on slightly different levels, up or down a few steps. Each one led out of the next, and the boy unlocked each door, then locked it behind us. And there wasn't a window in the place; maybe they were blocked up, maybe none of the gallery rooms had outside walls—you couldn't tell. But at least the rooms were properly done up. The walls were painted and clean, the pictures and statues arranged and lit by spotlights from up near the ceilings.

The house just can't have been built that way; Fajjy must have had it done himself. But I suppose it was security, of a sort. A burglar would take a week to find his way out, let alone in.

Elizabeth set the pace; she looked at everything, but some

got just a glance, some got a polite frown, which took a little longer, and some she had a real shufti at. Fajjy started off reciting names, but she obviously wasn't listening so he shut up—apart from a cough or two just to remind us he was dying.

Finally, after three or four rooms, she got really interested. I could see why: it was a largish job, more than twice the size of the two I'd handled before, and it looked like a fancy-dress picnic where the guests had been cheap in hiring clothes. Just a brass helmet, a bit of drapery slung over a shoulder, a spear or two, and everybody—half a dozen—having fun in a sort of non-sexy way. Plus a couple of cherubs playing Spitfires-and-Messerchmitts in the top right. It was certainly Dona Margarita's meat.

Fajjy said: 'Poussin.'

She agreed. 'I think so. Fairly early.' She had her nose almost on the canvas.

When she stood back, I lifted the bottom of the frame away from the wall and felt round the back. I found a small, ragged metal tab.

I looked at Fajjy. 'What date?'

Elizabeth frowned and said: '1632, maybe. About then.'

Fajjy said: '1966.'

'What?'

I said: 'It's been imported. If you have it registered, they photograph it, stick a tab on it, give it a certificate. Means you can export it again without tax or anything for the next five years. You won't need me for this one—if you buy it.'

She nodded. 'It's a bit big for you anyway, I'd think.' Then she looked at Fajjy. 'I might make an offer for this. Have you got a photograph?'

'Yes. But this—I am sorry to sell this one. It is my only Poussin. It is so happy, so young. It makes me forget I am dying.'

I said: 'It makes you forget you're giving them all away.'

He coughed more or less in my direction. 'I will sell, of course. I am a seller of pictures. But . . .'

'But at a price.'

Elizabeth just nodded. 'We can see about that when I've checked with my client.'

Fajjy said: 'It is catalogued.' He knew she was going to check more than just the client.

We went on.

Two or maybe three rooms later we got into what might once have been a corridor. It was that shape, anyway. Pictures along both walls, a few statues and a glass case down the middle. Elizabeth strolled along the walls; I went to snoop at whatever Fajjy reckoned was worth keeping behind glass.

Most of it was antiquities—little twisted pots of blue glass, probably Roman. And scarabs, and bits of primitive jewellery. And a pistol.

I rammed my nose against the glass and stared at it.

It was a flintlock and a bit of a dog's dinner—I mean over-decorated with silver wire inlays, engraved lockplate and barrel, silver butt cap. But underneath, it was a real gun. The butt curved right down to give a proper grip, the barrel looked heavy. It hadn't been the maker's idea to wrap it in bright metalwork that could flash the sun into the shooter's eyes.

Fajjy looked at me, coughed, and said: 'Ah, I am forgetting you are a seller of guns. It is nice?'

'Not so bad.'

'You would like to see it more close?' He beckoned up the lad with the keys and opened the case. 'You must advise me what it is. I know nothing about guns. It is by Wogdon, about 1770.'

I picked it up, held it pointing straight down by my side, swung it up. I'd been right about the balance and grip: it locked itself into a true, steady aim. I found I'd got it pointed at the house-boy's tie; he gave me a sharp scowl and stepped aside.

'The code duello,' Fajjy said. He was trying to keep an eye on me and Elizabeth simultaneously.

I nodded. It was a duelling pistol, all right. Most of the decorated pistols from that time weren't even intended to be fired; just presentation jobs, *papier peint* from the day they were made. Even the military pistols weren't much cop—clumsy, unbalanced, old-fashioned. But a duelling pistol was a gentleman's life.

Fajjy said: 'You like it, no? I do not know about it, but I think perhaps it was presented by your East India Company to the Nabob of Oudh.'

My guess exactly. At any rate, it was the most likely bet. The old Nabob must have been a right nut about fancy pistols, and the Company was always keeping him sweet by giving him a new pair.

I checked it over, but I knew already. It said *Wogdon* inlet in gold along the top of the barrel, a London proof-mark on the side, the initials MB for Mark Bock on the silver butt cap. The lock was sweet, the ramrod slid down the barrel unobstructed. It was in near-mint condition.

'Are you selling?' I asked.

'For you—four hundred thousand lire. But I knew nothing about guns.'

'Stop saying that!' I snapped. Like hell he knew nothing. He might not know as much as me, but he knew this gun and he knew the top price he could hope for it. To the nearest lira. 'Three hundred quid? You're crazy.'

'It is one of a pair.' He was watching Elizabeth, and arguing with me over his shoulder.

'So where's the other one?'

'If I am having the other one, you are buying for perhaps two and a half million. But now you buy this, then you find the other, and *you* will have that money, no?' We both knew how likely you are to re-match a pair of pistols once they've been split. The second might not even exist any more. 'So then, you have cheated poor Faggioni once more. But I do not care; money is nothing. I am—'

'You said that before. I'll give you two hundred thousand.'

He shook his head. Just then Elizabeth called: 'Is this *right*?'

Fajjy waddled over. I followed.

She was staring at an old portrait, head to tummy of a bearded gent with a fancy tin hat and metal breastplate. And that was all; it was as dull a picture as I'd seen the whole trip.

Not even in good condition; it was on wood which had curved and got a few thin splits, plus some worm-holes near the edges. The paint was pale and flaky.

But it meant something to her. Her finger was on—no, almost on—a line of faint lettering running across the top, split by the bloke's helmet. It said:

FRANCISCO HERNANDEZ DE CORDOBA.

She said: '*Is* it him?'

Fajjy shrugged. 'It says so. I do not know.'

'Have you tried to check it out?'

'What can I check? It is very old; the words are also old. I can hear of no other portraits of this man. So . . .' he shrugged.

This was all way beyond me. I thought of asking, but with such a Spanish name, it looked like we'd soon be mentioning Dona Margarita.

Elizabeth was ploughing up the paint with her nose. 'It's been damaged at the top and bottom. There's probably an inch or two missing.'

'I believe also. What do you expect? Probably it was made in Mexico. You have the ants, the banditti, the hurricanes, everything—you are knowing a rich Mexican, then?'

'Rich?' she seemed affronted. 'It isn't worth much. You might sell it to a Latin-American historian, that's all.'

He shrugged. 'Or a rich Mexican. I will wait.'

'All right.' She turned away. 'But the likely markets are on my side of the Atlantic. How much are you asking?'

'One hundred thousand of your dollars.'

She winced, then shook her head and walked on.

I said: 'I made you an offer for this . . .' and held up the pistol. But Fajjy was waddling after her.

'It is not the art, as the art it is nothing. But if it is right, then it is most rare—unique, you say. For the proper man, it is more than Raphael, Botticelli, Titian—anybody.'

She stopped and turned, then nodded. 'Yes, well—I'll see.'

I took my own snoop: no import tag on the back. And he'd said it probably came from Mexico, hadn't he? I wasn't going to enjoy taking that job out of the country; unless it was wrapped like a new-born baby I'd end up with a handful of firewood and a few flakes of old paint. Probably even a change of climate would make it fall apart.

I said loudly: 'This gun—will you take two-fifty?'

Without turning, he said: 'For you—three-fifty, You bring me customers, perhaps. I like you. Three hundred and fifty thousand.'

'Oh hell.' Then I said: 'All right—hold it until I collect anything here. Cash, I presume?'

'What you like.'

So I'd bought a gun—if I could raise two hundred and sixty pounds in the next few days.

But we didn't buy anything else that day. Ten minutes later we were back in Fajjy's study, waiting while he sorted through his files somewhere else for photographs of the Poussin and the old portrait.

'Is it a good gun?' Elizabeth asked politely.

'Very nice. You wouldn't like to lend me two hundred pounds, would you?'

'Well—I . . . I don't think I've got it right now.' She seemed a bit flustered.

'Never mind. I could give you a very nice rate of interest, though.'

'You're going to make a profit on it? When?'

'Not for a while. Come the summer, probably.'

'You could see if Carlos will give you an advance.'

'I'll try that.'

After a little while, she asked: 'What was that about your state-financed holiday?—does it mean what I think it means?'

'I got slung in jail up in Milan for six weeks.'

'What for?' She wasn't looking at me, just fiddling with a pile of art magazines on the corner of the desk.

'The usual. The Customs unwrapped my dirty shirts one day. But I never got charged in the end. The bloke I was working for paid a ruddy great fine and got me out.'

'Oh. What did Faggioni have to do with this?'

'He'd sold the bloke the picture—and then tipped off the Customs.'

She turned, frowning. 'Are you sure? Why should he do that?'

'He sold it at an export price, about twenty-five per cent over the odds—well, you know all that. And when I got nicked and the picture got a bit of publicity, there wasn't a hope in hell of *anybody* getting it out of the country. So my bloke had to sell it off again. But of course, he couldn't get the export price. Fajjy bought it back. He cleared twenty thousand quid on that little deal.'

'And your man had to pay a big fine as well. I don't suppose you got much more custom from him.'

'You're damn right. He never really believed it was Fajjy anyway. Just thought I'd bollixed things myself.'

'Umm.' She turned back to the magazines. 'Was it a good idea you coming up here, then?—letting him know you'll probably be smuggling out some items?'

I shrugged. 'That's rather what I wanted to talk to him about.'

We didn't say any more until Fajjy came back with the photographs and a handful of papers about the Poussin.

As we were about to go, I said: 'I'll see you about the pistol soon, then. I'm interested in all sorts of guns, you know. I mean, the modern ones as well, the ones that really work. I'm pretty good with them, too.'

Fajjy was watching me quietly.

I said: 'And you don't move very fast any more. I mean not fast enough to make it worth trying any export swindles.'

He turned silently and led the way to the front door. As we went out he gave one last explosive cough.

TWENTY-THREE

OUTSIDE, I SAID: 'Well—was I subtle enough?'

She buried her face in her tomcat collar and muttered: 'If you'd waved a machine-gun in his face he might have got the message a bit clearer, but otherwise it was fine. If he sells us anything after *that*—'

'He'll sell.' We were walking back down the narrow side roads towards the main street, the wind pouncing on us from every corner.

There wasn't any taxis, of course. But a hundred yards down there was a small restaurant, and it was already past one o'clock. She ordered prosciutto and a veal cutlet; I just had lasagne—and the wine *now*, before the food, *per favore*.

When I'd got the first layer of chill off, I said: 'Well, what's this portrait bit? I mean, who's this Cordoba?'

'Cordoba or Cordova. Francisco Hernandez, or Fernandez, de. He was with Cortez.'

'Yes? And who was he?'

She stared. 'Oh, come *on*. You must know something. Stout Cortez on a peak in Darien.'

'Oh, that bastard. He put the boot into Mexico and so on, didn't he?'

'That's right. And Cordoba was one of his lieutenants— the one Cortez sent to conquer what's now Nicaragua.'

'Ah, I get it. Noble founder of the noble nation and all that.'

'They were a bunch of Gestapo thugs.'

I raised an eyebrow; just then the food started arriving. It was rough but at least cheap. After a couple of mouthfuls, I said: 'Still, Madam Presidente ought to like it. D'you think it's genuine?'

'For age, yes. But if it's really Cordoba . . .' she frowned,

'. . . I doubt we'll ever know. It's probably *some* Cordoba, but there was a Gonzales de Cordoba back in Spain about the same time, and another Francisco Cordoba out in Cuba. And there must have been others.'

'You didn't have to rush from shop to shop to find one with a Cordoba still in stock?'

'Anything but,' she said gloomily. 'I'll need help, on the historical side. You don't know anything about armour, as well as old guns?'

'Some. That helmet looked about the right period. But I wouldn't try dating a picture on that. I mean, armour lasted a long time; you didn't buy a new suit every six months. And fashions didn't change very fast. But why don't you chuck the whole problem back to Managua? If anybody knows about Cordoba, they ought to.'

She nodded. 'I'll ask Carlos to do that. Oh *heck*.'

'What's the matter?'

'This whole thing . . . the whole trip. We're always having to buy the wrong pictures or for the wrong reasons and in too much of a hurry—*and* having to smuggle them out. Then Henri getting killed and you getting beaten up . . . It's all just a *mess*. You shouldn't be dealing in art this way.'

I gulped wine. 'You've had too much to do with museums. A lot of art dealing's always been this way.'

She looked up from the rather half-hearted attack she'd been making on her veal. 'How much d'you know about it?'

'Art, nothing. But something about art dealing. I mean, it isn't always quite as hectic as this, but you get anything that's worth big money and you'll get funny business going with it.' I pointed at her plate. 'If somebody—enough people—suddenly decided Padua forks were worth collecting, the next day you'd have fork-stealing gangs, fork smugglers, little men in Paris forging Padua forks.'

She smiled wanly. 'Forks aren't art.'

'Well, art ain't forks. You can't eat veal with a portrait of Cordoba.'

'You can't eat it with a fork, either. It's a pity you didn't get that pistol: it might have helped.' She shoved her plate

146

away and stared gloomily out through the leaves of some potted plant at the grey street.

Time to change the subject slightly. I asked: 'How did you get into the art biz?—if it isn't a silly question.'

'My father. I just about lived in the National, when he was there. I saw more da Vincis than I did comic books. I suppose perhaps I'm trying to keep up with Daddy, or do better . . .I don't know, though. If you've lived with art like that, you can't just give it up. It'd be like a musician cutting off his ears.'

'So you're hooked.'

'I guess so.' She smiled wanly. 'It's a bit un-American really, if you think of. America produces everything, just a bit bigger and better than anybody else, but we can hardly produce any old masters.'

'Oh, I don't know. I'm sure Harry could put you in touch with a couple of boys if you asked him nicely.'

She suddenly went quite pale. 'I'm *sure* he could. And if he does I'll probably kill them with my own hands.'

Blimey. I stopped with a forkful of lasagne in the air and my mouth hanging open for it. Then I pulled myself together. 'Oh, come off it, love. Like the man said—just a man I met —if you think you've bought a genuine Whatsit but really it's a fake, then as long as you don't know you don't get any less fun out of it—do you?'

'*Yes!*' I got the word straight between the eyes. 'You don't buy a . . . a Poussin because you already know all about it, understand it all. You buy because you *want* to understand. You want to sit and look and learn. And if it isn't a real Poussin then you aren't learning. Selling forgeries is like bringing up a child on deliberate lies.'

I took a quick swig of the wine. 'I suppose so . . . in a way. But I mean, aren't most art forgeries by artists who just can't get recognition for their own work?'

She almost spat. 'So they say—and so what? Do you justify a bank robber by saying he couldn't get a job as a bank president?'

I sat back and stared at her carefully—and, in a way, for the first time. Somewhere under the dull clothes and the schoolgirl

147

face there was sheer stainless steel. It was odd. A bit disturbing, too. Like a song you can't quite remember and can't quite forget.

But it felt like a bit too much deep water for Bert Kemp. Time to change the subject again. 'Well, we seem to have finished the day early. Feel like going to the pictures—the moving ones? There's a John Wayne western on, back in Venice. Now there's a boy who knows about guns. Always carries the same one, same place, high on his hip, every picture. He's not just acting.'

'You're not the first person to say *that* about John Wayne.' Then she suddenly smiled, bright and cheerful again. I liked that. 'Maybe. But while we're in Padua I want to see the Giottos in the chapel.'

So in the end I went along as well and we wandered round the cold narrow Cappella degli Scrovegni and stared at the stiff, worn figures acting out the life of Christ as they had done for nearly seven hundred years. I don't go a bundle on that sort of stuff; it's a bit early for me. But it's got something, apart from the formal expressions, the sexless saints, the out-of-scale castles, the lions and camels drawn from a police description. Maybe the sheer size, the amount of work it all took. But maybe that glimpse of Hell, too; far more real than the Brigade-of-Guards Heaven above it. The simple certainty that there *would* be a fat blue devil stuffing naked sinners into his mouth like hot dogs. Giotto didn't paint that just for the money; he *knew* that big blue bastard was waiting down there.

Finally Elizabeth said: 'Well, do you like it? Or were you just thinking it'd be a problem to smuggle out?'

I grinned. 'It's not bad.' I said some of what I'd been thinking.

She nodded. 'Yes, Hell was one thing they were sure about, then. The Church made sure about that—and nobody but the Church commissioned painting. The real thing behind the Renaissance was the upper-middle classes getting into the act —rich Venetian merchants commissioning stuff for their own homes. That started everything: non-religious subjects, the size of pictures, and new materials. It made the artists pretty rich, too—and independent. You know, the idea of the artist starving in a garret and not being recognized in his own time —that's only come up in the last hundred years. For most of art history the artist's been fairly well off.'

'I suppose that's because your patrons—your Venetian merchants—are gone, now.'

'Heck, no—they aren't gone, but they're not buying *new* art so much. It's the same as Dona Margarita: old masters and Impressionists. And look at the prices; Faggioni will ask over two hundred thousand dollars for that Poussin—and we'll pay it; it's the market price. But it's nonsense.'

We were walking fairly briskly in the direction of the station; still no taxis.

I said: 'Didn't I read the Mona Lisa was insured for something like fifty million dollars?'

She stopped abruptly. 'Right. And *that's* crazy. No picture in the world is worth that much more than all the rest. And anyway—who's going to buy it? Suppose France went broke and the Louvre was told to sell it off?—who to? Maybe Washington or the Met could raise that sort of money, but nobody else. And they'd *know* there wouldn't be anybody else, so why pay that price? They'd get it for half or less.'

She started walking again, her face almost angry against the wind. 'The trouble is, the ordinary buyer reads that and takes art at that valuation. He sees a picture he likes, at five hundred dollars, and then he works out five hundred against fifty million and figures it can only be one-hundred-thousandth as good as the Mona Lisa and so he must be crazy to like it at all. So he buys an electric barbecue instead. At least nobody can have a barbecue a hundred thousand times better than his.'

Then she added: 'Or they turn the argument around and buy a picture they *don't* like because they hope it'll one day be worth fifty millions.'

'You're sounding a bit anti-capitalist today.'

'Maybe . . . Oh well, at least it gets the best art into the museums, where people can see it. In a hundred years I don't suppose there'll be a single old master or Impressionist in a private collection.'

'We'll be back before the Renaissance—except the State instead of the Church.'

'Something like that.'

By now we were in sight of the station—and of course a couple of empty taxis cruised past.

I patted her elbow. 'Come on love. John Wayne awaits.'

'So does Dona Margarita. I'll have to see them. And don't you want to try and raise a loan?'

Well, come to think of it . . . So I rang them from the station and fixed a board meeting for six o'clock.

TWENTY-FOUR

WITH HARRY IN TOWN I was back to being security-conscious. Hotel rooms were a bit too obvious and the posh restaurants—there aren't many, anyway, apart from the hotels—would be so empty that we'd stand out like a bad fairy at a christening. So we met under the huge dome of the Salute, just across the Canal from the Gritti.

They were setting it up for a TV concert. They'd floated the big vans on barges down the Canal, then lifted them up onto the piazza outside. Inside, there were cameras and monitors and microphones lousing up the nice clean lines of the pillars, lights glaring down, cables and junction boxes all over the floor—and in the middle a TV technician in a red shirt picking out *Honeysuckle Rose* on a grand piano.

I was late, of course, so Elizabeth had explained all about the new pictures before I got there.

Dona Margarita was holding the photo of the Poussin and giving it a careful look; Carlos had the photo of the Cordoba or whoever.

Dona Margarita looked up and smiled. 'I understand you have discovered us a good engraving, Senor.'

'He did,' Elizabeth said grimly.

'It was well done,' Dona M assured me. 'I like it much. Many thanks.'

Carlos said: 'Miss Whitley was telling us ye had a little trouble with the Italian Customs a while back. Ye might have told us yeself.'

I shrugged. 'What's the odds?'

'If they know ye as a smuggler ye might have trouble with *our* pictures.'

'Maybe. Let's wait and see what has to go out.'

Dona Margarita put one of her long cigarettes delicately between her teeth. A uniformed attendant zoomed out from behind a pillar and told her this was a house of God and *non-fumare*. She glared at him, but put it away again. All around us the TV men went on puffing away like five-alarm fires.

'If the picture is truly of Cordoba,' she said, 'it will have to be taken by Senor Kemp?'

Elizabeth looked thoughtful. 'I don't know . . . The Italians might not think it's valuable to them at all. Trouble is, once we ask permission, we're stuck if they say no.'

Carlos said: 'Ye'd better start thinking of some clever ways, Mr. Kemp.'

'Down to Brindisi and take a boat to Greece and fly it in from there. I mean, nobody expects you to smuggle art to Greece, do they?'

Elizabeth looked doubtful; probably she was thinking of a picture that fragile bouncing around the winter Adriatic for a couple of days. Come to that, I didn't fancy the bouncing much myself, but it *was* a safe route.

Dona Margarita said: 'One hundred thousand dollars . . . It is much. You are sure this Senor Faggioni does not know you are working for me?'

'Pretty sure,' Elizabeth said, 'but he must guess I've got some Mexican or Central American client in mind. A picture like that wouldn't make anything like that money in Europe or the States.'

I said: 'Fajjy didn't push it. I mean, he wasn't claiming much for it.'

'He hung it and lit it. And asked a hundred thousand for it. I don't call that being exactly shy.'

'No, but he boasts about his pictures—like the Poussin. This time he didn't.'

She went back to looking thoughtful. 'I'd guess he wants us to buy entirely on our own judgment—then we can't kick later if somebody proves it isn't Cordoba. A dealer like him can't afford to get in bad with somebody like me.' She said it quite straight, quite innocently. Well, she was good, all right, so why shouldn't she know it?

She went on: 'Because if it isn't Cordoba, then it's nothing. Quite worthless.'

Dona M nodded. 'Carlos will cable Basle tonight, and air-mail the photograph to Managua. Si?'

The 'si' came out with a crisp, military snap. Carlos jerked, then said tonelessly: 'Si, Dona Margarita.'

'And do not forget the . . . the Poussin.'

'Si, Dona Margarita.'

There was an embarrassed silence. We started to walk slowly round the rim of the floor, behind the pillars and cameras. Somewhere a bit of TV equipment fell with a crash and a blast of swearing that echoed through the dome.

Elizabeth said: 'Well, if that's everything . . .'

Dona Margarita gave her a royal smile. 'You are doing most well. Is there much more to find in Venice?'

'There's a couple more people to see, but there isn't much in Venice. It isn't Florence or Rome. I assume we're going on there?'

'Perhaps. But I do not like Florence in winter. It has no atmosphere.'

'It's got some big dealers.'

'If you wish, then. But you must not work too hard, Senorita. This journey should also be for the fun.' She swung round on me. 'Senor Kemp—you should take Senorita Whitley for dinner, or the cinema.'

Elizabeth and I looked at each other. She smiled suddenly.

I said: 'By royal command. Okay?'

'All right. I've got to go back to the hotel first.'

'Meet you in Harry's Bar at seven.'

She said: 'I suppose it *does* have to be a western?' but didn't wait for an answer.

Dona Margarita smiled again, satisfied she'd kept the kiddies happy. So maybe this was the moment.

I said: 'I suppose I couldn't have a little advance on salary?'

Carlos woke up fast. 'What for, man? Ye got paid the other day.'

'Well, Faggioni's got this gun . . .'

Now Dona Margarita stared, as well. 'A *gun*?'

'Antique pistol. You know.'

'Ye are not here to carry on your own business,' Carlos said sternly. 'We're already paying the overheads for ye.'

'Hell's teeth, I'm just borrowing a couple of hundred quid for—'

'Ye are not.'

And so I wasn't.

But damn it, my credit should have been pretty good, what with finding that Dürer for them.

Dona Margarita gave a little sympathetic but helpless smile. 'Perhaps is best as Carlos says. You would probably have to smuggle the pistol also, and that would be complicated.'

Well, she had a point there; I probably *would* have to smuggle it. But I was still bloody well going to.

I just nodded gloomily.

Dona Margarita turned back to Carlos. 'Now, you must send the cables. Senor Kemp will find me a boat.'

Carlos gave me a last sharp glance, then bowed and trotted off, zigzagging between the cables.

We started to walk slowly back to the door.

After a few yards, she said: 'Senor—when we are finished, you are going back to London, si?'

'Yes. I mean, that's where I work.'

'You like being a smuggler and dealer in guns?'

'I'd prefer to stick just to the guns, but . . .' I shrugged.

'I am thinking; perhaps you would like to work for me always?'

'What, back in Nicaragua?'

'Ah no. But in Europe I have interests also.'

'Doing what? I mean me.'

'The work . . . like Carlos.'

'Blimey.' If she meant booking hotel rooms and air tickets and standing to attention and kiss-my-arse, then not bloody likely.

Or did she think I'd be hot stuff in bed?

'Well,' I said slowly, 'if there's anything special you want —well, you know where I live . . . But a permanent job, hell, I'm an antique-gun dealer.'

'Ah yes. Never mind; it is not important.' We arrived at the top of the steps. 'Now, a water-taxi to the hotel, please.'

'There's a vaporetto stop here. It crosses the Canal. I mean, it's only a hundred yards to walk, the other side.'

'A taxi, please,' she said firmly.

Well, it was her money. I just wished the bitch would spend it on financing Wogdons instead of water-taxis.

TWENTY-FIVE

I GOT TO HARRY'S BAR about ten to seven—and there was Carlos, sitting quite obviously waiting for me. I asked the bar to bring me a Scotch, then sat down beside him.

He started straight in. 'Were ye talking to Dona Margarita?'

'Yes.'

He waited for me to tell him what we'd said. I didn't. 'Well, man—what did she say to ye?'

'Did you get that stuff off to Basle and Managua?'

He got as angry as I expected. Anyway, he went hard-mouthed and pale. 'I did, not that it's your business. Well—what did she say?'

'Not that it's your business—she offered me a job.'

'Doing what?'

'Dunno, really. Didn't ask.'

'Ye're not taking it, then?'

'No.' And that was all he wanted to know. He leant back in his chair and smiled—a bit thin, but nice and relaxed.

The waiter brought my Scotch. I said firmly: 'My friend will pay.' And to my surprise, he did, so I must have brought him good news. Hell's teeth, had he really thought I was likely to do him out of a job? Or a bed?

'Aye,' he said, slowly and contentedly, 'ye wouldna have liked it much. So ye'll be going back to London when this is all over?'

'Yes.' Just then Elizabeth came in. Wearing a red suit, a bit bright for her pale face and fair hair and a bit low at the knee, but at least it was a change.

Carlos stood up. I said: 'Stick around and buy another drink.' Partly it was that he'd got me a bit niggled, but partly it was Harry's Bar prices.

He gave me another thin-but-happy smile. 'I'll be leaving ye now. Have fun.' And he nodded at Elizabeth and went out.

She sat down, a bit puzzled. 'I didn't know you were on drinking terms with Carlos. Outside of business conferences.'

'I'm not. He was trying to find out what Dona Margarita had said to me. I mean, he'd pushed off soon after you did.'

'She was a bit sharp with him this afternoon, I thought.'

I shrugged. 'Lover's tiff.'

'Oh *really* . . .' The waiter came over and she ordered a Cinzano. 'Really, Bert—she's not sleeping with him. I don't say she's not sleeping out, but she's on the town every night —without Carlos. You've never tried to get in touch after eight in the evening or before noon: she's never available. She's probably looking up old friends she made on the tennis circuit.'

I hated to let a good dirty idea go. 'Maybe she sort of nibbles him between meals.'

'You've got a very nasty mind.' The waiter brought her drink. 'By the way—did you get your loan?'

'No I didn't. Bloody Scotsman.'

She smiled sympathetically. 'What are you going to do now?'

'Dunno. Borrow it off Harry Burroughs, maybe.'

Her eyes opened wide. 'You're joking.'

'I'm afraid so.' But the thought of Harry reminded me of another rich American. 'Still, there's always Harper.'

'Who?'

'You don't know him. Edwin Harper, probably related to Harper's Ferry. Met him in Amsterdam, then again down here. I mean, he's loaded. He might spring a loan.'

He might, too. On a business basis. Anyway, it was him or Paulus Boemack, and I preferred that relationship the way it was. I glanced at the phone by the bar.

She caught the look. 'Go on, ring him.'

'I'll just make sure he'll still be here tomorrow.'

'Why not tonight? I'd rather watch anything than a western. Even you borrowing money.'

I was feeling a bit guilty, but much more than a bit anxious to get my hands on some spending money. 'D'you really mean that?'

'Sure. Anyway, you always know how a western's going to end.'

The Bauer Grunwald was obviously the road-transport convention's HQ. The big modern lobby was hung with gold banners, crowded with little booths labelled with manufacturers' names, and jammed with big men in snazzy suits wearing lapel badges and slapping each others' backs and saying that was the funniest thing they'd heard in years. We fought our way through the mob and came out with no more than two handshakes and a four-colour brochure on Leyland trucks before anybody noticed I wasn't wearing a badge.

As we got to the bar, I said to Elizabeth: 'A word of warning: this bloke might be in a state of liquidation, and I don't mean money.'

She nodded. But if our Edwin was as hooted as a fog-horn he wouldn't be lonely: the bar was near as jammed as the lobby, and they were all sucking up the hard stuff like bilge pumps. But Harper was still the biggest and ugliest of the lot. He saw me, raised a hand, then shouldered his way through the crush like one of his own long-distance trucks.

'Hi, there, Bert. This is once again a great pleasure.' He crunched my hand, then looked at Eizabeth. I introduced her.

'Most pleased to meet you, ma'am. You come from a little further north than me, I'd say. Are you in the same business as Bert, here?'

She gave me a cool glance. 'In a way. A different branch of it.'

I said: 'She means she's honest.'

Harper creased himself with laughter. 'Well, now how about a drink? Ma'am?'

She asked for another Cinzano; I chose Scotch. Harper passed the word to a harassed waiter, brushed a few minor trucking executives away from a small table, and got us installed.

'Well, Bert, I'm really sorry Mrs. Harper isn't here to meet you. But I guess there must still be some shops open in this town, and if that's so, well you can bet Mrs. Edwin Harper is visiting them.'

By now I was beginning to wonder if she really still existed. I mean, she might have dropped dead years ago, and he was keeping her alive just as a tax deduction or something.

We chatted until the drinks arrived, mostly Harper asking Elizabeth how she got on in this place Europe, and her tactfully saying she liked it fine except for the plumbing.

Finally I said: 'Well, as I said on the phone, this is a bit of a business visit . . .'

Elizabeth said: 'I'll take a walk.'

I said: 'Stay as far as I'm concerned.'

Harper nodded seriously. 'I'm in agreement with you, Bert. I believe women should understand business matters. Many of my associates think I'm a dangerous liberal, believing that, but . . .' He gave a big ho-ho. And got one of Elizabeth's cool looks. Come to think of it, she'd probably arranged as many million-dollar deals as he had, even if she wasn't doing it on her own money.

Anyway, she stayed.

I said: 'Suppose I give you the story and you pick the holes in it?'

'That's always the best way, sir.'

'There's a dealer who's got a gun—an antique pistol. Getting on two hundred years old. Perfect condition and so on. I can get it for . . . about seven hundred dollars. The trouble is, I don't have that much, and I can't get it without going back to London and selling some stuff. I mean, I told you I was a small dealer. Well, I am.'

His big, ugly face was still. Quite, quite still.

I went on: 'So I'm trying to borrow some money. The point about this pistol is it's one of a pair. Most fancy pistols were. Separately, they're worth about what he's asking: seven hundred. Together, they're worth maybe three or four times the total. I mean, I could sell the pair for at least four thousand dollars.'

159

Very calmly, he said: 'And you know where the other one is?'

I nodded. 'A man offered to sell it me just a few weeks ago. In London. He was asking too much, and anyway, I didn't want just an odd gun. He's most likely still got it—but anyway, I can always find it.'

Elizabeth said: 'You're sure they really match?'

Harper smiled appreciatively. 'A very good question, ma'am.'

'I'm sure,' I said. 'I've handled them both; they're the same. And I mean, I know guns.'

'Very well, Bert—so you want me to finance this pistol? And back in London you buy the second one and sell them as a pair?'

'That's the idea. I mean, it might not work, but . . . well, if he won't sell, then I'll sell this one to him. And not for seven hundred dollars, neither. I can ask three times that at least. We just can't lose.'

They both smiled. Harper said: 'Forgive me—but I guess I've heard that remark before.'

That got me a bit niggled. 'Well, we *can't*. I mean, the damn thing's worth seven hundred just by itself. If the other one's got lost, I can sell this one without a loss.'

'And without a profit. But let's say you make the profit—then we split that down the middle.'

Like hell we did. I said: 'Not quite. I mean, I can put up some of the money myself—I'm not asking for the whole seven hundred—and it's my expertise and my shop and all that.'

He clinked the ice in his glass. 'I guess it's normal to pay interest on a loan. And—again you'll forgive me—but financing deals is regarded as kind of risky. So maybe we'll say a fifty-fifty split on the profit and I finance the whole purchase of this gun.'

'And you say small men make good deals.'

He smiled gently. 'I'd say you were doing all right. After all, I don't think you're offering any security?'

'You can keep this gun, when I've bought it, if you like.

Take it to London if you're going home that way, give it to somebody you trust until I've bought the other one.'

He shook his head. 'No, sir. I prefer to trust you. But one thought does happen: you could have made a profit simply by putting the owners of these guns in touch with one another —or tipping off one of them. And you wouldn't have needed any capital at all.'

I put my glass down, hard. '*I* found this pair. *I* matched them. They're going to be sold through *my* shop.' And not in too much of a hurry, neither. Give it a little time for the word to go round that Bert Kemp had matched a pair of fancy Wogdons all by his clever little self. A couple of classy dealers I could name were going to feel a bit sick about *that*. And give it time to act as bait, too. I mean, if I had that pair in stock, then the rest of my stuff must be pretty good, too—no?

Harper grinned. Or, anyway, his great ugly pan creased in all directions. 'A touch of pride. I like that.' He stuck out a hand. 'We'll do business. I guess you'd like the money tomorrow. In cash?'

I shook his hand. When you did business with Edwin Harper, you certainly did business.

TWENTY-SIX

WHEN WE GOT OUTSIDE, Elizabeth said: 'Well, you got your loan.' She sounded faintly surprised. 'At the expense of your profit, of course.'

'The racketeering bastard.'

'Oh, come on. He's just a man you met in a bar. Would you hand over seven hundred dollars just like that?'

'He can afford it.'

'I'd say he got that way by *not* handing out loans to people he meets in bars.'

I just grunted. But if our Edwin thought he was actually going to see a full fifty per cent of my profit, then he was a bigger mug than even she took him for. I mean, if he got a return of something like two hundred per cent on his investment, he'd be happy, wouldn't he? He wouldn't come across and check my books to see if it should have been three hundred, would he? And I wasn't going to sell them at an auction, where the price gets into the papers, neither.

She said cheerfully: 'So now you've got your gun and not had to spend your own money, you can afford something better than a western, can't you? Like a good dinner.'

I looked at her. She was still a bit of a mouse, but a mouse that had a way of getting its own way. Oh well; John Wayne would still be around tomorrow.

But if we were going for a big dinner, it was going to be my choice: the Gritti Palace.

Elizabeth objected: 'But we can't very well go in *there*.'

'Why not? You just told me the boss lady's out every evening. Anyway, there's nothing specially suspicious about it. They can't stop me eating where I want to.'

'Well . . .'

So we walked back through the cold, empty, misty alley-ways, our feet clattering in the silence. And into the nice warm dining room of the Gritti. That was pretty empty, too. Partly the time of year, partly that Venice eats earlier than most Italian cities. Near eight o'clock meant near the end of dinner.

'What d'you recommend?' she asked.

'Parma ham, then Scampi Gritti. It's the best in the world.'

'I didn't know you'd eaten all over the world.'

'I just know. It came to me in a dream. But don't take my advice; go ahead and make a mistake.'

'Strong, forceful character,' she murmured. 'All right. I'll take it, too.'

We were halfway through the paper-thin wisps of ham—they give you a good helping, at the Gritti; well, at their prices they ruddy well should—when she said: 'So now you've got a nice pair of guns—almost. I thought there must be something like that, the way you were so keen to get it.'

I stared. 'There wasn't anything crooked about *that*. There isn't a dealer or collector in the world who'd've done any different.'

'Oh, sure. But I just knew there must be something extra behind it.'

'Christ, you think everything I do must be crooked.'

'Well,' she said sweetly, 'an awful lot of it is, isn't it? Look at when we first met: you started straight off suggesting I should certify a fake old master and split the profit.'

'Hell, I was just trying you out. I mean, if you'd been at all interested, I'd've denounced you to Carlos.'

She chewed ham thoughtfully. 'Yes, I think you probably would have. You did the same thing to Henri in Amsterdam, didn't you? I know he was mad at you.'

'He didn't love me much. But it's sort of my job, you know? I mean, I'm a kind of security guard and all.'

'Yes, I suppose so.' She put her knife and fork down and sipped the wine. 'Tell me—d'you get much faking in your business? Of old guns?'

'Not much, not nowadays. You might get somebody knocking up an old horse-pistol on a garage lathe, but that's strictly for the peasants. The decorated stuff like these Wogdons, and that's what costs the real money, it would take the same sort of skill to fake as the real thing did. And where d'you get that skill these days? A few places like Purdey's—and they're making shotguns for a thousand pounds a time. Hell, that's more than most antique guns cost and you can shoot birds besides.'

I finished my own ham, and added: 'You get quite a lot of improving, of course. You know, if a gun's been bashed around or a spring's broken, you put it right and pretend it never went wrong.'

'*You* do, you mean?'

I shrugged. 'Nobody's proved it.'

She smiled wryly. 'Oh, I'm sure. But you said "nowadays". Did there used to be a lot of faking?'

'The end of the last century, it was quite an industry. I mean, you'd got a lot of skilled craftsmen on low wages and half of them out of work anyway. In the last century guns changed more than ever before—or ever will, unless they invent a ray-gun or something. You started with flintlocks; a hundred years later you'd got percussion ignition, then cartridges, then revolvers and repeaters and automatics—*and* mass production.

'The factories, that was what put all the craftsmen on the streets. But all those changes made quite recent guns into antiques. I mean, before that you could be using a gun a hundred years old and it'd hardly be different from the latest thing. Well, just suppose everybody today was still painting like Leonardo only better because paints and brushes and canvas have got better. I mean, then you couldn't give away the Mona Lisa free in a box of cornflakes, could you?'

'Well . . . I'm not sure that's quite a fair parallel.'

I shrugged. 'Maybe. But it's what happened with guns. Stuff less than a hundred years old suddenly became valuable historic monuments, and with craftsmen standing around out of work, well, they naturally started up faking. One bunch in London used to turn out Napoleon's personal carbine once a year. Took 'em all year, but it was worth it, every time, every year. Christ, I should know: I bought one once. I really thought I was in the money, then. I was younger in those days.'

She grinned. 'How much did you lose?'

'Well, actually, as far as I know, it's still Napoleon's one-and-only carbine—somewhere.'

'But whoever bought it—didn't *he* find out?'

'Could be—later. But *he'd* discovered it. I mean, there it was in a cupboard at the back of my shop, along with a bunch of tatty old muskets and Mausers and all covered in muck and dust. *He* spotted Napoleon's crest on it; I didn't tell him.'

'My God,' she said softly. 'It's that easy, is it?'

'Easy be damned. I spent a week putting all that muck on it.'

She sighed and shook her head. But just then our scampi arrived and we got stuck into that.

After a time, she said: 'You're right: it is the best in the world. I've just had the same dream.'

Afterwards we sat in the bar, me nibbling at a Strega, her with coffee. Outside the big windows, vaporettos and water-taxis crawled hooting and gurgling through the mist.

'I just don't see,' she said, 'how you can drink that stuff. It makes me feel I've got a crust of sugar round my mouth.'

'Same for me, really. But if I drink much after dinner, I feel like death in the morning. So I drink something I don't like.'

'Logical, I suppose.' Then: 'Bert—are you married?'

'Me? No. Was once.'

She didn't say 'What happened?' but she looked it.

So I said: 'The usual thing. I'm a small shopkeeper—that isn't very exciting. And when I had to travel I couldn't afford to take her. She got sort of left out all round. So . . .' I shrugged. The bitch. But did I really mean that, any more? Fifteen years. You're different, she's different—probably. It doesn't hurt any more—well, not much. And I suppose that's just pride—that you failed, once.

Bitch.

Elizabeth asked suddenly: 'Are you going to go on doing this—smuggling, I mean?'

'I'd rather stick to the shop. But you need capital—you know, to be able to buy stuff like a Wogdon, or hang on to it until you can match it. This is a way of building it up.'

She nodded. 'But how d'you get started at something like this? It doesn't seem a very obvious career. Were you another sort of crook before?'

'For Christ's sake!'

'I'm sorry.' She seemed genuinely surprised at the way I'd taken it.

I calmed down. 'Well, when I started dealing I was handling some art, as well—'

'You?' She laughed merrily.

'Yes, me, damn it.'

'I'm sorry,' she said again. 'But after all, you're always saying you don't know anything about art.'

'Well, that was how I found out,' I growled. 'Anyhow, there's this bloke Charlie Good. He's a bit of a crook—' and Charlie would send the boys round on the double if he heard me say that. The 'bit of', I mean—'and he wanted to invest in some art, so he bought some off me, then he started buying in Paris, and suddenly found out about art export laws. Well, he didn't want to get nicked for smuggling—he'd've really lost face; I mean like Al Capone being done for shop-lifting— so he tried me. And the Paris dealer knew, of course, and offered me another client and . . . well, there you are. How I made my first million.'

She grinned, then: 'But it's crazy, you know. Smuggling art.'

'You mean it devalues it?'

She looked surprised again. 'You know that?'

'Of course. You smuggle a picture out, you brand it a bit of an outlaw. That's one country you can't sell it back to without trouble. Cut your possible buyers, you must cut your price. But that's their problem, not mine.'

'Yes. It's funny they never think of that.' She stood up. 'Bert, let me go half on this dinner.'

I shook my head. 'No. Buy me a pizza when we get to Florence.'

She almost argued, then just nodded.

We walked back. And as we got near her hotel, she said quietly: 'You know—Henri was right. I shouldn't get high-minded about what you're doing. We both work for the same people—and I knew what I was getting into. Their morals are mine.'

'Well, Charlie Good's ain't mine, I'll tell you. And a few other clients, neither.'

'Aren't they?' she said thoughtfully. 'Can we really say that?' Then she smiled and held out her hand. I shook it, a bit surprised. 'Good-night, Bert. It's been fun.'

And I was alone in the quiet alleyway.

TWENTY-SEVEN

THE NEXT DAY, I made myself wait until half past ten before I called Harper and then went round with him to pick up seven hundred dollars. And I do mean dollars—Fajjy would like that. So then we had to have a snifter in Harry's Bar to celebrate our business partnership—and then at last I was free to ring Fajjy and tell him the deal was on. Only, in view of the dollars, I thought we might settle it at six hundred. He didn't agree.

I got a Zurich paper after lunch and Henri had faded away completely. Though that didn't mean the police had dropped it. Then I checked with the management and got Dona Margarita; Carlos was out of town for the day somewhere. No word from Managua yet, of course. She asked kindly how me and Elizabeth had got on, and was happy the girl was having some fun. We ought to do it again; Senorita Whitley was too serious.

I'd let her ring off before I thought of saying that if she wanted me to play gigolo then I ought to be able to put it on expenses. Still, I was going to anyway, wasn't I?

And finally I caught up with John Wayne. And he *was* still wearing the five-inch-barrelled Colt high back on his hip. Sort of gives you a feeling of security in a changing world, though there was one snap-shot at fifty yards, shooting uphill from the top deck of a horse, that I didn't quite believe in.

Still, when you fire a gun the bullet's got to go *somewhere*, hasn't it? I mean, all these stories about Wild Bill Hickok knocking down a man at eighty yards or people blowing birds out of the air from a fast draw, well, they're all likely true. What isn't true is that they could do it every time. If you shoot often enough, you'll sooner or later get lucky.

And on that bit of deep thought, I treated myself to a couple of Stregas and an early bed.

168

The day started off quiet. I rang Elizabeth and suggested lunch, but she had a last dealer to see. But she sounded sorry about it. I was, too, but I wasn't sure why. Something about her, that hard core, a tough innocence, professionalism . . . something. Hell, she *cared*, and most birds don't care more than if their shoulder-straps are showing and often not even that.

I liked that, but it scared me, too, a bit.

So I lunched early and alone, checked through the *Zeitung*, and got back to find a message to ring Carlos.

'We'll be leaving Venice in a couple of days,' he started. 'Provided we've heard from Managua, of course. So ye'd best be thinking about . . . your problems.'

'All right. I can still go via Greece.'

'Take too long, man. We've got something important to see.'

'Where are we going next, then? Florence? Rome?'

He paused, then: 'No. Vienna.'

'Oh?' Well, that didn't make any odds to me. 'All right. I'll start thinking, then.'

'Ye don't have any . . . little troubles in Austria, do ye?' he asked, a bit nastily.

'Not that I know of.'

'Verra good. I'll arrange one more meeting as soon as we hear from Managua.'

And that was that.

So I sat and thought, as promised. It didn't help much. Still, I ended up with one idea. Not bright, exactly, but at least a faint glow. Which was lucky, because twenty-four hours later Carlos was on the blower saying Managua had given the go-ahead and we were all to meet in an hour's time.

This time I made it the Naval Museum, down near the Arsenale. It was conspicuous, but off the beaten track and a pretty unlikely place for such as us. Anyway, I'd kept meaning to drop in there on my own account; it's mostly ship models and anchors and so on, but there's some nice early machine-guns and torpedoes and things.

Elizabeth and I arrived together; Carlos and Dona Margarita about five minutes later.

'D'you mean,' Elizabeth started off 'that Managua's approved both the Poussin *and* the Cordoba portrait?'

Dona Margarita nodded. 'That is true. They say it is a chance, but a chance we should not miss.'

Elizabeth nibbled her lip thoughtfully. 'Well, I suppose they know what they're doing . . . And I don't suppose anybody'll prove it *isn't* the right Cordoba.'

Carlos added: 'It might provide a wee touch of controversy. Get the museum talked about, ye know.'

'Oh well . . . as long as they know I can't certify anything but the approximate age. So I'd better ring Faggioni and tell him I'm buying. Is the money here?'

'It's being cabled through immediately. It should be here this afternoon.'

We started to stroll past the exhibits—including one of those two-man submarines like an oversize torpedo and you put on frogman's gear and rode them like a horse. The Italians invented them, I remembered.

'Now that would really make a secret meeting-place,' I said. 'Hire a couple of those and make a date twenty feet down in the lagoon.'

Dona Margarita smiled. 'At this time of year I would prefer not, Senor. But have you considered your own problem of reaching Zurich?'

Come to think of it, a sub like that wouldn't do badly in the smuggling business; I mean, just pop across the corner of the Adriatic to Jugoslavia or Trieste. I wonder if anybody ever tried it?

I said: 'The Cordoba's the only problem, isn't it? I mean, the Poussin's legitimate—Fajjy can fix to send that on to Zurich himself in a few days.'

Elizabeth nodded. Then added gently: 'Of course, there is the little problem with the Dürer. They probably wouldn't object to it going out, but unfortunately we don't seem to have any paperwork to go with it. Not even a receipt to show it wasn't stolen.'

170

Ouch. Still—'It isn't big. I can hide that easy enough.' Maybe, anyway. *And* the Wogdon?

We wandered on past a model of a Venetian rowing galley and Dona Margarita observed: 'Did you know that when they went on trading voyages to the East, even the rowers, the slaves almost, were allowed to take along some goods to barter, Senor?'

'Nothing like a bit of profit-sharing to keep the unions happy.'

'Ah yes. The democracy of profit. Now, Senor—have you thought of a way to travel safely to Zurich?'

Here we went. 'Well—if the Customs *are* going to search me, and I suppose there's a good chance they might, why don't we use me as a sort of diversion? I mean, we all go on the same train but you carry the Cordoba, and if they go for me then they won't bother with anybody else.'

Carlos was looking shocked. 'Ye canna ask Dona Margarita . . . Man! Ye're hired for this job yeself!'

I shrugged. 'All right, *if* I can do it my way. And that's some roundabout route like Greece. I don't see why you want *me* in Vienna in such a rush anyhow.'

'We need ye as a security guard.'

'Okay. But that doesn't leave me much choice, does it? I've *got* to go out north and I've *got* to go by train. I mean, you can't have a picture that old slung around by airline baggage blokes. So I'm back on exactly the route I got pinched on before.'

Dona Margarita said abruptly: 'I will take the picture. I am not searched, ever. It is best.'

For a moment, Carlos was bewildered, baffled. Still, he picked up fast. 'Well, ye willna be asking any extra pay for *this* journey,' he growled. 'And I'll take your pistol, if we're doing all the work ourselves.'

I turned to Elizabeth. 'You can tell Fajjy I'll collect the . . . the stuff tonight. Then we can take a train before lunch tomorrow and if it all goes okay we'll be in time to fly from Zurich to Vienna.' I glanced at Carlos. 'Is that quick enough for you?'

Dona Margarita said firmly: 'It is good, Senor. Carlos will

arrange the tickets, si?' And again there was a little touch of the sergeant-majors. Carlos made a stiff little bow.

Then for a while we just walked between the glass cases with neat models of cruisers and battleships from the 1900's.

Elizabeth said: 'Funny how they look like floating factories, isn't it? All those smokestacks and the vertical lines and the pipes all over them. The industrial society going to sea.' She turned to Dona Margarita. 'What is it we're supposed to see in Vienna?'

Carlos answered: 'A friend—a certain Captain Parker, he lives there—and he's been keeping his ear to the ground. He thinks he's on the track of something pretty remarkable.'

'Is it my period?' Elizabeth asked.

'Aye, he says so.'

'You've no idea. . . . ? Oh well, we'll see when we see. If there's nothing else, shall I go and start phoning?'

Dona Margarita nodded. 'Carlos will ring you to tell of the train.'

So Elizabeth pushed off. I only stayed long enough to arrange to pick up the money and one of Dona M's suitcases (I reckoned it would be easier to pack the Cordoba straight into that at Fajjy's, so it needn't be repacked until Zurich) and tell them roughly when I'd be back with it.

Outside, a slow fog was crawling in off the sea, and somewhere a ship hooting resignedly.

TWENTY-EIGHT

I GOT OFF a slow, cold train at Padua just after five, and by then the fog had climbed up there, too. It rolled in through the station doors like big puffs of winter breath, and the traffic outside was squawking like frightened hens.

It took me ten minutes to find a taxi and another three to persuade the driver even to get started in Fajjy's direction. I don't think he thought it was a bad direction; he just wanted to sit where he was and complain. Fog does that to people.

And we didn't get nearer to Fajjy's than the main road, leaving me a couple of hundred yards to walk up the narrow streets and alleys. He wasn't going up *there*, signore, it was impossible to reverse and if there was a runaway truck coming down the other way without lights, then . . .

I paid the bastard the flat fare, no tip, and felt a little better about the walk. Fog does that to people.

By then it was probably almost dark, except that the fog made it seem lighter. I bounced from one patch of street lighting to the next, lost my way once, and finally reached the big castle-type front door. I heard the bell purr faintly, deep inside the house, and after the usual long time, the crisp young man opened the door.

This time there wasn't any waiting around; by myself, I wasn't worth impressing. I was shunted straight through into the study. The Poussin was sitting there, totally unwrapped, and the Cordoba (or whoever) half-wrapped in a shell of cotton wool, plastic sheet and sacking.

Fajjy gave a cannon-like cough and crawled out from behind his desk. 'The mist—it is making me die. You bring it from England, no?'

'Naturally. Anything to kill you off. How about the pistol?'

'Ah yes. You have the money?'

I dealt Harper's seven hundred dollars onto the desk. He watched me, his mouth moving silently as he counted. I held the last ten-dollar bill in my hand. 'The gun, Fajjy.'

He smiled blearily, then took it out of the drawer.

I didn't take it. 'The other gun, Fajjy. The Wogdon.'

He patted his forehead. 'I'm getting old. I forget all the time. I am dying. Yes.' He put the cheap French horse-pistol back into the drawer and handed over the real thing.

And I'd got it. I'd got *them*. Well—almost. But even by itself, the weight, the balance, the feel of sheer craftsmanship . . . Something must have showed on my face, because he said 'You will sell it for much more, no?'

I shrugged. 'Maybe. Where did it come from, d'you know?'

Now he shrugged. 'I cannot know. I never ask these things.' Like hell. He'd certainly tried back-tracking to find its twin; anybody would. And he knew I knew. But his way was to wear you down with small lies, little attempts to 'forget', until you just got tired and let him get away with something. Only not me.

'Oh well—maybe I'll be lucky.' But I already *was*, you twisting old bastard. So I opened my overcoat and jammed the Wogdon down in my waistband. It was far too big—it wasn't no short-barrelled Detective Special—but it would have stuck a good six inches out of any pocket. And anyway, I already had a gun in one pocket.

I turned back to the pictures. 'Now I'll accept these.'

He held out a trembling old hand. 'The ten dollars, if you please.'

'So sorry. Must have forgotten.' I gave him the last bill. Oh well. Doing business the Edwin Harper way would get pretty dull after a while.

He pressed a button on the desk and the boy came in and went on wrapping up the Cordoba. Fajjy sorted some papers on his desk and came up with two envelopes. 'You wish the receipts, no?'

'Yes.' I took the two bank drafts out of my pocket and we swapped and settled down to a little mistrustful reading. On the Poussin receipt there were a few blank spaces—there had to be, since he didn't have the exact address it was to be sent to, but there didn't have to be quite this many.

'You're getting forgetful again, Fajjy. Delivery within three weeks and at *your* risk. That's what Miss Whitley agreed.'

He looked up, blankly innocent, the ragged stub of a cigarette shivering in his mouth. 'But no—she did not say that.'

'Don't bother to try it, mate. I was listening at her end.' I hadn't been, of course, but I knew she wouldn't make that sort of mistake.

He shrugged again. 'So, if you wish me to walk the way to Zurich carrying the picture myself. Through the mist—'

'And the snow on the Alps. Don't forget the snow.'

'So I am dying anyway. It does not matter when. Write the address, please.'

I tried writing in the new clause as well, but there wasn't room. 'It'll have to be typed again.'

'More cost, more cost.' He sighed, relit the cigarette, and coughed. 'It is making me poor.'

Just to niggle him, I took out a handful of coins and tossed him a five hundred lire piece. Like hell it niggled him; he just pocketed it calmly. I should've known better than to try and insult him that way. Now *I* was niggled.

The boy in the white jacket was still sewing the sacking. We waited; Fajjy obviously didn't do his own typing—there wasn't a typewriter in the room.

After a time, he said: 'And the pistol, you sell it to a rich American, no?'

'Perhaps. Or maybe I'll keep it until I can match it.'

He smiled. 'But of course. You will find its brother most easily.'

'Don't you be too bloody sure I won't.' It was a stupid thing to say, but probably I was still a little angry. I wanted to get under his skin. And I had, all right. His face went deep-frozen, except for the flash of his eyes.

I tried to cover up by making it seem I was just boasting. 'I'm a serious antique-gun dealer. A lot more serious than a lot of the over-capitalized little twerps you get in the trade now. If

175

that gun's around Britain, I stand a bloody sight better chance of finding it than most.'

'But of course.' He nodded, but I couldn't tell if I'd managed the cover-up.

Then the boy stood up, waving a hand at the finished packaging. I went and checked it over; it was good enough.

Fajjy said: 'If you excuse—I will tell Alfredo to do the typing.' He and the boy went out. So I started easing the picture into Dona Margarita's case. I suppose it would've been more comfortable to stick the Wogdon in, too, but I might not have a chance to take it out before I handed the case over.

That didn't take long. Then I just stood around and lit a small cigar and thought about having a quiet peekaboo at the old bastard's private papers. I didn't, though. Most of them would be in Italian anyway.

He came back with the retyped receipt, and I read it through again. This time he'd got it right. I signed his copy per pro Miss Elizabeth Whitley and he signed mine. And that was that. Over a quarter million dollars' worth of business signed, sealed and half delivered.

'Well,' I said, 'that's that until next time.'

'By next time I shall be dead. But it does not matter. I shall telephone the taxi, no?'

'You won't get one to come up here in this fog. I'll pick one up.'

'You must be careful, with that so-expensive picture. The . . . the banditti.'

I waggled the case; it wasn't very heavy. 'Just between us, d'you think it really is old Cordoba?'

He shrugged. 'I never meet him.'

'Sorry. I forgot.'

He showed me to the door himself.

By now the fog had a cold, cutting edge on it, freezing where it touched. I shivered, turned up my coat collar, took up the case in my left hand and stumped off down the slope towards the first patch of hazy light.

At the second corner I paused, uncertain. Then I realized

that anywhere downhill would bring me to the main road and it didn't matter where. I could even park in a café until a taxi came.

Something slammed around my throat and something else, cold and hard, pushed in under my right ear and a voice said: 'Put down the case.'

I said: 'Why?' A bit bloody silly, but you have to say *something*.

The pull on my throat tightened. 'Put down the case and raise the hands.' He had his left arm around my neck and a gun, it could only be a gun, rammed up under my ear.

So what would John Wayne have done in a situation like this? Had the script rewritten, probably. But I had one advantage over him: my gun—the useful one—wasn't high in sight on my hip.

I said: 'I am putting down the case.' I bent forward to do it—but the gun under my ear didn't shift. I straightened up again.

He loosened my throat and his hand started exploring, feeling my chest—for a gun, probably. He touched the outline of the Wogdon and then pulled at my coat, wrenching it open. And the gun under my ear slipped.

I spun right, slamming back with my elbow, and it landed. A hydrogen bomb touched off beside my ear, but then I was throwing myself away from him and grabbing in my pocket.

When I came around with the Browning in my hand, he was a silhouette against the hazy light of a lamp up the alley, doubled over but with the gun still clear in his hand. And it looked as big as it sounded.

I squeezed.

Low and left, and I knew it the moment I pulled the trigger, the way you do when it really matters. So I walked them up and across, two-three-four, at the line of his knees.

He might even have fired again himself, but I wouldn't know. All of me was down at the front end of that little gun, throwing hollow-point .22's as fast as I could hold an aim.

I didn't fire the fifth; he was going down. As he landed, he screamed. I stepped quickly aside, against the wall, but the gun slid clear of his hand. I walked carefully forward and picked it up. A Colt .45 automatic. Big, all right. And not for fun, and not for scaring innocent art-smugglers, neither. I dropped it in my pocket and bent and lifted his face.

Fajjy's boy, Alfredo. Well, of course it was. The bloody twerp. How many profits did he have to make on one deal?

The boy groaned and I saw the shiny wet patch on his right knee. Must have been my third that got him—the fourth had gone between his legs and the fifth would've popped his other kneecap. So then I picked him up and wrapped one of his arms back around my neck and half-carried, half-walked him back up the slope.

I was panting like a Derby winner when I reached Fajjy's front door again; even my finger felt tired against the bell. But he must have been waiting just inside, because the door opened straight off, and I staggered up and shoved in past him.

I dumped the boy in the study, on an old red plush divan, and he rolled over sideways and started groaning again. A shot kneecap hurts, all right.

Fajjy leant over my shoulder and I could smell his breath. 'What did you *do*?'

I waved the little pink-pearl-handled gun and thought of a lot of things to say, but ended up with: 'He fired first.' Wayne would have been proud of me.

The decayed old face fell apart in horror. 'But—you have spoiled him!'

'I've done *what*?'

'He is never the same again! And he was so perfect. And you spoil him.'

Tears trickled out from under his glasses.

I found a voice; it didn't sound like mine, but it would do for the moment. 'You nasty old bastard,' I croaked. 'Get a doctor—and one that won't talk to the police.'

Police gave him an idea. 'For this, you are in the jail—for all the time!'

'Get a doctor!' I yelled. I shoved him towards the desk and the telephone. But when he lifted the phone, I grabbed his hand. 'And if the police *do* get in on this, you can explain why he jumped me outside waving a bloody great .45. I mean, they might not believe *I* started a fight when I was carrying a hundred thousand dollar picture.'

He stared sadly at me. 'You should not have had a gun.'

'Yes. Him and me, neither and both.'

The boy on the divan moved and shrieked. More tears started down Fajjy's face. I took my hand away. 'Now get a doctor.'

While he dialled, I tore open the boy's trousers and looked at the knee. At least I could tell the bullet wasn't in there—and hadn't gone through. It must've hit at an angle, maybe cracked the bone, and gone its way. There wasn't even much blood; no tourniquet needed. But it was still a professional job patching it up. And he'd still remember me every time he put his right foot down.

Fajjy came across the room. 'He is coming. What shall I say?'

'Anything he'll believe, if he has to believe anything. Say you were fooling with a pistol, he got jumped by the Mafia—anything. Just forget he was in a gunfight, that's all.'

The small, wet eyes looked at me carefully. 'I will not forget some things.'

'Yes. Well, don't forget I wouldn't be here at all if I didn't have rich friends.'

Then Alfredo moaned again and Fajjy looked at him and murmured: 'But you have spoiled him.'

I took a deep breath. 'And it wasn't even for that damn Cordoba, was it? You wouldn't dare try *that*, mate. It'd look too sticky, even for the police. It was for the Wogdon. No receipt, no proof—and just little old Bert Kemp's business, not his client's. Just because you thought I knew how to match it, and you'd lost a few thousand lire. You bastard.'

'He was like a son to me.'

'Stuff it. He was born luckier than *that*.'

Then I went out into the fog again.

When I found nobody had stolen the suitcase I remembered to be surprised. Then I spent a couple of minutes routing around for the cartridge cases; I couldn't find one of the .22's nor the one—or maybe both—of the .45's. But the hell with them; if the police started looking seriously, they'd turn up the spent bullets and I wasn't going hunting for *those*.

I had a stiff drink at the station and while we were crossing the causeway back into Venice I slung the Colt out of the train window. I met Carlos in the lobby of the Gritti just before eight, not even much later than I'd told him.

He took the suitcase and the receipts. 'Ye didna have any problems, then?'

Well, not with his end of the business. I shook my head. 'Nope.'

'Aye. Well, I'll have the gun as well, please.'

I'd forgotten I'd promised him the Browning. So I wrapped it in a handkerchief in my pocket and slipped it across to him so neatly that any badly retarded two-year-old moron might have missed that we were passing over some secret. I only hoped he wouldn't bother to smell the muzzle for the next few hours.

I said: 'It's not fully loaded. I think there's only six in it. Helps keep the tension off the magazine spring.'

Either he believed me or didn't care. He just nodded. 'I left the ticket at your hotel. Eight-o-eight tomorrow. We'll meet in Zurich—I hope.' Then he headed for the stairs.

I groaned at the train time and headed back to the fog.

And it had all been so bloody stupid. I mean sending that kid up against me. I'd *told* him I was good with a real gun, hadn't I? I ought to have killed the boy and dragged *that* back and stuck it in his lap. All so bloody stupid.

Well, I'd be out of Italy tomorrow.

With an early train time, I had to do most of my bill-paying and packing that evening. And suddenly I realized I'd got a problem. So I rang Elizabeth after dinner and invited myself round for a last Strega at her hotel. I mean, why have friends and be selfish with your problems?

'How d'you think we've done in Italy?' I asked.

'Italy? We haven't done Italy yet. Only Venice. It's ridiculous not to go down to Florence and Rome as well.' She was back to Gloomsville.

'They'll probably let you come back after Vienna.'

'I hope so. I just don't see what they think we'll find in Vienna. It isn't much of an art centre.'

That wasn't quite true, though probably true enough from her moral standpoint. There was one way a fair amount of art got handled through Vienna . . . Well, never mind.

Suddenly she asked: 'How did you get on with Faggioni, this time?'

'I had to get one of the receipts rewritten,' I said carefully. 'He'd forgotten he was carrying the risk on the Poussin.'

She shook her head impatiently. 'Why does he *do* it? These silly little swindles he tries to pull . . . It must lose him business.'

'Yes, but he can't count the business he doesn't even see. What he likes is screwing the last lira out of every deal he does. If he doesn't, he's failed. I mean, it's not the money itself, he's not a spender like Dona Margarita. It's a sort of scoreboard. He'd rather do two deals and cheat on both than to do ten and make an honest profit on nine of them.' And it doesn't only lose him business, love, it sometimes gets people popped knee-caps. But how did he count up *that* deal? If he reckoned I'd cheated him, he wasn't going to let it rest. But what could he do? Well, one thing he'd done before . . .

I said: 'All of which reminds me—I'm taking the Dürer tomorrow, aren't I?'

'I suppose so. D'you want to?'

'Well, I'd better take *something*. My job and all that. But I wonder if you'd take a few little things for me?'

'The pistol, I suppose.'

'Yes—and a box of .22 cartridges and a few bits and pieces off the other gun.'

She stared. 'My God. And what if *I* get searched?'

'You won't be. I meant to give 'em to Carlos, but I forgot. Can't very well go round there again now.'

After a moment, she said: 'Oh, all right then. I suppose you wouldn't just happen to have them with you?'

I grinned. 'Well, by an odd coincidence—yes.' I gave her the parcel.

She weighed it in her hand; heavy, of course. 'I'll get the Dürer.' She went a couple of steps, then turned back. 'How are you going to get *that* through?'

'Tell you in Zurich.'

TWENTY-NINE

AT CHIASSO they threw me off the train with a crash that probably started that avalanche you read about.

If you're being strictly geographical, I was already in Switzerland; they use Chiasso as a Customs and passport point just because it's the closest town to the border, on either side. But I wasn't going to argue about technicalities. That's for people with guilty consciences.

The Italian Customs officer was a thick forty-year-old with a heavy face and a big bandit moustache, wearing a well-cut uniform in the usual sloppy way Italians do to show their individuality or pride or sometimes just their sloppiness. But not this boy.

He started off formally enough: 'Your passport, please.'

I handed it over and he checked it through carefully—date, name, everything—just to see if there was any irregularity that he could hold me on. There wasn't, of course. I mean, I'm not that sort of bloody fool.

'You have been in Italy how long?'

'About a week.' In theory, you need a visa if you're there more than a month.

'You have how much money?'

I turned out my pocket. Officially, you can export fifty thousand lire in cash—about forty quid—or as much as you declared to them on the way in. I hadn't made any flipping declaration, of course—but when he counted up my change, I had only just over thirty quid.

No currency offences. He didn't seem bothered.

'You came to Italy for what?'

'Tourism.' Prove I didn't, you bugger.

'You are in what business?'

'Company director.' My passport said so. It was even true: I turned my shop into a private company years ago, when it was a useful tax dodge and I thought I was going to need to dodge. Bloody optimist.

'What business is your company?'

'Sell and buy antiques.'

'But you have not bought any in Italy?'

I shook my head. 'Your prices are too high, it's too difficult to export them, there's a restriction on how much money I can take out of Britain, and anyway, I haven't got much money.'

'But enough to come to Italy for tourism.'

I just shrugged.

Another Customs officer had drifted into the cold concrete half-office, half-shed where all this was going on. He was a sharp-faced boy who was still unsure enough of himself to wear his uniform smartly. He asked a question and my First Friend spat back a long, fast answer. The boy looked at me with a new interest.

I said: '*What* did you say?'—not that I'd understand a word of it, but I might get him to tell me, that way. But he was a professional, too.

Then he said: 'And you have nothing to declare for exporting? No objects of art or antiques?' Now he was pinning me right down, making me tell a flat lie—if that was what I was there for.

I said: 'Nothing.'

'Please to open your luggage.'

I unzipped the airline bag, unlocked the suitcase. The new boy leant in, hungry for a piece of the action. Obviously the boss had told him I was a pro smuggler, and probably I was the first one he'd come across. After a moment, the first one handed him my airline bag and he took it a few yards along the big concrete bench running up the middle of the room.

It took time, much longer than you'd think. But it always does. A friend of mine who did some intelligence work told me it took several hours to do a real 'body search' of just a man and his clothes—seeing if he'd got a microfilm shoved up his backside or hidden in a hollow tooth, stuff like that. A man and his luggage would take them all day.

They weren't going to be that thorough, of course, but I was still getting the three-star treatment.

While they were busy I wandered around, keeping more or less warm, peering out of the grimy windows and rereading the sports page of my yesterday's *Daily Mail*. My train was long gone but there was another in about an hour and a half, and one a quarter of an hour after that. I'd taken the trouble to check.

A little later, a Swiss customs man wandered in and asked what was going on. The bandit moustache gave him the word on me, and he looked me up and down—officially but not very concernedly. I wasn't breaking any of *his* rules. Anyway, you'd have to do a pretty good body search to find a Swiss Customs law—I mean apart from stuff like drugs and firearms.

A few minutes after that, the young one came across with my airline bag, looking a little sad that he hadn't found the Sistine Chapel roof stuffed inside the lining. Big brother just nodded and went on working over my clothes—laying them out along the bench, peering at the seams, fingering the lapels and the shoulder padding.

'You have bought much clothes in Italy,' he commented. 'And the suitcase also.'

'Yes—I lost a case here.'

'Ah?' He thought that over, but couldn't make anything suspicious out of it. 'I hope it is insured.'

'Me too.'

Finally he got down to the case itself—running his fingers along the lining, looking for loose threads, tapping it all over. A dead waste of time, and he must have begun to realise it. But he had to go through with it, now.

And so they came to me.

'Now your own clothes please, Signor.'

'For God's sake—how can I have any antiques on me?' I stretched my arms wide. 'What the hell are you looking for, anyway?'

Impassively, still politely, he said: 'Your clothes, please, Signor.'

'In here? I'll bloody freeze.'

'We will be quick.'

He was, fairly anyway. He gave my overcoat, jacket and trousers the treatment, then made me strip right down so he could see there wasn't anything taped to my body. He left my backside alone, so he didn't think I was carrying diamonds or drugs.

And that was it. He sat down on the bench and lit a Nazionale while I got dressed and repacked my stuff. The young one went on looking disappointed.

I asked just one question: 'Why all this?'

But he only shrugged again. So I'd probably never know whether it was on my past record or that bastard Fajjy giving another tip-off.

'And I can catch a train now?'

He just waved a hand at the Swiss Customs man, who asked: 'Do you have anything to declare, sir?'—and nearly split himself laughing. Then they both got out their little pocket immigration kits and stamped my passport. So I shoved my newspaper under my arm, picked up my bags and went out to wait twenty minutes for the train, leaving the young officer still looking as if he'd read a detective story with the last page torn out.

He was right, of course, but I waited until I'd been on the train a quarter of an hour before I unrolled the *Daily Mail* and took out the engraving to make sure it was still okay.

The train stopped just about everywhere it could find an excuse, and it was well past dark when I got into Zurich. *And still that creepy, nagging memory that I couldn't remember . . . how the hell had they got me, that night?* Then suddenly Elizabeth appeared.

She looked pale and worried and, probably, cold; she'd been waiting the better part of two hours. 'What happened?'

'Customs wanted a strip-tease.'

'Did they . . . did they find it?'

186

'No.' I gave her a reassuring grin. 'What happened to the ruling classes?'

'They went straight round to the bank. Carlos did, anyway. I suppose they're off to Vienna by now. He gave me a number you can ring and somebody'll be at the bank.'

'We'll do that first. Do they want us to try and get to Vienna tonight?'

'No—he said leave it to tomorrow. There's a plane that gets in about five in the evening and he'll meet us.'

Five o'clock meant about dusk; maybe Carlos was getting security conscious in his old age. 'All right. Have you booked a hotel here?—or shall I?'

She hadn't got anywhere, so I sorted through my pockets until I found some Swiss coins and called the Central and got a couple of rooms, then rang Carlos's bank number. They said somebody would be waiting in ten minutes—could I describe myself? Just a precaution, you know.

So I described Elizabeth instead. I suddenly didn't want to start pushing my luck and maybe reminding the bank about when I was in there—with Henri.

It didn't look as if it had snowed again since I'd last been there, but it hadn't thawed properly either. The pavements were edged with dirty scabs of old snow, and occasional piles like burnt coals swept into the corners. The whole city was grey, cold and grimy, like one big railway station.

We got a taxi and on to the old familiar route to the National Bank. I wasn't particularly nervous—apart from still trying to bring back that blank hour when I'd been jumped. If anybody got us now, they'd only get the engraving, and they probably wouldn't try that with the taxi-driver around. Still, I was keeping an eye open. And just before we reached the bank I saw them.

Two headlights that had been behind us just too long.

I leant forward and said: 'Stop. Stop here.'

We stopped. So did they.

Elizabeth asked: 'What is it?'

'We're being tailed.' What the hell did I do now? I couldn't very well ask the taxi-driver to start a chase scene. But were they really going to try and bounce us, with witnesses and everything?—it wasn't yet eight o'clock. Anyway, nobody had got out of the car behind. It was just sitting there, two unblinking eyes thirty yards back up the street.

I decided. 'Go on. Bank Nazionale. *Schnell.*' Then, to Elizabeth: 'You dive out and press the bell and get the hell inside. I'll hold 'em off if they try anything.' I gave her the rolled *Daily Mail*.

'It's in here?' She wanted to unroll the blasted thing and make sure it was still okay.

'For Christ's sake—yes, it's there and it's all right. Don't argue, just *go*.'

We turned the last corner and so did the headlights behind. Then we were pulling up in front of the bank.

She'd got the message finally, I'll say that. She had the door open before the taxi was stopped and dived for the big door, skidding on a patch of snow. I piled out behind her.

Now I was going to know. I was going to meet them. And for a moment I was sorry Carlos still had the .22 and the hell with witnesses. Then I was back to their car—a small green Opel—and I had my hand on the driver's door and yanked it open.

Polizeileutnant Lindemann leant across the driver and said calmly: 'Good evening, Herr Kemp.'

THIRTY

SO TWENTY MINUTES LATER the three of us—Lindemann, Elizabeth and me—were sitting in a corner of the bar at the Central drinking beer, and me for one feeling hungry.

I'd worked out how he'd got on to me. That Swiss Customs cove must have rung in to say that a man the Italians suspected of smuggling was on his way to Zurich. And Lindemann had seen my name on the sheet and his little carved-wood mind had thought: 'Ah-hah, I'm on duty this evening anyway, so why don't I enjoy it by going along and scaring the daylights out of Bert Kemp Esq.?' So he'd got down to the Bahnhof in time to tail me off the train.

I mean, if he'd actually got anything on me, we'd have been round at the Polizei-pen making statements in triplicate, not boozing it up in a hotel bar.

'Herr Kemp,' he said, 'can you tell me what you are doing in Zurich?'

'Travelling through. Going on to Vienna tomorrow.'

'And Miss Whitley also?' I'd had to introduce her at the beginning.

She said: 'Yes,' in a small but firm voice.

'You went to the National Bank. For what?'

She glanced at me. 'Put something in for sake-keeping.'

'Please say what.'

I nodded, and she said: 'An engraving, a valuable one.'

'It is yours?'

'No-o. It belongs to a client.'

'What client?'

I said: 'You can ask the National Bank.'

'But I am asking you.'

'Yes, I know. But we don't have to tell you unless there's a crime involved, do we? What crime are you investigating?'

His face got even more wooden. 'You are refusing information to the police!'

'You notice everything you cops. Tell you what to do, mate: you slap a charge on me and we'll go up in front of the magistrate and let *him* ask you why you're putting the boot into a couple of innocent visitors. And I'll call the Bank as my witness—all right?'

The banks aren't quite God in Zurich, but you can't get God to come along as a character witness, neither. And Lindemann must have been remembering that whoever we were working for had enough pull to get the National to open its doors at a quarter to eight of an evening.

Anyway, he switched his tack. 'When you were here before, when you had the *accident*—' he gave me a hard official stare '—I told you to leave Zurich. But you have come back.'

'Observant as ever. But you don't have the power to keep me out. I mean, under Zurich canton law a Polizeileutnant can't just say to a bloke "Out you go and stay out".'

'You have come back before?'

Henri.

This was the crunch. If he'd checked the hotel registers he'd know I'd been here that night. Now he was inviting me to lie about it—and then he'd know he was on to something.

So I went ahead and told him a lie. 'Yes—a couple of times. I'm always coming through Zurich.'

That shook him; so he *had* known I'd been here that night. 'When did you come?'

'Couple of days ago—didn't stay overnight, then. And a few days before that.'

Elizabeth was looking at me, a little perplexed and a bit worried, too.

'Did you know a man called Henri Bernard?—an expert of art?'

I frowned, as if I was trying to remember, and looked at Elizabeth. 'Yes, I think so. French, wasn't he? I think I met him once.'

'He is dead.'

190

'Yes, I thought I read that somewhere. Got himself murdered, didn't he?'

'The night you were here.' Very heavily and significantly.

'Which night was that?'

He sighed.

I said: 'Well, come *on*, mate. *I* didn't murder him. Why the hell should I?'

'He was robbed.'

'Well?'

'We believe he was robbed of a most valuable picture.'

I gaped at him. I'd never thought of that. I mean, *I* knew there hadn't been a picture pinched—but why should they know? There Henri was, an art expert, with my picture-sized suitcase and obviously not enough clothes to fill it up—so why not jump to the conclusion that somebody had swiped a picture from him? And all my bloody cleverness in nicking his money had been a sheer waste of time. They probably assumed the thief had done it for exactly the reason I had: shifting suspicion from the art angle.

I said feebly: 'I don't steal pictures either.'

Elizabeth said in a clear, crisp voice: 'What picture are we talking about?'

Lindemann frowned. 'We do not yet know.'

'Hasn't anybody reported one stolen?'

'We are checking to find out.'

'Valuable pictures don't get stolen without somebody *noticing*. It couldn't have been Bernard's picture—I knew him a bit, too, and he didn't have that sort of money. Art experts never do. It must have belonged to a client. Well, who was he working for?'

'We do not know.'

'My God, you don't know much. I'll bet there wasn't a picture at all.'

'Fraulein—we must check on every possibility.'

'That's exactly what you're *not* doing, you're only considering one possibility: that he had a picture, that it was stolen, and that anybody with the faintest connection with art who was here at the same time must have something to do with it. Are you *really* a detective?'

He got red and stiff, holding his beer glass rigidly in front of him, like a sword at the salute. 'Fraulein, I must order you not to talk to me like that!'

Maybe it was time for me to pitch in a pennyworth. 'Well, you started it. I mean, you've been sitting here accusing me of murder and robbery and God-knows-what. Am I supposed to like it?'

'I am not accusing!'

'You could have fooled me.'

He took a careful, official sip of beer. Then, when his voice was under control again, said: 'You are a smuggler of pictures.'

'I'm an antique dealer.'

'But also you smuggle?'

I shrugged. 'Everybody smuggles.' Yes, he'd certainly got on to me through the Customs.

'But you do it all the time, for money,' he persisted.

'What's it to you? I don't break any Swiss laws.' Well, apart from sometimes carting that .22 around, of course. And concealing a bit of evidence and deliberately misleading the Kriminalpolizei and a few little things like that.

'So you do these things,' he said triumphantly.

'And so what? Stop trying to enforce other country's laws. What about all that gold in Switzerland?—you got any gold mines in this country? Half of that comes in illegally—by somebody else's laws. Are you going to start shaking down all the gold smugglers? Like hell you are, because Switzerland makes a nice fat profit out of it. Well, you make a profit out of art, too. Don't rock the boat; you might find yourself swimming home.'

Elizabeth opened fire from the flank. 'We shall of course have to report all this to our employer. He'll have to decide himself whether to take it up with your superiors.'

His triumph hadn't lasted long. He gave his beer a long, frowning look, just in case there were any useful clues floating around in it, then coughed and said: 'You are going to Wien tomorrow?'

'Yes.'

'I would ask your address there.'

'Don't have one yet. But I'll be back soon. D'you want me to ring you so you can come and tail me from the station again?'

He looked at me, and stood up. 'I will know. Good evening.' Then he bowed slightly to Elizabeth and walked away.

There was a long silence, which I spent wishing I'd chosen a double Scotch instead of beer and wondering if I was really still hungry. It had been rather an official day.

Then she said: 'The *next* time you get yourself tangled up with the police, d'you mind leaving me behind?'

'Funny, I was going to say just the opposite. I mean, I hope you'll be along next time as well. Thanks.'

'I just don't like policemen thinking they're gods,' she said firmly.

'You won't convince them—but thanks anyway.'

'Has he stopped suspecting you, d'you think?'

'Ah, he never really did. He was just pushing me around on general grounds. We wouldn't be going to Vienna tomorrow if he thought he'd learnt anything. Anyway, he isn't running the Henri case; not a crummy little Leutnant.' Hell, I *was* going to have a Scotch; I could eat tomorrow. I waved at a waiter.

Elizabeth said: 'Did you have to admit you were an art smuggler?'

'It still isn't against the law—here. And now he knows I'm a sort of professional crook, he's even less likely to think of me doing for Henri. I mean that was a really bloody amateur job. The chances whoever-it-was took . . . just one scream, one night porter prowling around . . .'

She nodded absently. The waiter rolled up and I ordered; she didn't want anything. When he'd gone, she said: 'But if too many people know, you're going to be out of business, aren't you? Won't the Italian Customs tell the French and the Dutch and everybody?'

'No—o. Customs services don't talk to each other much.

Their laws and methods and so on are too different; it's not like the police. And anyway, they're sort of competing with each other. I mean they're all profit-making—the service gets a cut of the stuff it confiscates. If you've got a gold smuggler coming from London to France to Italy and the Italians know they wouldn't tip off the French. They'd wait until he came into Italy; then they get the gold and the glory.'

She was looking at me thoughtfully. 'I suppose you rather trade on that.'

'I suppose I do.'

She yawned suddenly, then apologized. 'It's been a long day. And a rather exciting one. I was really frightened when they took you off that train.'

It hadn't been my idea of a pleasure cruise, neither. 'Ah, just part of the job.'

She nodded absently, and got up. 'I'll see you in the morning, Bert.'

I stood there awhile, sort of wondering whether to eat, have another Scotch, or just go on standing there until I'd raised the energy to make a decision. In the end a waiter made it for me by coming across to see if my feet had got glued to the deck. I shook my head and crawled away to bed.

The morning started slowly, and by the time I was up and about Elizabeth had wandered off somewhere. So I drifted across to the Landesmuseum behind the station and drooled over some of their Radschlosspistoles and Luntenschnapphahn-schlosses—wheel-locks and matchlocks. To me, German always sounds more like a specification than a language, but Zurich used to make some pretty nice old guns.

She found me in the bar of the Central at about half past twelve, and we went out for a good solid lunch—which wasn't a bad idea, as things turned out. We left for the airport at half past two.

194

THIRTY-ONE

AT VIENNA Carlos was waiting with some hired or maybe borrowed Mercedes 220 and drove us into town. It was past dark, and all the lights were on in the big oil refinery just down the road, making the geometric shapes into some cold, deserted space city.

'Did ye have any trouble in Zurich?' he asked.

'The Customs tipped off the police so we had a little chat with them. But we're clean. They think.'

'Aye,' he said thoughtfully. 'Well, I hope so. But this could be the last purchase anyway, so ye'll maybe only have the one more trip.'

Elizabeth sounded surprised. 'The last one? But we've—you've—got over three million dollars left, haven't you?'

'Aye. But if Captain Parker's right about this, we'll maybe be spending most of it.'

'My God, it must be good. Or thinks it is. What *is* it?'

'That's for ye to judge. We havna seen it ourselves yet.'

I said gloomily: 'I'll bet it's bloody big, anyway.'

'Ye'll maybe have a wee problem. Is Austria verra strict about these things?'

'No, but something that valuable . . . Well, we'll see.'

'Aye.'

Down the long straight road that splits the huge cemetery, under the railway and then in among the first trams and up to the Ringstrasse itself. I assumed we'd be turning along it; most of the big hotels are around the Ring. But we went straight across and into the old city. I don't know Vienna that well—I mean I could find my way around in daylight—but after a couple of turns along the narrow streets I was totally lost.

After a couple more turns I asked: 'Where the hell are we going?'

'Captain Parker's flat. He's away at the moment.'

Elizabeth asked suspiciously: 'Are we supposed to stay there? Both of us?'

'It's a big place,' Carlos said soothingly. 'And it's maybe only a couple of nights. We wanted a nice quiet place for ye to examine the picture for as long as ye like—and secretly.'

She nodded, seemingly resigned to it. Well, I suppose most art expertise is just looking, just living with a picture until you get a feeling about it: it's right or it's wrong. Same with old guns, really.

And at last we stopped. It was a narrow, dark, empty street lined with huge gloomy old houses and hardly a one showing a light.

Our house was the same: walls as thick as a castle, tall shuttered windows that didn't even start until the height of your head. The doorway was a big double affair that would once have taken a coach; Carlos opened the usual smaller door cut into it, and led the way in.

We went through the little tunnel of an arch, with the Hausmeister's office on the right—dark again—and out into a little courtyard covered with iced snow. Wide stone stairs led up to a part-open gallery around the level of the first floor. One more floor above that. And still not a light showing. Then he switched on a single naked bulb halfway up the stairs.

'The building's condemned,' he explained. 'They'll be pulling it down soon. So there's only the two flats still occupied.'

'Who's got the other one?' I asked. 'Dracula?'

Elizabeth shivered. '*Don't*, please.'

'Well, it's a secret, all right.'

'Captain Parker's place is cheerful enough. Ye'll be warm. Watch for the ice on these steps.'

We went on up. 'Where is he?' I asked.

'Out of the country. Over the border.'

Austria's got plenty of borders—six, I think—but only two count. The gallant Captain was in Czechoslovakia or Hungary.

They're neither of them more than an hour's drive from Vienna, just down the Danube.

Carlos switched on another light and we went along the gallery to a big solid door at the side of the house. He opened it and we went in.

It took me about thirty seconds to discover that Captain P. wasn't a teetotaller. There was a near-full bottle of Teacher's Scotch, half a bottle of Polish vodka, some slivovitz, a couple of bottles of hock that looked pretty classy—anyway, they had a name as long as a Kentucky rifle—and a few bottles of soda. I was halfway through the first whisky and soda when Elizabeth came in. I was in what was probably the living-room, warmed by an electric fire and an electric storage heater.

'What's it like?' I asked.

'Good enough. It's a weird layout, though.'

'Probably all chopped up from one big room. Look at the height of the ceiling.' It was far too high for the size of the room, and the fancy mouldings ended abruptly at the dividing walls.

Carlos said: 'Aye, it'd be the main dining-room, I dare say. Ye could seat fifty at least. Must have been a pretty sight. Is there enough food for ye in the kitchen, Miss Whitley?'

'D'you want us to eat here?'

'Aye, if ye don't mind. If we're being secretive about it, it's best to be as secret as possible, so I'd rather ye weren't seen out just yet. I'm sure Mr. Kemp will agree.'

I shrugged, then nodded. It was my own sort of idea.

'Oh, all right,' she said. 'But I'm not much of a cook.'

'Neither am I, but I eat a lot of my own cooking. We'll live.' She grinned. I said to Carlos: 'If I can't go out, you might bring me some small cigars—you know.'

'Aye, I'll do that. So I'll be back about eleven—I hope.'

She asked: 'With the picture?'

'Aye—if it's here by then.'

I said: 'It's coming across the border, isn't it?'

He paused, then said quietly: 'Aye.'

When he'd gone, Elizabeth asked: 'Did he mean the border I think he meant?'

I nodded.

She said: 'You've got rivals in business.'

'They can have it. I mean, I'm not messing about with the Iron Curtain.'

'Don't blame you. Can I have a drink?'

I poured her a Scotch, then wandered through the flat on my own snoop-about. It was long, just a string of rooms and a corridor stretched along one side of the building. All the windows were on the courtyard side because the house joined straight on to the next one; the windowless corridor ran along that wall, with the rooms opening off it. There was a narrow kitchen with an old-fashioned electric stove, a smallish fridge and the usual bits and pieces; a big bedroom with a double bed—Elizabeth had dumped her bags there—a bathroom with a gas geyser that dated from the great days of the Austro-Hungarian Empire (as a firearms expert I wasn't going to touch *that*) and a smaller bedroom with a desk in it. The drawers were locked. Guess how I knew.

I drifted back to the living-room, where Elizabeth was gazing rather vaguely at the bookshelf.

'Any Mickey Spillanes I haven't read?' I asked.

'No . . . there's a le Carré, though.'

'Not enough guns in le Carré. I mean, hardly anybody gets shot.'

She gave me a quick look, and I felt guilty until I remembered nobody knew about Fajjy's boy in Padua. Then she turned back to the books. 'If it's guns you want, there's plenty of it here.'

I went over and looked. There were only about forty books in all: a few novels, a couple of books about Vienna and Austria, a bunch of books about art, and a bunch about guns: *Firearms, The Age of Firearms, Firearms Curiosa,* Lister's *Antique Firearms, History of the Colt Revolver* and a 1960 edition of W. H. B. Smith's *Small Arms of the World.* Well, well, well; so Captain Parker yearned for the good old days when he was bounding around at the head of his company waving an outdated .38. I suppose I could have guessed that, seeing that he still called himself Captain.

Elizabeth asked: 'A good collection?'

'Standard stuff. I've got 'em all at home.' I poured myself another drink.

'Do you want anything to eat?'

'Not much. What is there?'

'A few tins. Bread. Eggs. Potatoes. Coffee. I'd better make some coffee for when they come, I suppose.'

'If there's anything that'll make a sandwich, I'll have one.' I followed her into the kitchen and leant against the sink while she sorted among the equipment ancient and modern. The whole flat was like that: a mixture of furniture handed on from past tenants, a few bits Parker had probably added (but only when he had to, and not spending too much even then). And too much gloss paint, giving the place the shabby shine of a government office.

You can find a flat like that in every run-down old mansion in every big city in Europe. And when you've found it, they throw you into the street and tear the place down and stick up a twenty-four storey building for the United Nations Hogwash and Leprosy Organisation. From one empire to another in less than sixty years.

Elizabeth was holding out a sandwich on a plate. 'What are you dreaming about?'

'Progress. Thanks.' It was some sort of liverwurst. Not bad. I took it back into the living-room—there was a connecting door—then called back: 'Should I stick a bottle of this wine in the fridge?'

'What is it?'

I took a deep breath and flexed my tongue. 'Niersteiner Oelberg Riesling Feine Auslese Edelgewächs—1959.'

She whizzed out of the kitchen. 'My God, that's expensive stuff. Perhaps we'd better not touch it.'

'Why not? Parker can claim it on expenses. Anyway, I expect Carlos brought it in. I mean, Parker can't be much of a wine connoisseur if all he's got is two bottles of the stuff.'

'Perhaps he was planning a little seduction party.'

'Well, hard luck Captain Parker. He'll have to fill her up with slivovitz. How d'you know about wines, anyway?'

'America isn't *all* Scotch-on-the-rocks, you know. And the art world's very conscious about being cultured. We even go to Wagner—unless we've remembered to be out of town.'

I grinned.

The doorbell gave a couple of tinkles and a throaty Faggioni-type rattle. 'The big picture,' I said, 'is about to start,' and went to open the door.

THIRTY-TWO

DONA MARGARITA hurried in, wearing her leopard-skin and bringing a blast of cold air with her. Then a character I didn't know, carrying the front end of the picture—which was sewed up in sacking—and about six feet behind him another unknown carrying the rear end. I damn sure wasn't going to get *that* picture into any suitcase.

Finally Carlos, who closed the door behind him—and locked it carefully.

I followed them through into the living-room and started offering drinks while Elizabeth offered coffee. The two unknowns propped the picture up on the sofa and started cutting the sewing along the top. They were both dressed in dark overcoats and homburg hats, a little shabby, with thick cheap shoes. Their faces were almost the same, too, or maybe it was the expressions: calm, closed, watchful. I knew what their job was, and I don't mean fine art dealing. Also I was ready to bet they were on the wrong side of the frontier.

Dona Margarita was sipping a small Scotch and gradually unwrapping her coat; the cold air outside had reminded me how warm the flat really was. Carlos was sticking to coffee. Elizabeth was just standing, weaving her fingers together nervously. Nobody said anything.

Then one of the new friends saw the bottle of slivovitz, pointed it out to his mate, and they both went on strike.

Elizabeth muttered: 'Oh my God . . .' and tied her fingers into a clove-hitch. Dona Margarita glanced at her and smiled sympathetically.

Actually it didn't take long. The slivovitz went down without touching the sides and they were back unwrapping in less than a minute.

Under the sacking the picture was protected along the edges with corrugated cardboard, and under that it was wrapped about in lengths of thick cotton wool. Whoever had packed it up (Captain Parker?) had known what he was doing.

Finally it was all off—and we could see the back of the picture. They each took an end, lifted carefully, turned it round and propped it back.

Then Elizabeth said: 'Good God!' Then: 'Giorgione.' And then, in an awed whisper: 'You've found the "Venus with Pistol".'

It was a nude woman, getting on for life size, half-lying on a crumpled red cloth, her back against a mossy rock. And holding a weird old pistol conveniently across her lap. Behind her, the summer afternoon faded away past a big fortress-type farmhouse and isolated trees to low blue hills. A sky with tall clouds and a golden haze that picked up the glow of her body.

And it was the most beautiful thing I've ever seen.

The woman—not a girl—was full, soft, incredibly lovely. She was awake, looking out at me with dark serious eyes. But the strange thing was, there was no emotion about the picture. She wasn't expressing anything: she just *was*. The whole thing was alive, but quiet, still, like the afternoon. You could hear a bird clear its throat and then stop, ashamed to break the silence.

This was what the Renaissance was really about. This was a million years from Giotto's strict saints and hungry blue devils—but just as certain about a different certainty: original beauty, not original sin.

Very quietly, Elizabeth said: 'And I suppose we've got to talk about *money*.'

I glanced at Dona Margarita and Carlos; they were still standing, hypnotized. Only the two helpers weren't impressed; they'd given it one glance to make sure it was still in one piece, then pushed off into the corner to keep the slivovitz from getting lonely.

Suddenly that didn't seem a bad idea; I'd found my hands

were trembling. I went and poured a fresh Scotch, and that seemed to break the spell.

Carlos said: 'D'ye *recognize* it, then?'

Elizabeth nodded. 'We'd always known it existed—once. Somebody did a lot of engravings of Giorgiones—and others —a hundred years after he died. The first sort of catalogue, really. The engravings survived, but a lot of pictures haven't. Or haven't been found. The "Venus with Pistol" is the big one, though.'

Dona Margarita asked: 'Does that prove it is correct . . . genuine?'

Elizabeth stared at the picture, frowning. 'No—o. If you were going to fake an old master you'd try and choose one that had gone missing. You'd paint something to match the evidence. Or the engraver could always have got it wrong, that it wasn't a Giorgione at all, but Titian or Sebastiano . . .' Then she shook her head. 'This wasn't, though. This *must* have been Giorgione.'

'Is there anybody else we can consult?' Dona Margarita asked tactfully.

'Nobody. There aren't any Giorgione experts. He didn't paint enough—or enough didn't survive—to make it worth being an expert on him alone. There's only about half a dozen that everybody accepts as his. Only twenty that are worth arguing about. He died young.'

I decided it was time to be helpful. 'This looks pretty fresh.'

'It's been cleaned, quite recently. Expertly, too. That's in its favour, of course. If you were faking one you'd try and dirty it up.' Then she suddenly burst out: 'But nobody could fake it like *this*. This is *real*.'

A moment's silence; then I said: 'It's great, I'll grant you that—'

'*Thank* you.'

'—but where's it been the last three hundred years?'

Carlos said coolly: 'Hungary, I'd presume, Mr. Kemp.'

Elizabeth went and carefully tilted the picture forward—it wasn't framed so it wasn't heavy—and studied the back. 'There's no marks, no labels. Well, we knew it hadn't been on the market in the last hundred years.' She tilted it back. 'I'd guess it's been hanging in the back bathroom of some Hungarian castle for God-knows-how-long. All covered in dirt; just a dim picture of some nude. Nobody knew what they'd got. There aren't many places in the world that could happen, but Hungary's one of them. It was practically feudal until the last war; nothing had changed in centuries.'

Carlos said carefully, almost reluctantly: 'Ye dinna think it could be stolen?'

She glanced at him. 'Don't you know who you're buying it off?'

'Aye—but there's no receipt for a previous sale.'

She stepped back from the picture. 'Well, it depends what you mean by "stolen". Like I say, I wouldn't think this picture's been moved in hundreds of years. Then, come 1943 and the Germans start taking over. They may have broken up the family, looted the picture. In 1944 you get the Russians marching in; *then* a castle-owning family wouldn't last long. Either way, there won't be much of the family left by now. But the big thing is that they didn't *know* what they'd got, so there'll likely be no record of them having it. You don't get the pictures in your bathrooms catalogued. So if somebody turns up in Paris or New York and says "Hey, that's the picture from my grandaddy's castle," he won't be able to prove it.

'In fact he probably won't even recognize it, after the cleaning,' she added.

Dona Margarita said: 'You believe the title would be valid in law, then?'

Elizabeth chewed this over, along with her lip. 'Well, I'm no lawyer—'

I said: 'I suppose everybody does know we're buying off the Hungarian government—*if* we buy?'

Carlos said stiffly: 'Captain Parker doesna seem to agree with ye.'

'Then Captain Parker needs his flipping head shrunk. I mean, Hungary's a Socialist People's Paradise, ain't it? A bit of the old all-for-one and what's-yours-is-ours, right? I mean no private property—well, nothing this pricey. Anyway, remember I know something about getting pictures across frontiers. *Not* a thing this size, mate, and *not* across an Iron Curtain border. Those two—' I nodded at the vanishing slivovitz '—they ought to stay in the West and run me out of business. They're bloody magicians.

'Then—you said it had been cleaned. Expertly. Well, I don't know much about Hungary, but I wouldn't think there'd be many expert picture-cleaners around. There just isn't the trade in the old pictures. And they'd be known; all be working for state museums and so on. They wouldn't risk touching an undercover job like this. No. It's the Hungarian government.'

Elizabeth was chewing at her lip again. I'd seen the same sort of thing with Henri, with every other expert I'd worked with. She *wanted* it to be right, to be legal. An expert who discovers a great picture shares a bit of the artist's feeling of having painted it. Hell I was going to *create* a pair of decorated Wogdons, wasn't I?

Finally she said: 'I suppose that makes sense . . .'

Dona Margarita asked crisply: 'How does this affect the legal position?'

'I don't know . . . I suppose they might sell it, then claim it had been stolen and sue for it back. After all, *they'll* have a record of it now.'

Carlos said: 'They canna verra well claim it's stolen if they havena reported it stolen. Could they just be wanting a wee bit of foreign exchange?'

Elizabeth said: 'Ye—es . . . Well, that side of it isn't really my business.'

I'd slightly dropped out of the chat. Now I was up close to the picture taking a shufti at the pistol. It was a weird one, all right: nearly two foot long, with hardly any break in the line between barrel and stock, so the overall shape was a half-bent boomerang. The trigger was long and curling and sloped well back (her fingers were well clear of it) and the lock was a fancy affair of a wheel, a coil spring, and several other bright ideas.

Dona Margarita asked: 'So, Senorita—now can you make an estimate for the price?'

At the mention of money, I turned around. 'What about our chums knocking back the slivovitz?'

'They don't speak English,' Carlos reassured.

'They don't look as if they speak at all, but if they're government thugs then they'll be damn good listeners.' I was watching them for a reaction. I didn't get a flicker, but not reacting would be part of their job.

Dona Margarita looked at me impatiently. 'We are certain they do not understand. Now, Senorita . . .?'

Elizabeth said slowly: 'It's one of the last Giorgiones. I'd say he did it just before the Dresden Venus, just before he died—'

'When was that?' I asked.

'1510.' Now Carlos joined Dona M. in giving me a snarky look. Elizabeth went on: 'It's almost as good as the Dresden one . . . I'd say, in a London auction, it would bring—' she took a deep breath '—three million dollars. At least that. Probably more. You just can't *tell*.' She threw up her hands. 'This is the find of the century. God knows who'll bid what for it. Washington, Cleveland, the Met, the Louvre—they'd cut each other's throats for it.'

Dona Margarita smiled, catlike and satisfied. 'But Managua will have it. You said three million dollars?'

Carlos said: 'We're being offered it for that.'

'Then take it. Quick.'

'Will ye give me a certificate on it so I can contact Managua?'

She thought about it. 'I ought to get some test run on it. And I'd like to just live with it for a day. Just look at it. But you can warn Managua that we've *probably* found something great.'

I said: 'If you're ever thinking of breaking it up, I'll give you five thousand quid for the gun—if I'd got five thousand, I mean.'

That got me all-round looks of Bert-Kemp-go-Home.

But I ploughed on bravely. 'Bet I'd get ten for it in London. Bit of real gun history, that is.'

Elizabeth said coldly: 'And what's so special about it?'

'It's an early wheel-lock, see? The first real flash-ignition sort of gun. You wound on a chain pulling in the spring, and when you pulled the trigger, it——'

'And what's that got to do with it?' Carlos snapped.

'Well, this picture proves all the gun experts wrong and they *did* invent the wheel-lock before 1517.'

It took a moment to sink in, and in the second moment I thought Elizabeth was going to sit down and cry. Instead, she just sat down. 'Oh God,' she whispered. 'And he died in 1510. Oh God.'

Carlos said: Are ye *sure* of this, man?'

'I've never heard of a wheel-lock dated earlier than about 1520, and the theory goes they were invented in Nuremberg in 1517. Well, I mean we could all be wrong. Maybe it was earlier—and maybe old Georgy-boy used to pop over to Germany on the cheap tourist flights——'

Carlos said: 'Ah shut up.'

And after that there was a long gloomy silence. So I went back to studying the picture—not just the gun. And it was still the most beautiful thing I'd ever seen. It wasn't young, fresh, dawn, Eden—all those sort of words Botticelli painted. This was a mature woman at the harvest time of the world. Not a hope—an achievement.

Well, maybe even God thought things were really going to work out that way, once.

Then Carlos said, a bit tentatively: 'Well—couldna somebody have finished it off after he was dead? Put the gun in then, maybe?'

She answered in a dull voice, as if she was reading from one of her father's books. 'Titian and Sebastiano did some touching up on Giorgione—Titian probably finished the Dresden Venus. But this one's earlier . . . anyway, Giorgione must have finished *some* of his own work. And he liked weapons; he was always putting in armour and swords and spears and things—he'd've put in that gun from the beginning, if it had been him. I'm sorry: it just *can't* be his.'

I said cheerfully: 'Well, at least it explains why they're selling it undercover. I mean, if they put it up at Christie's or

Sotheby's *some* gun nut would've seen it and *pouf*. So they do better selling it as a Giorgione to a mug than as a Titian to somebody who really knows.'

Dona Margarita asked: 'Are there no tests which can help, Senorita?'

'I'd like to make sure of the age, that's all. But I'm sure it's sixteenth-century anyway. A modern forger wouldn't have made that mistake about the gun. . . . But the tests are only negative. They just show something *could* be by the right man, or couldn't be. That gun, evidence like that—that's perfect proof. Better than any test.'

'Assuming Mr. Kemp is correct,' Carlos pointed out.

I blew up. 'Jesus Christ—I save you blowing three million dollars and all I get is bloody niggling! So don't take my word for it: there's a museum of arms in this town—go and get a second opinion from there.'

Dona Margarita said soothingly: 'Senor Kemp is being most helpful. We are truly grateful. But, Senorita, if it is not by Giorgione, then who is it?'

'Titian or Sebastiano. No—Sebastiano never did anything this good. Titian, early, when he was still under Giorgione's influence.' She got up and came forward to the picture. 'It's still good—still a great picture. As Titian, I'd price it at two million dollars. No more. If they sell at that, then buy it.'

Dona Margarita and Carlos glanced at each other. Then Carlos said: 'Aye—well, I can put in a bid. We'll see what they say.' He nodded at the two tough guys and they finished the slivovitz in one gulp each and headed for the door.

Dona Margarita pulled her faithful leopards tight around her. 'Senorita, then we will leave the picture here until to-morrow. Thank you very much—but I am sorry it was a dis-appointment. Good-night, Senor Kemp.'

I mumbled a good-night. Carlos said: 'Aye—I'll drop in tomorrow, but probably not until dark. I dinna want to be seen around here.'

I said: 'Did you get my cigars?'

Carlos fumbled in his pocket and passed them over. I didn't know the brand, but they were about my size and made of

208

something like tobacco. He held out his hand. 'They cost sixteen schillings.'

'Take it out of that million I just saved you.'

From the door, Dona Margarita called sharply: 'Carlos!'

He said: 'Ye'll stay inside, then?' and hurried after her. I went along to see them out.

THIRTY-THREE

WHEN I GOT BACK, Elizabeth was still staring gloomily at the Venus. I mixed myself another Scotch, then remembered my manners. 'Hadn't you better have a spot of something?'

'I rather think I will. Scotch and water, please.' She went on staring.

When I brought it across she took a real swallow, not just a sip. We stood side by side drinking and looking.

Finally I said: 'It's bloody beautiful, all right.'

She nodded slowly. 'If only it could have been by him. . . .'

'You still think it looks like him?'

'I'd've said by the time Titian was this good, he wouldn't have painted this picture. He had more action, more . . . bounce. But. . . .' She shrugged helplessly.

I nodded and sipped. 'It's a funny thing about guns. I mean, you could walk into the nearest toyshop and buy something that's a bloody sight simpler *and* works a sight better than any wheel-lock. Just a couple of springs and a catch, but it took 'em another seventy years to think of it. I mean, just look at that thing; it's a flipping clock, really. The chain and the wheel and the coil spring and the U-spring. . . . Mind, that isn't a *real* wheel-lock. More a sort of fire-raising machine slapped on the side of a converted matchlock, I'd say.'

'Yes?' she said dully.

'Well, no lock like that's ever survived. Frankly, I don't think a gun like that was ever built. It wouldn't work very well; I mean, the sparks would fly all over the shop. But I know that lock. I've seen a drawing of it.'

She was showing a bit more interest.

I went on: 'You ever hear of Il Codice Atlantico? The Co-dex Atlanticus? Old Leonardo Da Vinci, but you might not know it because it wasn't art. It was a bunch of plans and stuff, all for military machines, that he did for the Duke of Milan. That lock thing was one of them.'

Her voice was a whisper. 'What date was this?'

'1485.'

Very slowly: 'Twenty-five years. Twenty-five years before Giorgione died.'

'S'right. Maybe somebody made up a gun like that, but I still doubt it. Probably he just saw the drawing somehow. He'd be interested enough to copy it, but he wouldn't know enough to see it wasn't really supposed to be for a gun. It's on the same page as a proper gun-lock.'

Suddenly she caught fire. 'And you *knew* this all along? And went on proving it *wasn't* Giorgione? Why didn't you *tell* us?'

'Oh yes? *And* those two Hungarian yobbos who can't understand English, like hell they can't.' My own voice was coming out loud and clear. 'And shove the bloody price back up to three million?'

The echoes died slowly. Then she said quietly: 'Yes. I'm sorry. I was a bit. . . . But why don't the Hungarians know this as well?'

'Because they're not so bloody clever about art as you are, nor about old guns like I am. Only you want to learn to trust your own opinions a bit more.'

'You bastard.'

'Only my dear old mum ever called me that, and I won't hear a word against her.'

She grinned. 'You *are* rather good. You know a lot more than you pretend to. About art as well, I think.'

'Ah, stuff it.'

She grinned again, then turned back to the picture.

'We've found a Giorgione, we've found a Giorgione,' she chanted softly.

I put an arm round her shoulder. '*You* found it, love.'

She slid her arm round my waist and hugged me. 'We've found a Giorgione, we've found a . . .'

Then suddenly we were kissing, wildly, happily. Then dan-

211

cing round the picture and then kissing again, gradually more
seriously. . . .

Then she held me away, at arm's length, and said breath-
lessly: 'Bert—is this for real?'

'Feels like it to me.'

'Yes . . .' she seemed to be working out her own feelings.
'I think it is.'

'Maybe you ought to run a spectrogram and X-ray on me
first.'

'What?' Then she laughed. 'Do I always sound so—so
academic?'

I pulled her back against me and she tried to nestle her
head under my chin; it didn't work—it never does, not with
me as short as I am. But her hair in my eyes was fantastically
soft and fine, and her body against me was alive and . . .

She said: 'I think I'd better have a drink.'

I started to get one, then didn't. 'Not if you *need* it. I don't
want you to have to be drunk.'

'I don't want to be drunk,' she said indignantly. 'I just want
a drink.'

'What about the wine—the Niersteiner whatsit? Should be
cold by now.'

'That sounds appropriate.'

I went to get it, and it took a time to dig up a corkscrew and
then I could only find one proper wineglass. So I rinsed out
one of the whisky tumblers.

When I got back to the living-room, she wasn't there.

Hell's teeth. But I hadn't heard the front door open. Had
she locked herself up in her bedroom or something?

But the door was open, the room almost dark except for the
light in the hall.

She said quietly: 'You forgot the wine.'

'So I did.' But I didn't move; just stood there, looking at
her standing by the big bed. And the dark air between us slowly
started to hum like radio waves.

'Bert—are we in love?'

'We might be. It's just been a long time since . . .'

'Bert, I'm not very good at . . . this . . .'

'This is *us*. There's no rules, nothing to be good at. It's only us.'

I walked towards her.

The light from the hall threw a fan-shaped spread of reflections across the ceiling. Like long thin wedges. Like fields of fire from concealed gun positions. Like slices of those round diagrams that show you how the Government spends every percentage of your tax penny—or gives you the idea the Government knows how it spends it, anyway.

When I couldn't think of anything else it was like, I said quietly: 'Elizabeth?'

'Hadn't you better call me Liz?' she said sleepily.

'Liz . . .' I tasted it. I wasn't sure, though. Maybe one day I'd change it to Betty, or Bess. Good Queen Bess. When did she reign? End of the sixteenth century. When they invented the snaphaunce. Renaissance England. My thoughts drifted like smoke round to where they'd started.

'Liz . . . we never told them it *was* a Giorgione.'

She nuzzled my bare shoulder. 'There's no phone.'

'That's right, isn't it? Well, I can go out and phone tomorrow.'

'Carlos said to stay home.'

'Stuff Carlos.'

She gave a muffled chuckle. 'No, *let's* stay home. I like being home with you. It'll be a nice surprise for Carlos when he comes round.'

'Yes . . .' My thoughts still floated lazily around the ceiling. Then: 'Anyway, if he's doing any bargaining at two million, he'll do it better if he doesn't know it *should* be three.'

She lifted her head. 'Oh Lord. Trust you to think of a crooked angle. Perhaps we ought to tell him, then.'

'Come off it. They thought they were trying to cheat us, didn't they? I mean selling it undercover like that. I mean, if they'd been ready to sell it as what they thought it was—a Titian—they'd've sent it to London, wouldn't they?'

'I suppose. . . . You do say "I mean" a lot, don't you?'

'What? Do I? I mean . . . I suppose I do, a bit.'

213

She chuckled again. 'I don't mind. I like it. I like everything about you.'

We were quiet for a time, then she said: 'Why me, Bert?'

I was back watching the ceiling. 'I don't know. . . . Yes, I do, in a way. You sort of care. I mean about pictures, and just that there *are* good pictures, and the way you got angry about forgery . . . I thought I could feel that way, once. But I can't, not really. It makes you pretty fireproof.'

'What?'

'You're tougher than you think. People who believe in something are.'

'That's not so rare.'

'It is in my circle.' When she didn't answer, I said: 'And why me, if it comes to that? Like it has.'

She chuckled again, then lay back herself to watch the shadows above. 'I suppose . . . it's that you *cope*. You can get things done. You—well, think of the angles. That's rare in my circle, you know.'

'Two different circles, it sounds.'

'Yes, I guess so. . . . How did you ever get interested in art, Bert?'

'Sounds silly, but—in the army. I even went to art school for six months, when I got demobbed. But it didn't work. I couldn't quite . . ."

'Do you look at pictures much? Just look?'

'Not so much, I suppose. Bit more than I pretend.'

'You really like to own things, don't you? If you can't own them, you're not very interested in them.'

The idea was a small cold draught. And like a draught, it got me a bit annoyed. I propped myself up. 'Well, so what? I'm a dealer. That means buying and selling—and owning in between.'

'Sure, sure,' she said soothingly. 'I'll bet you're a good dealer, too.'

'Yes, I am.'

She lay down and I could feel her breath on my shoulder. But now I was awake. I reached for my cigars—and I'd left them in the living-room. So you lie there and wonder if you really want one that much, and the more you wonder . . . I climbed out and walked through and found them and lit one.

Then I stood and looked at a picture I didn't own, and never could. And gradually the peace of that long-ago Italian afternoon came out like the warmth from a fire and I started to calm down.

Once I'd been able to just stand and look. That was a long time ago, too. Paris, it must have been, in 1944. The first time I'd really been in a serious art museum. That's what had fooled me I wanted to go to art school. But at the time I was in the army, where you didn't have to own anything, even if they let you. Now—hell, you *do* have to own things. And maybe stop caring too much about the things you can't own.

I mashed out the cigar and went back. But the calmness of the picture was still with me, like a voice I'd never hear again but never quite forget.

Liz was asleep, peaceful as any Venus. I eased in beside her and she reached a hand and touched my face and sort of purred like a cat. I grinned at her in the dimness, then lay there and let my thoughts wander through quiet summer afternoons. . . .

THIRTY-FOUR

I WOKE AT AROUND ELEVEN, and for a moment I felt sad because I knew it had been a dream and I'd never get back to it. Then I remembered it wasn't.

Liz had gone, so I just lay there and gloated for a while. Then I hauled myself up and took a squint inside the big wardrobe. She'd hung some of her clothes there, but separate to one side there was an old raincoat, a pair of slippers and a dressing-gown in some red artificial fabric. Captain Parker's I presumed, and the dressing-gown didn't seem to smell, so I put it and the slippers on. I don't carry such things with me; in fact, I don't usually wear them. But this morning it seemed right.

She was in the kitchen, sipping coffee and browsing through one of Parker's art books—Berenson on the Italian Renaissance.

She grinned at me—and then, damn it, she blushed.

'Hello there.' I went across and kissed her.

'You haven't shaved.' She put up a hand and touched my cheek. 'It's funny, all the little details about a person . . . you suddenly want to know . . . it's all so important. . . .'

'How about a little detail like coffee?'

'I'm sorry.' She poured me a cup. 'I can't even remember if you take sugar.'

'I do.' Then I propped myself against the sink and drank.

She said: 'Are we going to get married? Or not?'

'Jesus.' I slopped coffee into the saucer. 'I dunno—I mean, do you want to?'

'I don't know. Isn't that odd? Do *you* want to?'

I thought of my own flat in London; a bit like Parker's but smaller, colder, dirtier. The narrow dark shop. The dusty cupboards full of old, worthless guns.

I said: 'I've got damn-all money. Are you rich?'

'Hardly. I've got a bit, that's all.'

'We're going to be bloody poor.'

And that had done it; the night was over. The mood was busted and neither of us was skilled enough to put it back together. Not right away, anyhow. We smiled at each other bravely and I finished my coffee quickly and went to shave and dress.

When I got back she had a row of tins and stuff—just about all the food there was—lined up for inspection. 'D'you want any breakfast? Or shall we make it a sort of brunch a bit later?'

'That's fine. Anything.'

'Well, you choose then.'

'Whatever you like.' Now we were being overpolite, not wanting to make any mistake, not cause any hurt. 'Hell, let's have some eggs. Any way you can cook 'em.'

'Okay. I'm making some more coffee.'

So I wandered through to the living-room, turned on the second bar of the electric fire, and said good morning to more than a million quid's worth of Venus and her absurd alarm-clock pistol. I mean, it's crazy—you paint a picture so perfect and simple at the same time that somebody else, just as bright and (come to think of it) just as good an artist, is inventing something as inefficient and over-complicated as a wheel-lock. She should've been holding my Wogdon, say, or even a Colt single action. Still, I suppose it takes time to invent something simple.

But, God, she was still lovely.

I went over to the tall windows and stared out at the day. Or tried; all I could see was the other tall, shuttered windows across the courtyard. The second gallery above us cut off the sky and most of the light; Parker lived almost as much in year-round dimness as Fajjy did. And there was a thin layer of fresh snow on our gallery balustrade. I shivered and went back to the fire.

Liz came in with the coffee, and I said: 'You know, you've never even seen our friend by daylight?'

'Yes. We'll take her for a breath of air after lunch. If it isn't snowing again. How about scrambled eggs on toast?'

'Fine.'

When she'd gone I poured myself more coffee—then added a jolt of Scotch to it. Hell, it was nearly noon. Then back to wandering around the room, snooping at things, just for something to do.

We ate in the kitchen. The eggs were a bit leathery and the toast a bit soggy and Liz a bit over-apologetic. I told her to shut up and pass the salt and pepper.

'I can't find them.'

'Hell's teeth.'

She suddenly burst out: 'I can't find anything but a bag of flour! The first meal I cook for you and it's . . . it's like this.' Then she just sat staring at her plate, and tears began to trickle gently down her face.

I got up and put an arm round her shoulders. 'It's all right, love. Not your fault; it's that bloody Captain Parker.' I picked up a saucer and tossed it into a corner and it made a nice ringing smash. 'Revenge. That'll show the bugger.'

She started to laugh through the tears, then put up her face and I kissed her. After a time I went back to my eggs, which were now cold along with their other problems.

When I'd finished I lit a cigar. That hadn't improved with time, neither.

'I wonder what sort of bloke this Parker is.'

She considered. 'Bachelor. Ex-Army. He doesn't eat in much. And he's probably got this apartment on a short lease, so he hasn't made much of a home of it.'

'Yes. But if he's so proud of once being an army captain—and they're not much—why doesn't he have any souvenirs around as well? Regimental photographs or crests and things?'

She got up and started clearing away the dishes. 'He was probably in the Cookhouse Corps or whatever you call it. Isn't it the soldiers who never got near a battle who're the most proud of it?'

'Yes, maybe. But he wasn't in Catering, not stocking a kitchen like this.'

'He's probably got a whole den of souvenirs back at his

218

parents' house in England, all carefully arranged. He wouldn't break up a collection just to bring a few things abroad for a few months.'

'Hadn't thought of that.' I went across and helped with the washing-up. Yes, me, Bert Kemp.

A bit later we drifted back into the living-room. I poured myself a Scotch and soda. 'Well, he's got a good taste in whisky, I'll say that for him. But he's not too bright about the price; he got this in a shop.'

'Why shouldn't he?'

'Most foreigners in Vienna get themselves International Atomic Energy Agency privileges. They run a sort of duty-free shop at their headquarters here, sort of like a PX. You can wangle a contact easy; cheap whisky, English cigarettes and stuff. I mean, I was going to do it myself if we'd been here a week.'

Liz nodded, looking out of the window. 'Will you help me take the picture outside in a minute?'

'Sure.' I ran a finger along the back of the books. 'What's the gallant Captain really interested in? What's his hobbies?'

'I don't know. What does it matter?—we'll probably never meet him anyway.'

'Just general snoopiness. Trying to work out what sort of man he is. I just can't do it, somehow.'

She shrugged, then smiled. 'All right, let's have a go, then. He comes of a fine old English family—the Hyde Park Parkers, you know—and he served twenty years in India*h*.'

'Twenty years and didn't get past Captain?'

'Ah, you're forgetting that unfortunate affair with the Colonel's wife. They hushed it up for the honour of the jolly old regiment, don't you know, but it ruined his chance of promotion. So finally he resigned.'

I grinned. She was doing a nice imitation of a certain London art dealer who never let you forget he'd had a jolly good war in a jolly good regiment.

'Why doesn't he like salt and pepper, then?'

'He contracted a rare Eastern disease. Two, in fact. Salt catches him under the liver and pepper catches him under the kidneys. But he's still a bit of a lady's man, you know, ha ha?'

'The double bed. Yes.'

'*And* those two bottles of wine, remember. Then, after the uncultured life of the army, he's trying to catch up by reading up on *great* art. But his real passion is still guns.'

'Balls. Not with that collection of books it isn't.'

She looked surprised. 'I thought you said you'd got them all?'

'Yes, I've got most of them, but they're pretty pop stuff. Except the Smith. I mean, if he was a real gun nut he'd have Greener or Pollard or Jackson or somebody. I thought art was his real love.'

'Never. They're just pop, too. Coffee-table stuff; just reproductions. The Berenson's the only serious one.'

I got a bit thoughtful and took down the W. H. B. Smith *Small Arms of the World*, and looked inside the covers. He'd bought it second-hand, in Paris. Now, Smith's a reference book and it's all about modern weapons. They bring it up to date every few years. I keep my out-of-date editions, but mostly because who wants to buy an outdated reference book second-hand? Captain Parker, it seemed.

I put it back. 'He's also crazy.'

But she'd lost interest in Captain P. 'Well, let's get that picture outside.'

'In a minute. What's he really interested in? Music?—there's no record player. History? Poetry? Chinese vases? Photography? Hindu sex habits? Fast cars? There's nothing just nothing.'

'He sounds a pretty dull character.'

'He can't be all that stupid, not if he's fixing up fancy undercover deals with the Hungarian Government.'

'Yes. Well, so you've finally deduced something about him. I want to get that picture out to the daylight.'

'Wait a minute.' I was prowling round the room, puffing smoke and worrying. 'He buys expensive art books but doesn't hang up any pictures. He doesn't use salt or pepper. He does clever deals with the Hungarians and hasn't got the sense to buy his Scotch on the cheap. He's just about cleaned out the flat when he left. Only the raincoat and the dressing-gown and the slippers.' I stopped. 'There's nothing *private* of his around. No old toothbrushes or papers.'

'He'd keep his papers locked up—in that desk in your room.'

'That's right, isn't it? Get the biggest kitchen knife and anything else you can find.'

'*Bert!* You can't go breaking into people's desks!'

'*I* can.' I took out the flintlock screwdriver and pulled it apart to give me the wide blade, then headed for the small bedroom.

The desk was old and solid but not big nor valuable. Just a desk, with three drawers on one side, a drawer in the middle, and a cupboard on the other side. Everything was locked except the middle drawer, and that had just a couple of ball-point pens, a bottle of aspirins and a box of carbon paper.

I tried jamming the screwdriver into the crack of the top left drawer and prising. It hardly moved. So I shifted to the cupboard side.

That was a bit looser, what with the side panel of the desk being much thinner than the top. But I still couldn't move it enough with the screwdriver.

Just then Liz came in with a whacking great butcher-type knife, an old-fashioned tin-opener and an even more old-fashioned look on her face.

'Look, Bert, I just don't like this. You're going to leave marks on that desk, and——'

'I'm going to tear the bloody thing apart if I need to,' I said grimly. 'Give me that knife.'

It slid most of the way into the crack by the lock, then jammed; it was that thick. I worked it in a bit further, then gave the handle a sideways thump. There was a crack of a parting joint, but the door sprang open.

'Bert!' she wailed. 'You've broken it!'

The cupboard was empty. Just dust. I held up a grimy finger, then went round the back of the desk.

The panel hiding the back of the three drawers was even thinner; just plywood, probably, and only held on by panel pins. The knife went in easily, and I worked off the panel in less than a minute. I lay on my back and stab-kicked at the backs of the drawers.

At the second kick there was a tearing crash and the middle drawer jumped clear out on to the floor. The next kick got the top drawer. Liz peered down sombrely at them.

'Well?'

She shook her head. 'There's . . . nothing in them.'

I kicked out the last drawer, got up and went round to her. 'Well, there's Captain the bloody gallant Parker for you. Nothing. He don't exist.'

'But why? You mean Carlos just invented him?—just furnished up the apartment to look like it?'

'Probably got the furniture with the apartment. Just the books, the clothes, the food, the booze, that's all he'd need to get in.'

'Why should he do it, though? Is he pulling a fast one on Dona Margarita?—getting her to pay Parker a commission on the Giorgione and really keeping it himself?'

'Something like that, I should think.' I put the screwdriver together again and went out to wash the grime off my hands.

Liz was in the living-room. 'Are we going to tell Dona Margarita about this?'

'Maybe. I don't know; I haven't worked it out yet. . . . D'you want to get this picture outside?'

So we put on our coats and carried it carefully out on to the gallery. I took one quick look, then left her to it and walked back along the gallery. Just for fun I tried the door of the other flat I had to pass. It was locked, nobody answered the bell, the windows were shuttered tight. Down below, nobody had walked across the thin snow-fall in the courtyard.

So I went down and walked all round, trying doors and staring up at the flats above us. I couldn't see a sign of life; if Carlos was right and one other flat was still occupied, they were staying well wrapped up against the cold.

Far away, a bell tolled slowly, talking to other people in another world.

I tried the Hausmeister's door, and that was locked and dark, too. And so finally I tried the door on to the street. It was shut as tight as a tomb.

I walked slowly back upstairs, thinking. Worrying a bit, too.

When we'd got the picture inside, the first thing I did was pour another Scotch to help along the thinking.

Then I remembered to ask: 'Is it right? The picture?'

She nodded. 'As far as I can tell. . . . It isn't wrong, anyway. Have you decided what we should do—about Captain Parker?'

'I dunno. We're locked in, you know.'

'What?'

'The front gate; it's locked. Maybe it's just usually kept that way, without a concierge, and each flat has its own key. You haven't seen one lying about?'

'Maybe Parker took it. . . . Sorry. Carlos, though.'

'Yes. But let's have a look anyway.'

So we looked, although by then I didn't expect to find it. We didn't.

Liz said: 'It looks like Carlos wasn't trusting us not to take a little walk. Are you going to try with the kitchen knife again?'

'On that door? Christ, no. It's like a prison . . . I mean.' I said slowly, 'it really is like a prison.'

'What about the other apartment that somebody's in?'

'I'll give a hundred to one there *isn't* another flat occupied. Or they're away at the moment, anyway. You know—had you wondered why Carlos made such a lousy job of setting up this flat? I mean, not just forgetting the salt and pepper, that was just bloody stupid, but not enough books or clothes or anything? Not enough *real* Parker? Not really trying to create a character?'

She shook her head slowly. 'No—o. Anyway, he did it well enough to fool me.'

'Yes, well . . . but I mean, if somebody who didn't know us but knew a bit about us just walked in here, he could think everything here belonged to us?'

'*What?*'

'The furniture, sheets and stuff—they come with the flat.

223

But the personal stuff—your clothes, my clothes, and those books: a few novels, a couple of guide books, then art for you and guns for me. See?'

Oddly, she got offended. 'They'd think I carried around *that* collection of art books?'

'Hell's teeth—not another art expert, no, but just . . . just anybody who knew *you* were an art expert.'

After a time, she said: 'Those clothes he left, though . . .'

'Raincoat, dressing-gown, slippers. They haven't got names in—and we know the dressing-gown and slippers more or less fit me. Or he could carry them all away in an airline bag, afterwards.'

'After *what*?'

I shrugged.

'Do you mean,' she said carefully, 'that he's planning to frame us for something? Stealing the Giorgione or something like that?'

'I don't know . . . I don't see how. We'd be here to swear we didn't. Just setting us up in a love-nest that we're supposed to have rented for ourselves doesn't prove—' Then I got it. Love-nest. Of course. And he couldn't know, maybe couldn't even have hoped, how true it would work out.

I said: 'It's a great setting for a suicide pact.'

After a while, she whispered: 'You aren't serious.'

'Somebody is. If we're being set up to carry the can for something, then we're sure as hell better off dead. For them, I mean.'

After another while, she said: 'I never thought I'd say this —but now I'm rather glad you've got that gun.'

'But I haven't. Carlos never gave it me back, after Italy. Jesus.'

'My God.'

So I suppose if somebody had been around to say 'the Holy Ghost' we'd have drawn three-of-a-kind.

'But why? But *why*?' she asked. Then, more sensibly: 'What do we do then?'

I glanced out of the window to the slow-fading afternoon gloom. It was past two o'clock. 'First I'll check every flat to make sure there *isn't* anybody else around. You lock the door after me. He said he wasn't coming till after dark, so he probably won't but. . . . And shut all the shutters, too. I won't be long.'

I wasn't, neither. And there wasn't any good news.

I carefully locked and bolted the flat door from the inside. 'It'll take him an age to kick that in. But he can smash in the window and shutter fairly easy.'

'Couldn't we hide in one of the other apartments?'

'We'd have the same problem: we'd have to smash in a window. All he has to do is come looking for a busted window.'

'But what *can* we do?'

'I'm trying to think.' I put an arm round her shoulder. It didn't help the thinking much. I mean, it just made me think about her, and if we shouldn't spend the last few hours. . . . Why in hell didn't I ask Carlos for that gun back? Well, he'd have forgotten to bring it, of course.

But we did have a gun.

'Look,' I said, 'get out my old pistol—and the box of .22 cartridges.'

THIRTY-FIVE

WHILE SHE WAS DIGGING THEM out of her luggage, I sorted around in the kitchen for anything useful. There wasn't much, of course. But I collected a big old pair of scissors, a small saucepan with a lip, and my trusty flintlock screwdriver.

Liz came back with the gun and cartridges. 'Are you really going to make this work?'

'I'm going to try.' I spilled the cartridges on to the table; out of the original fifty I'd fired—how many? four?—and left six in the gun, so I should have forty. That was good enough.

Then I took the gun and gave it a careful check. Before, I'd only looked it over to see if it was, or wasn't a nice antique worth two hundred and sixty pounds. Now, I wanted to know about it as a gun.

I cocked it and pulled the trigger—just what any dealer doesn't do to an old gun. The lock was still sweet, the trigger pull a bit heavy. Was I going to try messing about with it? No. I could hold an aim anyway. Then I lifted the frizzen and squinted at the touch-hole.

'Got a pin or something?'

She took off the brooch at the neck of her blouse and passed it over, then sat down to watch with a calm, serious expression. I poked at the touch-hole—it was framed with gold—until I was quite sure it was clear. I'd've liked to do a bit of enlarging on it, too, but if I tried that with just a pin then I'd probably end up blocking it.

Liz asked: 'How does it work?'

'You stick a piece of flint in those jaws there'— I tapped the top of the cock, with its tightening screw '— shove the powder and ball down the barrel, then more powder in the flash-pan.' I lifted the frizzen and showed. 'Then you shut it down again. That kept it more or less waterproof. When you pulled the trigger, the flint hit the frizzen, that caused sparks, the frizzen was knocked up out of the way, the sparks hit the priming powder, that caused a flash through the touch-holed —and bang. Coffee for one.'

'And it'd really kill somebody?'

'By Christ it would. With the right amount of proper powder, and a proper ball, this is probably more accurate than any military pistol today. And it's throwing a ball the size of a heavy machine-gun, too.' I hadn't measured the bore, but I reckoned it was near-as-dammit half-inch diameter.

'Umm.' She stared sombrely at the gun. 'But have you got a flint?'

'No, not a proper one. But I've got a small one in my lighter. That might work.' Or might not.

Using the scissors as pliers I started pulling the bullets out of the cartridges, and carefully pouring out the charges into a saucer.

Liz stared. 'Is that all there is in there?'

'About a grain and a half. It'll push a bullet over a mile.'

She'd been going to poke the little grey-green granules with a finger-nail; now she took her hand away rather sharply. I said: 'Stub out a cigarette in it and all you'll get is a little flame. An explosion's only a flame in a compressed space.'

There weren't any scales in the kitchen, of course, and even if there were, they'd have been no use. I mean, I needed a jeweller's or chemist's balance if I was going to weigh this stuff. So reckoning on one and a half grains per cartridge, four cartridges would give me six grains. I stopped there. How much would you really need to work up a head of steam behind a .50 calibre ball?

Then I remembered W. H. B. Smith; *he* gave a table of cartridges and propellant weights at the back, didn't he? And he did, too. A .45 automatic cartridge was factory-loaded to just 5 grains. Some .455's went up to 7 grains.

But only some. I sat down again puzzling. I still didn't know how heavy my bullet was going to be. And this was a black-powder gun; even if I could remember the relative efficiency of black powder and nitro-cellulose, black powder burnt far slower—so its pressure built up slower and never got as high.

And old Wogdon had been building for that and only that. I mean, shove a grain too much of this modern smokeless stuff in and I was liable to get a short-barrelled gun and a short-fingered hand all of a sudden.

And I didn't know how much of the pressure would leak out of the touch-hole.

Oh hell. Still, the flint ignition probably wouldn't work anyway. Smokeless powder isn't all that sensitive; I mean, the primer, just the primer, on a .22 gives a hell of a flash to get the main charge started.

But I had to try.

'Think of something I can cast a lead bullet in. You know, I want to get a ball about half-inch across.'

Liz frowned, then looked around the kitchen. I started to dismantle my lighter. The flint looked ridiculously small compared with the big lump you ought to have in a flintlock. Why didn't Fajjy sell his ruddy guns with a piece of flint in them? Well, neither did I, come to that. I mean, you just don't go snapping the lock of a decorated Wogdon making pretty sparks.

Liz said: 'What about a potato? Suppose you cut it in half, then scoop out a bit in each half, and bore a hole through into one half and shut it all up and pour—'

I nodded. I'd got it. It sounded good.

'We used to carve potatoes to make prints in art classes at school,' she explained. 'Have you got any lead?'

I picked up the .22 bullets. Thank God I'd chosen a .22. I mean, you can't melt down a cupro-nickel-jacketed .25 or .32. While she chose a potato, I pulled open another ten rounds—keeping the powder on a separate saucer.

Carving the spud wasn't too tricky, if you accepted that the ball wasn't going to be perfect in shape or size. I could trim it down with a knife and a nail-file after. Anyway, I'd probably wrap it in a bit of handkerchief or paper before I shoved it down, so as to make a reasonably smooth fit. Then I put the saucepan on the stove and dropped in all the bullets I'd got. I wouldn't need them all, but there'd be a wastage.

It took only a couple of minutes; suddenly each little grey bullet slumped and turned shiny-silver, then ran together in one bright puddle, clouding quickly over with scum. Didn't I read something about you mixed arsenic with lead when casting your own bullets? I never knew why. Still, unless Carlos had spiked the flour or something, there wouldn't be any arsenic around.

How was he planning to kill us? *How?* I mean, he wasn't going to walk in and say 'Drink this' and point a gun, was he? Or was he going to be subtle—I mean bring in a bottle for a celebration or something? Bloody risky. It would have to be the gun, the Browning. It would fit, with my background. Suicide pact—I shoot her, then myself. He could thump me on the head and then stuff the muzzle in my mouth and loose it off before the bruise had time to come up. Anyway, who's going to check on the obvious? Suicide pact. Hopeless love. Bingo.

Liz said: 'Aren't you going to pour it?'

The potato was standing on the rim of the stove—she'd chopped off the end to make it stand up. A funnel-shaped hole ran into it from the top. So here we went; I poured.

Maybe I poured too fast—but lead hardens fast, too. Anyway, what I got was a small fountain of molten lead spitting back at my hand. I dropped the saucepan and said something.

Liz said calmly: 'I suppose there's too much water in the potato. And if we baked it, it would go soft. How did they cast real bullets?'

I stopped checking over my hand for second-degree burns. 'Had a sort of thing like a pair of scissors, except the points were little cups. Half-round, each one, you know. I suppose you stuck it into a pot of hot lead, crunched it shut, and when it had hardened you'd got a ball. *Now* what?'

'You really need something like plaster of Paris. What about dough?'

'What about it?'

'Well, it's just flour and water, I *think*. I haven't made any since I was about ten. I don't mean bake it up, though: it'd probably just crack. But suppose I made some, thick? Could that make a ball?'

I started scraping little bright star-shaped splashes of lead off the floor. 'It doesn't really need to be like a ball. A bullet shape'll do.' And maybe carve a crater in the back end? I'd just reinvented the Minié ball. Grant and Lee would have been proud of me.

So while she got on with the pastry-making, I tried fitting the lighter flint into the jaws of the cock. It was still far too small, and it had to stick out a fair way, which didn't help the grip. But finally I had it in place.

Then I spooned a bit of powder into the flashpan, shut down the frizzen, cocked the lock and pulled the trigger.

And bugger-all.

I mean there was a nice shower of sparks and the frizzen whipped open, but the powder didn't take a blind bit of notice. I re-fixed the flint—it had got knocked squintwise in the jaws —and tried again. Results as per before.

I slammed the gun down and put my elbows on the table and my face in my hands. Oh *damn* it.

Liz came across and said: 'I don't think I can get the dough stiff enough. But I've put it in the freezer—that should do it. What's the matter?'

'The bloody thing isn't going to work. I was afraid of this. Smokeless powder just won't catch fire off a few sparks.'

'Oh.' She sat down across the table from me, and for a long time neither of us spoke.

At last she said, a bit irrelevantly: 'Bert, d'you think this apartment's registered in our names?'

'Probably. Or one or the other. I mean, whoever owns this dump, he wouldn't be too particular who he rented it to. Carlos could've done it by letter, signed my name. Send a couple of months rent and the bloke wouldn't bother checking up or asking for references or anything.'

'But would Carlos be able to get away with it—afterwards?'

'I dunno. I mean, we don't have to be found right off, do we? He takes away the Venus and next day he tells Dona Margarita we seem to have skipped out together. You wouldn't need to report anything like that, would you? Then, how long before we get found? Couple of weeks? Month, maybe? The evidence, time of death and all that, it'll all be so screwed up by then they'll shove us underground quick as they can and call it suicide.'

She shivered, thinking about lying there dead for a month.

I said: 'Anyway, it doesn't matter whether he can get away with it or not. I mean, he *thinks* he can—that's enough.'

'But why? Why kill us?'

I took out my cigars, then remembered my lighter was in pieces. 'Dunno. I've been trying to work that one out. He's pulling some fiddle . . . I just don't know.'

She looked at her watch; instinctively I looked at mine. Nearly four o'clock. With the shutters closed you couldn't see the darkness crawling up outside, but it would be there. And soon, so would Carlos.

She said suddenly: 'Couldn't you just point it at him? Threaten him—pretend it was loaded?'

I shook my head. 'He'd never believe me. I mean, you just don't believe in an old gun like this being loaded.'

'You could tell him. Tell him everything you've done, pulling the bullets to pieces and the flint, and pretend it really did work.'

I smiled, a bit gloomily. 'It sounds a bloody chatty sort of hold-up. No—he still wouldn't believe it. *I* wouldn't.'

And then she said: 'Couldn't you turn it into that other sort of gun?—the one in Amsterdam, in the "Nachtwacht"?'

'A *matchlock*?'

'Yes. You said if you put a cigarette into the powder it would burn; well, that's what you want, isn't it?'

I said slowly and faintly: 'Yes, that's what I want.'

But it took time. And cigars, which would have been a waste of good cigars if they'd been good cigars. I put my lighter back together in a hurry and started experimenting.

First I just filled up the flashpan and rammed a hot cigar-end into it. There was a vicious spurt of very bright flame.

That might have been good enough by itself; if the gun was

231

going to fire at all, it would fire that way. But the trouble would be using both hands, the gun in my left because the lock and flashpan were on the right.

So then I tried it with a cigar-stub clutched in the jaws of the cock—just like a matchlock and its 'serpentine'. That way, you couldn't actually get the cigar down into the powder. I mean, the flint of a flintlock never reached the flashpan; it stopped anything up to an inch short, after hitting the frizzen. The sparks could find their own way from there.

But the frizzen was so delicately balanced—for all its decoration Wogdon really had made a serious shooting gun, God bless him—that it flipped up even when a cigar-end squashed into it. And some nice glowing bits fell down into the pan. Another spit of powder flame.

I said: 'We're in business.'

Liz smiled and went to the freezer and took out a teacup of half-frozen dough. 'Is this good enough?'

Probably it was. Anyway I got the handle of a wooden spoon and shoved it into the dough, turning it carefully. Then I had a hole about an inch deep, somethin like half an inch diameter, and rounded at the bottom. But the dough down there hadn't frozen very much; it started to flow back. So we put the whole thing back into the fridge.

To pass the time, I pulled the remaining cartridges apart; I'd lost quite a bit of the first batch of lead anyway.

Liz asked: 'What actually are you going to do when he comes?'

'I dunno.' Or did I?

'Will you have to shoot him?'

'I dunno. I'm prepared to try and chat him up now—I mean now I can shoot if I want to. If he hands over his gun, then all right.'

She nodded. 'You can always shoot him in the shoulder or leg or something.'

'Ye-es.' I mean, they do it in the bad westerns all the time. Blow a gun out of a man's hand with a snap shot at twenty yards. I suppose you really might do it, though the bullet's as likely to ricochet off his gun into his gut. But the real thing is, you just wouldn't ever even try. The times I've told young soldiers messing about in my armoury: 'Don't point a gun at a man unless you mean to kill him.' Well, it's good advice, but it works two ways. I mean, when you point a gun, you really mean to kill.

But all I did was nod to Liz and say: 'We'll see how things work out,' and started to melt more lead.

This time there was no spitting: after a couple of minutes I had a bullet.

Well, nearly, anyway. It had some peculiar whorls and wiggles in it, from where the dough had flowed a bit, but it was distinctly bullet-shaped, about the right diameter and maybe three-quarters of an inch long. I sat down with Liz's nail-file and the sharpest kitchen knife.

After a time, I said: 'Look, why don't you get us packed up, love? Whatever happens, we want to get the hell out of here as soon as we can.'

She thought about this, then nodded and went away.

I carved and filed on. In the end I didn't really try to make it a proper Minié, with a hollow base. The 'Minny ball' was smaller than the calibre, so it just slipped down the barrel for loading, but the hollow base expanded with the blast so it made a tight seal and gripped into the rifling grooves and got a proper spin.

There wasn't any rifling on this pistol. There usually wasn't on English duelling guns, though the French had it. Supposed to be a bit unsporting, eh what? In fact a smooth bore wouldn't make an inch of difference at duelling ranges—twenty yards and under—and was a lot faster to reload. Besides, some part-time English gentlemen played it both ways by ordering pistols rifled just halfway from the powder end, so the rifling didn't show at the muzzle. But Wogdon hadn't been that crafty with his gun, and may he rest in peace for that, too. I had enough of a problem without having to screw this bullet down past rifling grooves as well.

So finally I tried it in, holding the gun upside down and pushing the bullet up. Gently. Very gently. Just my luck if it had jammed in place without a powder charge behind it.

It was pretty much the right size, but uneven. Back to the nail-file. And then back to the gun. It took another half-dozen tries before I was happy. Finally I let it go all the way down, and it slid smoothly out again.

Liz came back. 'We're all packed up. I don't know if I've got all your things in the right bags, but . . . . How's it going?'

The doorbell whirred and wheezed.

THIRTY-SIX

FOR A LONG MOMENT it was very quiet. I looked quickly
at my watch: five o'clock, so it would be mostly dark. But he
was still early, by my reckoning. If the street outside was very
busy, it would likely be so at this time, what with people going
home from work and so on.

Then I remembered that church bell. 'What's today?'

'Sunday, of course.'

'Hell.' And then I started to move. 'Kleenex, quick.' She
grabbed a handful from her bag.

One wrapped round the ramrod and pushed down and
screwed around to clean out the chamber. A wipe across the
flashpan. Then —'That brooch again.'

She dragged it off.

Touch-hole picked clean again—it had got bunged up with
the practice firings. Now the powder charge . . .

How much? *How much?* Five grains behind a .45, but this
ball was twice as heavy as a .45, but this gun wasn't built for
nitro-cellulose, but then again some of the blast would come
out of the touch-hole . . .

If there *was* any blast. I'd have to ram it tight as a Scotsman's wallet, and even then—

The doorbell rang again. And a heavy knocking as well.

Oh hell. I just spooned in the measured six grains I'd started
with, plus a pinch to make up what had trembled off the spoon.
My hands were acting as if they hadn't had a drink all day.

Then a wad of folded Kleenex rammed down, tight, tight,
tight. Another strip wrapped around the bullet, and that eased
down and rammed tight.

More bell, more knocking. A distant shout of 'Mr. Kemp!'

Powder in the flashpan, frizzen shut. Time to light a cigar.

I puffed it bright, chopped off the burning end and clamped it in the cock. Then, as a second thought, relit the rest. I could try slapping it in the pan if the first one didn't work. If I had the time.

I stood up, and my knees weren't much better than my hands. 'Here we go, love. Stay out of sight.'

'Bert—kiss me.'

For a moment she clung to me fiercely, trembling as badly as I was. Then I walked quickly out to the front door of the flat. As I got there he started thumping away again.

I shouted: 'All right, all *right!*' just in case he might believe he'd woken us. But unlikely. The locks, the shutters, the delay would have got him suspicious.

You bastard. You lousy murdering Nicaraguan Scottish bastard. I'm not scared of you, mate. I can kill you. I want to kill you. I really want to . . .

I eased back the bolts, unlocked the door, stepped back quickly, holding the Wogdon in front, canted up to keep the cigar high. It would be burning down, getting shorter—the old matchlock problem. *And covering itself in cold ash.* I snatched it to my face, blew the end to a bright glow, held it out again.

'It's open—come on in.'

Whatever it was, it would have to be fast, before the cigar burned down . . .

I want to kill you. I really want to kill you. And suddenly my knees heard me and weren't there any more and I was just a gun, pointing . . .

He came in, and he was suspicious, all right. He held the Browning by his side, not particularly aiming anywhere.

Then he saw my gun.

I said: 'It's loaded, Carlos. I made it work. Put down that gun.' My voice sounded flat and dull, and I was staring just at a point on his chest.

'Mr. Kemp—I dinna understand what this—'

'Put it down, Carlos. Then we'll talk.'

'Will ye tell me what—'

'I am going to shoot.'

236

He stared at the Wogdon, frowning, seeing the bright cigar end. And maybe then he believed me. But what he did was raise his own gun.

The flare from the flashpan was dazzling and then there was a million years for me to know it wasn't going to fire the charge and his gun coming to an aim . . .

I suppose subconsciously I'd been expecting the long *boom* of black powder, like the pistol was made for. The sharp *crack* shook me as much as the recoil.

Carlos was blown back against the half-closed door and its slam was like a second shot. He turned as it gave way behind him, fell face against the wall, slid to his knees, and just crumpled. The blood stopped coming out and he was dead.

But I'd known that from the moment I'd fired. At a range of five feet . . . The Wogdon was accurate, all right. So maybe I could've clipped his shoulder, but . . .

Through the ringing in my ears Liz said: 'Was he going to shoot?'

I just nodded.

'I suppose you had to . . . Is he dead?'

I nodded again, then went forward and picked up the Browning and worked the slide. There was one in the breech.

Liz asked: 'What are we going to do?'

At last I got the courage to look at her. She was very pale, very serious, but very determined, too.

I said: 'We're getting the hell out of here.'

'For the police?'

'We'll see . . . Get weaving.' Then I put my hands under Carlos's armpits and started dragging. He'd bled, but not all that much, and it was a lino floor. I got him to the bathroom and slid him into the bath. If he wanted to bleed any more, then that was the place. Then I went through his pockets.

Liz came in with her coat on. 'The bags are in the hall—My God! You're not taking *his* money, too?'

'Don't be silly. Key of the front door.' I held up a six-inch piece of Habsburg ironmongery.

'Bert, I'm sorry. I'm a bit . . .'

I nodded, but went on rifling through the papers from Carlos's pocket.

Finally I held one up. It was a typed document, and it started:

Giorgio da Castelfranco, known as Giorgione;

'Venus with Pistol'

—then a short description of the picture and its size, a bit about it matching in reverse an engraving by an unknown seventeenth-century artist, inscribed "Giorgione pinxit" ' and ending up:

In my opinion this is the work of Giorgione. Despite the lack of provenance, accounted for by the fact that it appears to have been in the possession of a Hungarian family for several hundred years, the style, tone values, the pose and expression of the figure correspond closely to other works accepted as being by this artist. I would therefore value this at $3,500,000.

It wasn't signed.

I passed it over; put the rest of the papers back.

When Liz had finished reading, I asked: 'What's "provenance"?'

'Oh, history of the painting. "In the collection of Jacob Astor, exhibited in Chicago 1912, described in a book by Berenson"—that sort of thing.'

'That's the normal sort of opinion you'd give for Managua?'

She nodded, puzzled. 'But I didn't write this. And nor did Carlos—he wouldn't know how.'

I got up off the side of the bath, went out to the living-room, and dug up the wrappings the picture had come in. Then started wrapping it up once more.

It took time. Liz came in before I'd finished.

'What *are* you doing now?'

'We're taking this, too.'

'Bert, we *can't.*'

'I think we're going to need it. I think I know what it's all been about now.'

But it was all one hell of a job. Liz had two sizeable suitcases, I had my big smuggling one and the airline bag, and even with that slung on my shoulder it only left us with one hand free among the two of us.

Outside, the pavement was patched with frozen snow and a wind whipped at the picture, sending me staggering like a drunken sailboat.

We turned one corner, then another, and hadn't seen a single person. Then there was a properly lit street ahead and we came out on to the Rotenturm Strasse. At last I had a rough idea of where we'd been the last twenty-four hours.

After another hundred yards—and three stops for breath —we found a small old hotel with a battered metal plate on the wall saying it had been awarded two stars by some touring organization three years ago. It would have to do.

They had a couple of rooms—hell, they probably had the whole hotel. We registered and handed over our passports. I didn't like doing that much; we were still a bit close to the scene of the late Carlos MacGregor. And I thought the picture was getting some curious looks.

'Our auto,' I explained, 'ist kaput.' I jerked a thumb in roughly the opposite direction from where we'd come. 'The battery ist kaput.' I made a few noises like a starter motor failing to start, and the old boy behind the counter got the message. He offered to ring us up a garage, but I said that tomorrow would do. He even managed a joke about how at least nobody could pinch the auto with the battery flat.

Maybe it all helped explain why we were walking around with too much luggage and a thumping great piece of (obviously) fine art.

The rooms were about one step better than the flat, and not a high step. Big brass-knobbed bedsteads and those huge fat Austrian eiderdowns. Cold running and lukewarm trickling water in every room. No telephones. But good enough.

We dumped our bags and the picture and then Liz said: 'Well, *now* the police, then.'

'Well, I don't know about that.'

'Bert, you *can't* walk away from this.'

'Look—I just killed a man. That's going to take one hell of a lot of explaining away.'

'You'll have to tell them what it was all about. You haven't even told me, yet.'

'Let's go round and tell the Boss Lady first, all right?'

She looked at me coldly. 'Bert, I don't understand what's going on.'

'No—o. Well, just trust me a bit, then. She's at the Bristol, isn't she?'

So I went downstairs and borrowed the desk phone and rang Dona Margarita.

'This is Bert Kemp'— I spoke quickly, not giving her time to interrupt or react— 'we've got a bit of a problem. I'm out of the flat and so's Miss Whitley. Carlos, I'm afraid he's been hurt. But I don't want to explain on the phone—can we come round now? I don't think I want to stay in Vienna much longer.'

A long pause, then, hesitantly: 'Of course, Senor Kemp, you will come . . . but what is it about Carlos? He is hurt, you say?'

'I'll tell you everything when I get there. What's the room number?'

She told me and I rang off fast.

Then I started the old familiar round, ringing the Imperial Sacher's, the Ambassador. And no luck. That began to bother me. I couldn't try every damn hotel in the place. Then, just on an off-chance, I rang the Bristol again and asked for Mr. Harry Burroughs.

They put me straight through.

THIRTY-SEVEN

IT WAS GETTING ON half past six when we reached the Bristol. The hall porter disapproved of my overcoat but let us march straight in and up.

Just before I knocked on Dona M's door, Liz said: 'Bert, you really do know what you're doing?'

'Yes. Well, probably.' I knocked. 'Just trust me, okay?'

She gave me a very small nod. I leaned across and kissed her cheek. Her smile was just a quick twitch.

Harry had beaten us to it. He opened the door and looked down at me. 'Bert—and Liz. Well, hi there. I didn't know you knew each other. What's this all about?'

I said: "You're a liar, Harry. But thanks for coming up. I'd've been here first except we had taxi trouble."

Liz dodged his handshake and scuttled inside. I followed.

There was a short passage with—probably—a bathroom opening off it. Then into the big main room, with other doors at each end. It looked like an antique showroom from one of the Knightsbridge tourist traps. The walls were panelled in primrose silk, the furniture was stiff armchairs done in petit point, a sofa in green Regency stripes, three-legged tables, original views of Old Vienna, marble fireplace—hell, *you* know. Mrs. Edwin Harper would have written a cheque on the spot.

Dona Margarita was on the sofa, looking as expensive as anything else in the room only a lot less antique. A gold lamé dress, or maybe housecoat, reached from a high Chinese collar down to her ankles.

"Senorita and Senor—good evening. What is the trouble?— but please have a drink."

I looked around but couldn't see any bottles. Then, smiling apologetically, Harry opened a cupboard panelled in the same silk as the walls, and it turned out to be a refrigerator jammed with booze.

'Liz? Scotch for you?'

She said yes and I seconded the motion, then turned to Dona M. 'Sorry I wasn't here to introduce Harry—'

'I have, of course, heard of him.'

'Yes, of course.'

'Please take off your coats. Now—what is the problem?—and what has happened to Carlos?'

I slung my coat across the back of an upright chair and sat in it. Liz took an armchair. Harry tiptoed selfconsciously across with the drinks.

'It's like this,' I said. 'I just killed Carlos.'

Harry's hand didn't even twitch as he passed me the Scotch.

Dona Margarita twitched, all right. 'You have done what? Why? How?'

'I sort of shot him. I mean, I had to. He was going to kill us.'

'Madre de Dios! This is . . . mad! Have you told the police?'

Harry was still standing beside me, like an over-helpful butler, and giving me a good close-up of an expensive checked sportscoat. It bothered me. I waved him away. 'Look, we can call the police later—I won't stop you. But I'd like to try and explain, you know?'

Her dark eyes were rigid on my face.

I said: 'I'm afraid there's been a bit of swindling going on about the pictures you've bought. I don't know about New York and London; I mean, I wasn't in on that, but over here—'

She said quickly: 'You are telling too much.'

I shook my head. 'No. We always thought Harry knew more than he was supposed to. I'm not giving anything away. Well, the first picture I know you got cheated on was the Cézanne in Paris.'

Liz sat up. 'But Henri was sure about that. It had a record —everything.'

'Oh yes—but it cost a bit of overtime as well, didn't it? I mean when I got thumped and you had to ransom it back again. Well, I'd say Carlos helped fix that. He didn't give the bank any instructions at all; he just tipped off some tough guys in Zurich and had them pick me up. So he cleared—what was it? a hundred and fifty thousand dollars on that one. Minus expenses, of course. But you can't pull that trick twice, you know? I mean. Managua's going to get suspicious even if *you* don't. So, you move on to stage two: planting a few fakes along the road.'

'Even assuming,' Liz said carefully and not very warmly, 'you could get forgeries past Henri and me, Carlos wouldn't have known how to do it.'

'Oh sure. I mean, that's why he'd need Harry, isn't it?'

Harry looked at me. 'This just isn't true, Bert.' He made it sound like an apology.

Dona Margarita glanced at him. 'Please go on, Senor Kemp.'

I guzzled some Scotch. 'Let's get down to cases. Take the portrait of Cordoba.'

Liz said quickly: '*I* didn't say that was Cordoba.'

'No. Somebody in Managua decided that. Probably it was fixed that he would, before you found it.'

'And it did *say* Cordoba. And the lettering wasn't new.'

'Yes, but it had lost a bit at the top and bottom, hadn't it? Suppose it originally said

FRED GONSALEZ A LIEUTENANT OF
FRANCISCO WHATSIT DE CORDOBA

in two lines'—I sketched them in the air—'and they just chopped off the top line, see? I mean, you didn't really check for any weathering on the break, did you?—because it wouldn't tell you anything about how old the picture itself was.'

She devoted a small thoughtful frown to the idea. 'I suppose . . . it might have happened. I was having to work so fast; too fast.'

'Of course. That and doing so much under-the-counter dealing and having me along—well, it was a perfect situation for a bit of fiddle-de-dee. I mean, Henri had the same thing with the Van Gogh, didn't he? Even *I* know Van Gogh's the boy you always do an X-ray on, the way he builds up his patterns

243

of paint. So Harry could have found an old Van Gogh copy, old enough, and fixed it with the bloke at The Hague and everything.'

Harry said politely: 'Bert, if you go on like this, I'll just have to sue you for a million dollars.'

'Better lend me a million first. Stuff it, Harry.'

Liz said thoughtfully: 'It's neat, but it's all *too* neat. Just suppose I hadn't recommended the Cordoba or Henri hadn't come across the Van Gogh, or hadn't believed in it? What then?'

'Then nothing. There couldn't've been half a dozen more fakes and mis-attributions they planted but you both missed. It wouldn't have cost them much. But you'd bite on some of them—and it had to be *you* two finding them, you know? Like Napoleon's carbine. I mean, they could've been fixing this for . . .' I looked at Dona Margarita. 'How long were you planning this trip?'

'Since—for almost five years.'

'See? They've had that long for Harry to pick up good fakes and fix things with people like Fajjy.'

'The Poussin?' Liz asked suddenly.

'No, that was genuine. I suppose, anyway. You've got receipts, his word on it, everything. You could sue on that.'

Then she said: 'But—suppose we'd had second thoughts. Suppose Henri had wanted to do an X-ray in Zurich—'

'He was going to.'

'Well, what then?'

'Then he'd have to be killed. And he was.'

Dona Margarita gave a gasp and looked at Harry. I said: 'No, not Harry. Harry wouldn't touch murder. He might know about it, but he wouldn't touch it. That was Carlos again. I mean, he *knew* we were going to Zurich—I phoned him before we left. Then Henri phoned from Zurich to say where he was staying. Carlos had nearly ten hours to get there—by plane —and knock him off before I found him. He could do it.'

Liz opened her mouth. I said quickly: 'Now, just let me tell it, love. Trust me.' I looked back at Dona Margarita. 'But *you'd* know. D'you know if he did get away that night?'

She frowned, blinking with concentration. Then, after a long time, she said slowly: 'He perhaps had done it . . . I did not see him for a long time, not the next morning.'

I wanted to take a deep breath; instead, I took a deep swallow of Scotch. Now I knew we were safe: she was on our side.

'So,' I said, 'we come to the big one: the Venus. So far I reckon they've cleared—what?—half a million dollars, about. Less a cut to the bloke in The Hague and Fajjy and so on. But this is the big one; if the Hungarians are ready to sell at two million, as a Titian, and you can pass it on for three million, as Giorgione—well, I mean, you're really cooking.'

Liz stared. 'Was *that* it, then?'

'Sure. Probably the Hungarians didn't even know it was being used as a racket. Just glad to get rid of it for two million in foreign exchange. All that stuff about smuggling it, the guards and so on—well, maybe, but it could've been imported quite legally. Though I bet Hungary hasn't been paid yet, so the guards may have been real.'

She just lay back and laughed.

Harry suddenly stopped being apologetic. 'And what's so goddamn funny, then?'

I grinned at him. 'It really is a Giorgione, see? I mean, last night Liz and me changed our minds about it. Not that that makes any difference really, so long as Hungary's still prepared to sell it as a Titian. You've got your million anyway—if somebody's prepared to certify it. And that's what nearly got us killed, see? Because Carlos thought Liz *wouldn't* certify it except as Titian. So—well, he'd thought that might happen, so he'd got us fixed up in a nice lonely flat all ready for a little suicide pact.'

Liz sat forward again. 'But supposing I *had* certified it last night—or said I probably would?'

'Then nothing. Big smiles all round and we get first-class tickets home.'

'But . . . with us dead, how could they get Managua to accept it as genuine? Was he going to torture us into signing that certificate?'

'I doubt it. But isn't it a nice coincidence? I mean, just the time when you've got a cheap offer of a really big picture and your own expert's gone missing or dead, surprise surprise; staying in the very same hotel is that world-famous expert, Harry Burroughs. Managua's heard of him, probably, but probably not too much. So, let *him* sign the certificate just for once. Hell, he must have drawn it up. You said Carlos couldn't.'

She looked at him, then said thoughtfully: 'You are a bastard, Harry.'

He stood up. 'Bert, I've had enough bedtime stories. Dona Margarita—will you excuse me now?'

Her eyes crackled dark fire. 'I will not! If you have truly done these things, then stay to hear of them. It is really my money you are stealing—and my career in politics you are spoiling. Sit down! *Sit down!*'

He didn't so much sit as get blown off his feet. Anyway, he stayed.

I said soothingly: 'Well, that isn't necessarily so, you know? I mean, the collection's *almost* okay. If you buy the Giorgione, it *is* a Giorgione; the Cordoba *might* be Cordoba—only Harry knows for sure and *he* won't talk—and all you have to do is stop anybody running tests on that Van Gogh. That shouldn't be difficult. And Liz and me—well, we're not going to talk either. All we want out of this is out of it."

Now everybody was looking at me.

I went on: 'Well, I mean—I've got to explain away Carlos, haven't I?—if I start talking.'

Dona Margarita said carefully: 'You do not want to go to the police?'

I shrugged. 'He was going to kill me: I killed him. No, I'm ready to let it go—if things can be fixed. And Harry's the great fixer.'

He said: 'Bert—just how much d'you think you can *prove*?'

'Just about bugger-all, I'd say.'

He was happy again; his full polite, timid manner was back.

'Bert, if you've really killed a man, there just isn't anything *I* can do.'

I wriggled on the chair and shoved my right hand into my

ide pocket, as casually as I could. 'Well, now, I'll tell you, Harry: this dealing in guns, it just gets you into trouble—you know? So I'm coming into your line of business. Art, I mean. You can be my first customer; I'll sell you a Giorgione.'

There was no polite apologetic smile now. Not a hint nor memory of one. After a time he said hoarsely: 'You'd never get it out of the country.'

'I've got pictures out of countries before. So, maybe it'll take a little time, *but* if I can't get it out, then so help me God, I'll send it for a swim in the bloody blue Danube.'

He leaned forward, tensed. Just as precaution, I took the Browning out of my pocket.

He said: 'I can pick up that phone and have a stolen picture report on you before you're out of the hotel.'

'Yes? Can *you* prove ownership? Can you prove I had anything to do with it? Can you prove it even exists? And one thing I know about that picture, Harry—it ain't insured. It just couldn't be, the way it's been shunted about under cover. So you'll just have to go back to your little friends in Budapest and say "Sorry, comrades, but it sort of got away from me. Let's say we forget the two million I owe you".'

Briefly, there was just a ghost of a smile—but not an apologetic one.

'The comrades won't forget *you*, Bert.'

'Maybe. *If* they believe some little creep like me could get it away from a big bad wolf like you. No—you're the one they trusted to sell it for them, *you're* the one they'll take the value out of. They'll open a birthday box of rubber truncheons for you, chum.'

It was like when you're snap-shooting at a bottle at fifty yards and you shoot and shoot and nothing happens and then suddenly it isn't there any more. He just turned ten years older.

'Okay, Bert, so what's the deal?'

I took a long breath, then glanced at Liz. She was watching, bird-like, her head on one side.

'Well—we're going to need Dona Margarita's co-operation

on this, so it'll only work if she agrees. First off, you get rid of Carlos. He's got a big lump of lead in him, so you can't turn him into a traffic accident. Just get rid of him. I mean, nobody's going to miss him, in Europe, are they?'

Dona Margarita was frowning thoughtfully. 'Perhaps not, but—'

'Look, you can pack his bags here and send them on and check him out of the hotel here, okay? I mean, you can keep him alive for a long time like that; maybe send some cables in his name. Then, in a week or two, you tell Managua he's quit on you; walked out. How much can they worry, at that distance?'

She went on looking rather suspicious. Well, it wasn't every day she got asked to help paint over a killing. Though, come to think of it, it was the second time in two weeks.

I turned to Harry. 'Then I want that flat cleared out. I think you fixed that up—Carlos didn't know Vienna like you do—so now you can unfix it. I mean, if our names are on any register or anything, I want them *off*.'

He nodded heavily, wearily.

'And one more thing: fifty thousand pounds, please.'

'Hey?'

So I said it again. Liz was also sitting up straight and startled. Harry growled: 'Like hell.'

'A dealer takes a percentage, doesn't he? Well, that's ours.'

'*Jesus*. I'm getting you off a murder charge and now you want to make a profit on it.'

'Who got me mixed up in it? Suppose I'd been a good little boy—where's the profit in ending up a phoney suicide? You can call it restitution or damages or what you like, but call it fifty thousand quid, in cash, as soon as the banks open to-morrow. I want to be out of Vienna by lunchtime.'

He looked slowly around the room—not at anybody, just looking hopelessly for a miracle the last guest might have left in an odd corner. Then: 'Oh hell—all right.'

Dona Margarita smiled coldly. 'You are a hard bargainer, Senor Kemp. I expect Senorita Whitley approves?'

I said quickly: 'Of course she does. Now, if you don't mind, we'd like to resign. I mean, I think you'll see why. So we call it all square as of now—right?'

She nodded. 'I understand.'

'So we'll be going now.' I nodded at Liz; she stood up obediently. 'I'll ring you in the morning, Harry. This is the key to the building.' I handed it over. 'You'll find Carlos in the bath.'

At the door, I turned back. 'Harry—just how *did* you get me, that first time in Zurich? With the Cézanne?'

The apologetic smile flickered. 'You really don't remember? And we were so damn careful that you wouldn't think it was all fixed from the inside.' He sighed. 'We could have used a phoney bank messenger after all . . . We just had three boys walk up to you in the station and stick guns in your back and tell you to get into the car. That time of night, nobody noticed.'

'As simple as that?' I shook my head. 'Yes, I'd've done what I was told. It's the way I'd've fixed it myself. Thanks, Harry.'

I smiled at Dona Margarita for the last time and led the way down the passage and out.

THIRTY-EIGHT

IN THE LIFT, I SAID: 'Well, that could have gone a sight worse.'

I was beginning to feel pretty chuffed with myself.

But Liz just grunted.

It wasn't until we were in a taxi crawling carefully back over the snow to our hotel that she said: 'What you said in there—was it all true?'

'Most of it. But I did say I couldn't prove it.'

'And the whole truth?'

'Well . . .'

'About getting from Amsterdam to Zurich: I don't know much about European airlines, but I don't think they'd have a flight around midnight, in the middle of winter, like you said Carlos took to kill Henri.''

'But there'd be one in the afternoon, though, after I'd rung to say we were on our way. Then all you have to do is wait in Zurich until Henri rings Amsterdam to say where he is, then Amsterdam rings you.'

Her face glowed intermittently in the passing street lights. She said quietly: 'So she knew, all the time. She was in it: they all were.'

'Of course. I mean, that's why she didn't get really mad at Harry—just an act. If he'd really been cheating her, she'd've killed him right there.'

She nodded. Then: 'So why didn't you accuse her? Why blame just Carlos and Harry?'

'Hell, we had to have her on *our* side. I mean, we can't cover up on Carlos unless she helps. I had to give her a way out. If I'd told her she was sinking, she's the sort of captain that takes the whole ship down with her, and us still on board.'

'I suppose so . . . Then the whole thing, the whole art museum idea, was just to get some of her money out of Managua. What about her political career, though?'

'Who says she wants one, apart from her? I mean, d'you see her as a politician? And we always said the museum was crazy, politically. No, what she wants is Paris and Rome and Monte Carlo—maybe a new rich husband, too. Meanwhile a million and a half dollars'll last even her a good time. But she never planned going back to Nicaragua."

'But won't they sue her? Get her extradited?'

'Can you see a Swiss court backing a Nicaraguan land grab against a millionairess? It *was* her money, after all.'

We crept around St. Stephan's church, a black Gothic crag stretching up out of reach of the street lights, and turned down the Rotenturm Strasse. A few slow snowflakes drifted down.

Liz said: 'And I suppose now she'll get it; all she wants. She's got away with it.'

I shrugged. 'I suppose so. But I told you: if I start anything, the whole ship goes down.'

'But you don't really mind, do you?' she said thoughtfully, almost to herself. 'You're not really angry that she's getting away with it, that she got Henri killed, she tried to get us killed?'

I shrugged again. 'I dunno . . . I mean, what good'll getting angry do?'

She looked at me carefully, for a long time. 'So she gets her cut—and Harry gets his—and Faggioni got his—and you got yours.'

'Hell, *we* got it. We deserved something out of that.'

The taxi slid gently to a stop outside the little hotel.

Liz said: 'Not *we*, Bert. Tell the cab to wait. I'll take it straight on to the airport.'

But I didn't get it. Not right away. 'Hell, you don't know if there's a plane to where you want, tonight. Just wait till tomorrow and we can go anywhere we like.'

She shook her head. 'Not *we*, Bert. I'm going home. By myself.'

I rode to the airport with her. She didn't want it, but she couldn't exactly sling me out of the taxi.

For a long time we didn't say anything. Then I tried. 'Look —now we've got it made. I mean with that fifty thousand. Change my shop. Make it an art gallery as well, if you want to. Or just move, travel. I mean, now there's no problems.'

She glanced at me, smiled sadly. 'No problems.'

Maybe my voice sounded a little desperate. 'But I did it for you—for us. That's what I wanted it for.'

'Maybe . . . Yes, I think you really did. But you'd have done it anyway, if I hadn't been there, wouldn't you?'

Well, I suppose . . . I said: 'Hell, she deserved to lose *something;* it's her money we'll be getting, not Harry's.'

'What she *deserved,*' she said firmly, 'is to be stuck in court on a conspiracy to murder charge.'

'Or murder,' I said—rather absent-mindedly.

'What?'

Hell. I hadn't meant to bring it up, really. But now I was stuck with it. 'Maybe it wasn't Carlos killed Henri. She could've gone to Zurich just as easy.'

'But she couldn't . . .' Then she stopped.

'It was all about *her* money, wasn't it? She's certainly an activist, if that's the word. I just can't see Carlos doing it— well, not that way. If he'd used a knife, he'd've used it better. But her . . . I mean probably Carlos was supposed to go, but he just got cold feet. So she did. Just my guess; I still can't prove anything. But it could be why she went sour on him in Venice. Why she offered me a job.'

'She did what?'

'Offered me Carlos's job—I think. When I turned it down, she just went ahead on Plan A: throwing you and me together.'

After a time, she said: 'You mean it was just her setting us up for a suicide pact?'

'No. You don't think that, neither.'

After another time, she said: 'No. I'm sorry. But . . . why did Carlos even agree to any of it, then?'

'Dunno. Suppose he was in love with her, or something.'

She looked at me quickly. Then said: 'Yes. Or something. So you were right about all that—in a way. The poor bastard.'

'Poor bastard? He was still going to kill *us*!'

'Would he, though? If he got cold feet once . . . And I think he'd've tried to get me to certify the Giorgione first. He did have the certificate with him.'

'He had a gun with him—in his hand.'

'Oh yes. But you know—you didn't have to kill him. Not really. We could have run away somehow. Broken into a ground floor apartment, then broken out through a street window—'

'They were barred. Probably, anyway.'

'You see?' she said gently, almost sadly. 'You didn't even try. We could have done *something*. But he was coming to kill you, so you were going to kill him first. That's the way you think.'

And why bloody well not? But I didn't say anything.

'Bert—it *is* only the way you think. I'm not really blaming you. *I* could have thought of something. I guess I was just too frightened. And I could go to the police now and tell them everything, if I really wanted *her* in court. But I'm running away. I know. And neither of us will change, Bert—but I just can't live with it.'

We were passing the refinery, the lights still glittering all over it and nothing moving, not a man, not a flame, nor a puff of steam—nothing. Alive but dead.

Then we were turning in for the airport. She said suddenly: 'Bert—last night . . . I won't forget it. I'll always . . . Don't think it was just . . . one of those things.'

Christ Almighty. Don't try and forget and don't try and remember. Just hang it on the wall and don't try to fire it again and don't get it valued or sell it.

We stopped and she got out fast and she and the taxi-driver got her luggage out of the boot. Then she just lifted a hand at me and almost ran into the terminal. The driver looked at me and shrugged sympathetically. Screw him.

I jerked my head backwards. 'Hotel, *bitte*.'

And down the road the cold lights of the refinery and the

big cemetery where they don't feel anything, not anything, any more.

I'd better get the Wogdon cleaned. I mean, the residue of the firing would be eating into the barrel and flashpan. Knock half the value off it.